THE READER'S LIBRARY

THE works of literature that have been selected and edited for this series are not alone of a character and standard that make them interesting to all readers; they are issued in well made volumes, substantially and attractively bound, so that they may take their place on the library shelves at home, or be carried in the pocket and read at odd moments. They are easily held in the hand. They go naturally into the pocket.

The series contains romances and stories of adventure, poetry and essays, biography and travel, philosophy and science, for the entertainment and instruction of old and young. The type, the size, the weight, the binding, make them available to those who read at all hours of the day or night. They are books to be read, to be used, to be kept close at hand.

To place such literature within everybody's reach under any and all circumstances is the reason for the creation of THE READER'S LIBRARY, to which new titles by famous authors will be constantly added.

LUCAS LEXOW,
Editor.

SHERLOCK HOLMES
DETECTIVE STORIES

BY

A. CONAN DOYLE

J. H. SEARS & COMPANY, Inc.

PUBLISHERS

NEW YORK

Set up, Printed and Bound at the
KINGSPORT PRESS
Kingsport   Tennessee
United States of America

CONTENTS

CONTENTS

SHERLOCK HOLMES
DETECTIVE STORIES

SHERLOCK HOLMES
DETECTIVE STORIES

THE SIGN OF THE FOUR

CHAPTER I

THE SCIENCE OF DEDUCTION

SHERLOCK HOLMES took his bottle from the corner of the mantel-piece and his hypodermic syringe from its neat morocco case. With his long, white, nervous fingers he adjusted the delicate needle, and rolled back his left shirt-cuff. For some little time his eyes rested thoughtfully upon the sinewy forearm and wrist, all dotted and scarred with innumerable puncture-marks. Finally he thrust the sharp point home, pressed down the tiny piston, and sunk back into the velvet-lined armchair with a long sigh of satisfaction.

Three times a day for many months I had witnessed this performance, but custom had not reconciled my mind to it. On the contrary, from day to day I had become more irritable at the sight, and my conscience swelled nightly within me at the thought that I had lacked the courage to protest. Again and again I had registered a vow that I should deliver my soul upon the subject, but there was that in the cool, nonchalant air of my companion which made him the last man with whom one would care to take anything approaching to a liberty. His great powers, his masterly manner, and the experience which I had had of his many extraordinary qualities, all made me diffident and backward in crossing him.

Yet upon that afternoon, whether it was the claret

which I had taken with my lunch, or the additional ex-
asperation produced by the extreme deliberation of his
manner, I suddenly felt that I could hold out no longer.

"Which is it to-day?" I asked. "Morphine or cocaine?"

He raised his eyes languidly from the old black-letter
volume which he had opened. "It is cocaine," he said;
"a seven per cent. solution. Would you care to try it?"

"No, indeed," I answered, brusquely. "My constitution has not got over the Afghan campaign yet. I cannot afford to throw any extra strain upon it."

He smiled at my vehemence. "Perhaps you are right,
Watson," he said. "I suppose that its influence is physi-
cally a bad one. I find it, however, so transcendently
stimulating and clarifying to the mind that its secondary
action is a matter of small moment."

"But consider!" I said, earnestly. "Count the cost!
Your brain may, as you say, be roused and excited, but
it is a pathological and morbid process, which involves
increased tissue-change, and may at last leave a permanent weakness. You know, too, that a black reaction
comes upon you. Surely the game is hardly worth the
candle. Why should you, for a mere passing pleasure,
risk the loss of those great powers with which you have
been endowed? Remember that I speak not only as one
comrade to another, but as a medical man to one for
whose constitution he is to some extent answerable."

He did not seem offended. On the contrary, he put
his finger-tips together and leaned his elbows on the
arms of his chair, like one who has a relish for conversation.

"My mind," he said, "rebels at stagnation. Give me
problems, give me work, give me the most abstruse
cryptogram, or the most intricate analysis, and I am in
my own proper atmosphere, I can dispense them with
artificial stimulants. But I abhor the dull routine of

existence. I crave for mental exaltation. That is why I have chosen my own particular profession—or rather created it, for I am the only one in the world."

"The only unofficial detective?" I said, raising my eyebrows.

"The only unofficial consulting detective," he answered. "I am the last and highest court of appeal in detection. When Gregson, or Lestrade, or Athelney Jones are out of their depths—which, by the way, is their normal state —the matter is laid before me. I examine the data, as an expert, and pronounce a specialist's opinion. I claim no credit in such cases. My name figures in no newspaper. The work itself, the pleasure of finding a field for my peculiar powers, is my highest reward. But you have yourself had some experience of my methods of work in the Jefferson Hope case."

"Yes, indeed," said I, cordially. "I was never so struck by anything in my life. I even embodied it in a small brochure with the somewhat fantastic title of 'A Study in Scarlet.'"

He shook his head sadly. "I glanced over it," said he. "Honestly, I cannot congratulate you upon it. Detection is, or ought to be, an exact science, and should be treated in the same cold and unemotional manner. You have attempted to tinge it with romanticism, which produces much the same effect as if you worked a love story or an elopement in the fifth proposition of Euclid."

"But the romance was there," I remonstrated. "I could not tamper with the facts."

"Some facts should be suppressed, or at least a just sense of proportion should be observed in treating them. The only point in the case which deserved mention was the curious analytical reasoning from effects to causes by which I succeeded in unraveling it."

I was annoyed at this criticism of a work which had been specially designed to please him. I confess, too, that I was irritated by the egotism which seemed to demand that every line of my pamphlet should be devoted to his own special doings. More than once during the years that I had lived with him in Baker Street I had observed that a small vanity underlay my companion's quiet and didactic manner. I made no remark, however, but sat nursing my wounded leg. I had had a Jezail bullet through it some time before, and though it did not prevent me from walking, it ached wearily at every change of the weather.

"My practice has extended recently to the Continent," said Holmes, after a while, filling up his old brier-root pipe. "I was consulted last week by Francois le Villard, who, as you probably know, has come rather to the front lately in the French detective service. He has all the Celtic power of quick intuition, but he is deficient in the wide range of exact knowledge which is essential to the higher developments of his art. The case was concerned with a will, and possessed some features of interest. I was able to refer him to two parallel cases; the one at Riga in 1857, and the other at St. Louis in 1871, which have suggested to him the true solution. Here is the letter which I had this morning acknowledging my assistance." He tossed over, as he spoke, a crumpled sheet of foreign note-paper. I glanced my eyes down it, catching a profusion of notes of admiration, with stray "magnifiques," "coup-de-maitres," and "tours-de-force," all testifying to the ardent admiration of the Frenchman.

"He speaks as a pupil to his master," said I.

"Oh, he rates my assistance too highly," said Sherlock Holmes, lightly. "He has considerable gifts himself. He possesses two out of the three qualities necessary for the ideal detective. He has the power of observation and that of deduction. He is only wanting in knowledge; and that may come in time. He is now translating my small works into French."

"Your works?"

"Oh, didn't you know?" he cried, laughing. "Yes, I have been guilty of several monographs. They are all upon technical subjects. Here, for example, is one 'Upon the Distinction Between the Ashes of the Various Tobaccoes.' In it I enumerate a hundred and forty forms of cigar, cigarette, and pipe tobacco, with colored plates illustrating the difference in the ash. It is a point which is continually turning up in criminal trials, and which is sometimes of supreme importance as a clew. If you can say definitely, for example, that some murder has been done by a man who was smoking an Indian lunkah, it obviously narrows your field of search. To the trained eye there is as much difference between the black ash of a Trinchinopoly and the white fluff of bird's-eye as there is between a cabbage and a potato."

"You have an extraordinary genius for minutiæ," I remarked.

"I appreciate their importance. Here is my monograph upon the tracing of footsteps, with some remarks upon the uses of plaster of Paris as a preserver of impresses. Here, too, is a curious little work upon the influence of a trade upon the form of the hand, with lithotypes of the hands of slaters, sailors, cork-cutters, compositors, weavers and diamond polishers. That is a matter of great practical interest to the scientific detective —especially in cases of unclaimed bodies, or in discovering the antecedents of criminals. But I weary you with my hobby."

"Not at all," I answered, earnestly. "It is of the greatest interest to me, especially since I have had the opportunity of observing your practical application of it. But you spoke just now of observation and deduction. Surely the one to some extent implies the other."

"Why, hardly," he answered, leaning back luxuriously in his armchair, and sending up thick blue wreaths from his pipe. "For example, observation shows me that you have been to the Wigmore Street Post Office this morning, but deduction lets me know that when there you dispatched a telegram."

"Right!" said I. "Right on both points! But I confess that I don't see how you arrived at it. It was a sudden impulse upon my part, and I have mentioned it to no one."

"It is simplicity itself," he remarked, chuckling at my surprise; "so absurdly simple that an explanation is superfluous; and yet it may serve to define the limits of observation and of deduction. Observation tells me that you have a little reddish mold adhering to your instep. Just opposite the Wigmore Street Office they have taken up some earth which lies in such a way that it is difficult to avoid treading in it in entering. The earth is of this peculiar reddish tint which is found, so far as I know, nowhere else in the neighborhood. So much is observation. The rest is deduction."

"How, then, did you deduce the telegram?"

"Why, of course I knew that you had not written a letter, since I sat opposite to you all the morning. I see also in your open desk there that you have a sheet of stamps and a thick bundle of post cards. What could you go into the post office for, then, but to send a wire? Eliminate all other factors, and the one which remains must be the truth."

"In this case it certainly is so," I replied, after a little thought. "The thing, however, is, as you say, of the simplest. Would you think me impertinent if I were to put your theories to a more severe test?"

"On the contrary," he answered, "it would prevent me from taking a second dose of cocaine. I should be delighted to look into any problem which you might submit to me."

"I have heard you say that it is difficult for a man to

have any object in daily use without leaving the impress of his individuality upon it in such a way that a trained observer might read it. Now, I have here a watch which has recently come into my possession. Would you have the kindness to let me have an opinion upon the character or habits of the late owner?"

I handed him the watch with some slight feeling of amusement in my heart, for the test was, as I thought, an impossible one, and I intended it as a lesson against the somewhat dogmatic tone which he occasionally assumed. He balanced the watch in his hand, gazed hard at the dial, opened the back, and examined the works, first with his naked eyes and then with a powerful convex lens. I could hardly keep from smiling at his crestfallen face, when he finally snapped the case and handed it back.

"There are hardly any data," he remarked. "The watch has been recently cleaned, which robs me of my most suggestive facts."

"You are right," I answered. "It was cleaned before being sent to me." In my heart I accused my companion of putting forward a most lame and impotent excuse to cover his failure. What data could he expect from an uncleaned watch?

"Though unsatisfactory, my research has not been entirely barren," he observed, staring up at the ceiling with dreamy, lack-luster eyes. "Subject to your correction, I should judge that the watch belonged to your elder brother, who inherited it from your father."

"That you gather, no doubt, from the H. W. upon the back?"

"Quite so. The W. suggests your own name. The data of the watch is nearly fifty years back, and the initials are as old as the watch; so it was made for the last generation. Jewelry usually descends to the eldest son, and he is most likely to have the same name as his father. Your father has, if I remember right, been dead many years. It has, therefore, been in the hands of your eldest brother."

"Right, so far," said I. "Anything else?"

"He was a man of untidy habits—very untidy and careless. He was left with good prospects, but he threw away his chances, lived for some time in poverty, with occasional short intervals of prosperity, and finally, taking to drink, he died. That is all I can gather."

I sprang from my chair and limped impatiently about the room with considerable bitterness in my heart.

"This is unworthy of you, Holmes," I said. "I could not have believed that you would have descended to this. You have made inquiries into the history of my unhappy brother, and you now pretend to deduce this knowledge in some fanciful way. You cannot expect me to believe that you have read all this from his old watch! It is unkind, and, to speak plainly, has a touch of charlatanism in it."

"My dear doctor," said he kindly, "pray accept my apologies. Viewing the matter as an abstract problem, I had forgotten how personal and painful a thing it might be to you. I assure you, however, that I never even knew that you had a brother until you handed me the watch."

"Then how in the name of all that is wonderful did you get all these facts? They are absolutely correct in every particular."

"Ah, that is good luck. I could only say what was the balance of probability. I did not at all expect to be so accurate."

"But it was not mere guess-work?"

"No, no; I never guess. It is a shocking habit—destructive to the logical faculty. What seems strange to you is only so because you do not follow my train of thought or observe the small facts upon which large inferences may depend. For example, I began by stating that your brother was careless. When you observe the lower part of that watch case you notice that it is not only dented in two places, but it is cut and marked all over from the habit of keeping other hard objects, such as coins or keys, in the same pocket. Surely it is no great feat to assume that a man who treats a fifty guinea watch so cavalierly must be a careless man. Neither is it a very far-fetched inference that a man who inherits one article of such value is pretty well provided for in other respects."

I nodded to show that I followed his reasoning.

"It is very customary for pawnbrokers in England, when they take a watch, to scratch the number of the ticket with a pin-point upon the inside of the case. It is more handy than a label, as there is no risk of the number being lost or transposed. There are no less than four such numbers visible to my lens on the inside of this case. Inference—that your brother was often at low water. Secondary inference—that he had occasional bursts of prosperity, or he could not have redeemed the pledge. Finally, I ask you to look at the inner plate which contains the keyhole. Look at the thousands of scratches all round the hole—marks where the key has slipped. What sober man's key could have scored those grooves? But you will never see a drunkard's watch without them. He winds it at night, and he leaves these traces of his unsteady hand. Where is the mystery in all this?"

"It is clear as daylight," I answered. "I regret the injustice which I did you. I should have had more faith in your marvelous faculty. May I ask whether you have any professional inquiry on foot at present?"

"None. Hence the cocaine. I cannot live without brain work. What else is there to live for? Stand at the window here. Was ever such a dreary, dismal, unprofitable world? See how the yellow fog swirls down the street and drifts across dun-colored houses. What could be more hopelessly prosaic and material? What is the use of having powers, doctor, when one has no field upon which to exert them? Crime is commonplace, and existence is commonplace, and no qualities save those which are commonplace have any function upon earth."

I had opened my mouth to reply to his tirade, when, with a crisp knock, our landlady entered, bearing a card upon a brass salver.

"A young lady for you, sir," she said, addressing my companion.

"Miss Mary Morstan," he read. "Hum! I have no recollection of that name. Ask the young lady to step up, Mrs. Hudson. Don't go, doctor. I prefer that you remain."

CHAPTER II

THE STATEMENT OF THE CASE

MISS MORSTAN entered the room with a firm step and an outward composure of manner. She was a blonde young lady, small, dainty, well gloved, and dressed in the most perfect taste. There was, however, a plainness and simplicity about her costume which bore with a suggestion of limited means. The dress was a somber grayish beige, untrimmed and unbraided, and she wore a small turban of the same dull hue, relieved only by a suspicion of white feather in the side. Her face had neither regularity of feature nor beauty of complexion, but her expression was sweet and amiable, and her large blue eyes were singularly spiritual and sympathetic. In an experience of women which extends over many nations and three separate continents I have never looked upon a face which gave a clearer promise of a refined and sensitive nature. I could not but observe that, as she took the seat which Sherlock Holmes placed for her, her lip trembled, her hand quivered, and she showed every sign of intense inward agitation.

"I have come to you, Mr. Holmes," she said, "because you once enabled my employer, Mrs. Cecil Forrester, to unravel a little domestic complication. She was much impressed by your kindness and skill."

"Mrs. Cecil Forrester," he repeated, thoughtfully. "I believe that I was of some slight service to her. The case, however, as I remember it, was a very simple one."

"She did not think so. But, at least, you cannot say the same of mine. I can hardly imagine anything more strange, more utterly inexplicable, than the situation in which I find myself."

Holmes rubbed his hands and his eyes glistened. He leaned forward in his chair with an expression of extraordinary concentration upon his clear-cut, hawk-like features. "State your case," said he, in brisk, business tones.

I felt that my position was an embarraassing one. "You will, I am sure, excuse me," I said, rising from my chair.

To my surprise, the young lady held up her gloved hand to detain me. "If your friend," she said, "would be good enough to stay, he might be of inestimable service to me."

I relapsed into my chair.

"Briefly," she continued, "the facts are these. My father was an officer in an Indian regiment, who sent me home when I was quite a child. My mother was dead, and I had no relative in England. I was placed, however, in a comfortable boarding establishment at Edinburgh, and there I remained until I was seventeen years of age. In the year 1878 my father, who was senior captain of his regiment, obtained twelve-months' leave and came home. He telegraphed to me from London that he had arrived all safe, and directed me to come down at once, giving the Langham Hotel as his address. His message, as I remember, was full of kindness and love. On reaching London I drove to the Langham, and was informed that Captain Morstan was staying there, but that he had gone out the night before and had not yet returned. I waited all day without news of him. That night, on the advice of the manager of the hotel, I communicated with the police, and next morning we advertised in all the papers. Our inquiries led to no result; and from that day to this no word has ever been heard of my unfortunate father. He came home, with his heart full of hope, to find some peace, some comfort, and instead—" She put her hand to her throat, and a choking sob cut short the sentence.

"The date?" asked Holmes, opening his note-book.

"He disappeared on the 3d of December, 1878—nearly ten years ago."

"His luggage?"

"Remained at the hotel. There was nothing in it to suggest a clew—some clothes, some books, and a considerable number of curiosities from the Andaman Islands. He had been one of the officers in charge of the convict guard there."

"Had he any friends in town?"

"Only one that we know of—Major Sholto, of his own regiment, the Thirty-fourth Bombay Infantry. The major had retired some little time before, and lived at Upper Norwood. We communicated with him, of course, but he did not even know that his brother officer was in England."

"A singular case," remarked Holmes.

"I have not yet described to you the most singular part. About six years ago—to be exact, upon the 4th of May, 1882—an advertisement appeared in the *Times* asking for the address of Miss Mary Morstan, and stating that it would be to her advantage to come forward. There was no name or address appended. I had at that time just entered the family of Mrs. Cecil Forrester in the capacity of governess. By her advice I published my address in the advertisement column. The same day there arrived through the post a small card box addressed to me, which I found to contain a very large and lustrous pearl. No word of writing was inclosed. Since then, every year upon the same date, there has always appeared a similar box, containing a similar pearl, without any clew as to the sender. They have been pronounced by an expert to be of a rare variety and of considerable value. You can see for yourselves that they are very handsome." She opened a flat box as she spoke, and showed me six of the finest pearls that I had ever seen.

"Your statement is most interesting," said Sherlock Holmes. "Has anything else occurred to you?"

"Yes; and no later than today. That is why I have come to you. This morning I received this letter, which you will perhaps read for yourself."

"Thank you," said Holmes. "The envelope, too. please. Postmark, London, S. W., date, July 7. Hum! Man's thumb-mark on corner—probably postman. Best quality paper. Envelopes at six-pence a packet. Particular man in his stationery. No address. 'Be at the third pillar from the left outside the Lyceum Theater to-night at seven o'clock. If you are distrustful, bring two friends. You are a wronged woman, and shall have justice. Do not bring police. If you do, all will be in vain. Your unknown friend.' Well, really, this is a very pretty little mystery. What do you intend to do, Miss Morstan?"

"That is exactly what I want to ask you."

"Then we shall most certainly go. You and I and— yes, why, Doctor Watson is the very man. Your correspondent says two friends. He and I have worked together before."

"But would he come?" she asked, with something appealing in her voice and expression.

"I should be proud and happy," said I, fervently, "if I can be of any service."

"You are both very kind," she answered. "I have led a retired life, and have no friends whom I could appeal to. If I am here at six it will do, I suppose?"

"You must not be later," said Holmes. "There is one other point, however. Is this handwriting the same as that upon the pearl box addresses?"

"I have them here," she answered, producing half a dozen pieces of paper.

"You are certainly a model client. You have the correct intuition. "Let us see, now." He spread out the papers upon the table and gave little darting glances from one to the other. "They are disguised hands, except the letter," he said, presently, "but there can be no doubt as to the authorship. See how the irrepressible Greek *e* will break out, and see the twill of the final *s*. They are undoubtedly by the same person. I should not like to suggest false hopes, Miss Morstan, but is there any resemblance between this hand and that of your father?"

"Nothing could be more unlike."

"I expected to hear you say so. We shall look out for you, then, at six. Pray allow me to keep the papers. I may look into the matter before them. It is only half-past three. Au revoir, then."

"Au revoir," said our visitor, and, with a bright, kindly glance from one to the other of us, she replaced her pearl-box in her bosom and hurried away. Standing at the window, I watched her walking briskly down the street, until the gray turban and white feather were but a speck in the somber crowd.

"What a very attractive woman!" I exclaimed, turning to my companion.

He had lighted his pipe again, and was leaning back

with drooping eyelids. "Is she?" he said, languidly. "I did not observe."

"You really are an automaton—a calculating machine !" I cried. "There is something positively inhuman in you at times."

He smiled gently. "It is of the first importance," he said, "not to allow your judgment to be biased by personal qualities. A client is to me a mere unit—a factor in a problem. The emotional qualities are antagonistic to clear reasoning. I assure you that the most winning woman I ever knew was hanged for poisoning three little children for their insurance money, and the most repellent man of my acquaintance is a philanthropist who has spent nearly a quarter of a million upon the London poor."

"In this case, however—"

"I never make exceptions. An exception disproves the rule. Have you ever had occasion to study character in handwriting? What do you make of this fellow's scribble?"

"It is legible and regular," I answered. "A man of business habits and some force of character."

Holmes shook his head. "Look at his long letters," he said. "They hardly rise above the common herd. That *d* might be an *a*, and that *l* an *e*. Men of character always differentiate their long letters, however illegibly they may write. There is vacillation in his *k*'s and self-esteem in his capitals. I am going out now. I have some few references to make. Let me recommend this book—one of the most remarkable ever penned. It is Winwood Reade's 'Martyrdom of Man.' I shall be back in an hour." I sat in the window with the volume in my hand, but my thoughts were far from the daring speculations of the writer. My mind ran upon our late visitor—her smiles, the deep rich tones of her voice, the strange mystery which overhung her life. If she were seventeen at the time of her father's disappearance, she must be seven-and-twenty now—a sweet age, when youth has lost its self-consciousness and become a little sobered by experience. So I sat and mused, until such dangerous thoughts came into my head that I hurried away to my desk and plunged furiously into the latest treatise upon pathology. What was I, an army surgeon with a weak leg and a weaker banking account, that I should dare to think of such things? She was a unit, a factor—nothing more. If my future were black, it was better surely to face it like a man than to attempt to brighten it by mere will-o'-the-wisps of the imagination

CHAPTER III

IN QUEST OF A SOLUTION

It was half-past five before Holmes returned. He was bright, eager, and in excellent spirits—a mood which in his case alternated his fits of the blackest depression.

"There is no great mystery in this matter," he said, taking the cup of tea which I had poured out for him. "The facts appear to admit of only one explanation."

"What! you have solved it already?"

"Well, that will be too much to say. I have discovered a suggestive fact, that is all. It is, however, very suggestive. The details are still to be added. I have just found, on consulting the back files of the *Times*, that Major Sholto, of Upper Norwood, late of the Thirty-fourth Bombay Infantry, died upon the 28th of April, 1882."

"I may be very obtuse, Holmes, but I fail to see what this suggests."

"No? You surprise me. Look at it in this way then. Captain Morstan disappears. The only person in London whom he could have visited is Major Sholto. Major

Sholto denies having heard that he was in London. Four years later Sholto dies. Within a week of his death, Captain Morstan's daughter receives a valuable present, which is repeated from year to year, and now culminates in a letter which describes her as a wronged woman. What wrong can it refer to except this deprivation of her father? And why should the presents begin immediately after Sholto's death, unless it is that Sholto's heir knows something of the mystery, and desires to make compensation? Have you any alternative theory which will meet the facts?"

"But what a strange compensation! And how strangely made! Why, too, should he write a letter now, rather than six years ago? Again, the letter speaks of giving her justice. What justice can she have? It is too much to suppose that her father is still alive. There is no other injustice in her case that you know of."

"There are difficulties; there are certain difficulties," said Sherlock Holmes, pensively. But our expedition of to-night will solve them all. Ah, here is a four-wheeler, and Miss Morstan is inside. Are you all ready? Then we had better go down, for it is a little past the hour."

I picked up my hat and my heaviest stick, but I observed that Holmes took his revolver from his drawer and slipped it into his pocket. It was clear that he thought our night's work might be a serious one.

Miss Morstan was muffled in a dark cloak, and her sensitive face was composed, but pale. She must have been more than woman if she did not feel some uneasiness at the strange enterprise upon which we were embarking, yet her self-control was perfect, and she readily answered the few additional questions which Sherlock Holmes put to her.

"Major Sholto was a very particular friend of papa's," she said. "His letters were full of allusions to the major. He and papa were in command of the troops at the

Andaman Islands, so they were thrown a great deal together. By the way, a curious paper was found in papa's desk which no one can understand. I don't suppose that it is of the slightest importance, but I thought you might care to see it, so I brought it with me. It is here."

Holmes unfolded the paper carefully and smoothed it out upon his knee. He then very methodically examined it all over with his double lens.

"It is paper of native Indian manufacture," he remarked. "It has at some time been pinned to a board. The diagram upon it appears to be a plan of part of a large building, with numerous halls, corridors and passages. At one point is a small cross done in red ink, and above it is '3.37 from left,' in faded pencil writing. In the left hand corner is a curious hieroglyphic, like four crosses in a line with their arms touching. Beside it is written, in very rough and coarse characters, 'The sign of the four—Jonathan Small, Mahomet Singh, Abdullah Khan, Dost Akbar.' No, I confess that I do not see how this bears upon the matter! Yet it is evidently a document of importance. It has been kept carefully in a pocketbook; for the one side is as clean as the other."

"It was in his pocketbook that we found it."

"Preserve it carefully, then, Miss Morstan, for it may prove to be of use to us. I begin to suspect that this matter may turn out to be much deeper and more subtle than I at first supposed. I must reconsider my ideas." He leaned back in the cab, and I could see by his drawn brow and his vacant eye that he was thinking intently. Miss Morstan and I chatted in an undertone about our present expedition and its possible outcome, but our companion maintained his impenetrable reserve until the end of our journey.

It was a September evening and not yet seven o'clock, but the day had been a dreary one, and a dense, drizzling fog lay low upon the great city. Mud-colored clouds drooped sadly over the muddy streets. Down the Strand the lamps were but misty splotches of diffused light which threw a feeble circular glimmer upon the slimy pavement. The yellow glare from the shop windows streamed out into the steamy, vaporous air, and threw a murky, shifting radiance across the crowded thoroughfare. There was to my mind something eerie and ghost-like in the endless procession of faces which flitted across these narrow bars of light—sad faces and glad, haggard and merry. Like all human kind, they flitted from the gloom into the light, and so back into the gloom once more. I am not subject to impressions, but the dull, heavy evening, with the strange business upon which we were engaged, combined to make me nervous and depressed. I could see from Miss Morstan's manner that she was suffering from the same feeling. Holmes alone could rise superior to petty influences. He held his open note book upon his knee, and from time to time he jotted down figures and memoranda in the light of his pocket lantern.

At the Lyceum Theater the crowds were already thick at the side entrances. In front, a continuous stream of hansoms and four-wheelers were rattling up, discharging their cargoes of shirt-fronted men and beshawled, bediamoned women. We had hardly reached the third pillar, which was our rendezvous, before a small, dark, brisk man, in the dress of a coachman, accosted us.

"Are you the parties who come with Miss Morstan?" he asked.

"I am Miss Morstan, and these two gentlemen are my friends," said she.

He bent a pair of wonderfully penetrating and questioning eyes upon us. "You will excuse me miss," he said, with a certain dogged manner, "but I was to ask you to give me your word that neither of your companions is a police officer."

"I give you my word on that," she answered.

He gave a shrill whistle, on which a street Arab led across a four-wheeler, and opened the door. The man who had addressed us mounted to the box, while we took our places inside. We had hardly done so before the driver whipped up his horse, and we plunged away at a furious pace through the foggy streets.

The situation was a curious one. We were driving to an unknown place, on an unknown errand. Yet our invitation was either a complete hoax, which was an inconceivable hypothesis, or else we had good reason to think that important issues might hang upon our journey. Miss Morstan's demeanor was as resolute and collected as ever. I endeavored to cheer and amuse her by reminiscences of my adventures in Afghanistan; but, to tell the truth, I was myself so excited at our situation and so curious as to our destination that my stories were slightly involved. To this day she declares that I told her one moving anecdote as to how a musket looked into my tent at the dead of night, and how I fired a double-barreled tiger cub at it. At first I had some idea as to the direction in which we were driving; but soon, what with our pace, the fog and my own limited knowledge of London, I lost my bearings and knew nothing, save that we seemed to be going a very long way. Sherlock Holmes was never at fault, however, and he muttered the names as the cab rattled through squares and in and out by tortuous by-streets.

"Rochester Row," said he. "Now Vincent Square. Now we came out on the Vauxhall Bridge Road. We are making for the Surrey side apparently. Yes, I thought so. Now we are on the bridge. You can catch glimpses of the river."

We did indeed get a fleeting view of a stretch of the Thames, with the lamps shining upon the broad, silent water; but our cab dashed on, and was soon involved in a labyrinth of streets upon the other side.

"Wordsworth Road," said my companion. "Priory Road. Lark Hall Lane. Stockwell Place. Robert Street. Cold Harbor Lane. Our quest does not appear to take us to very fashionable regions."

We had, indeed, reached a questionable and forbidding neighborhood. Long lines of dull brick houses were only relieved by the coarse glare and tawdry brilliancy of public houses at the corner. Then came rows of two-storied villas, each with a fronting of miniature garden, and then again interminable lines of new staring brick buildings—the monster tentacles which the giant city was throwing out into the country. At last the cab drew up at the third house in a new terrace. None of the other houses was inhabited, and that at which we stopped was as dark as its neighbors, save for a single glimmer in the kitchen window. On our knocking, however, the door was instantly thrown open by a Hindoo servant clad in a yellow turban, white, loose-fitting clothes and a yellow sash. There was something strangely incongruous in this oriental figure framed in the commonplace doorway of a third-rate suburban dwelling house.

"The sahib awaits you," said he, and even as he spoke there came a high piping voice from some inner room. "Show them in to me, khitmutgar," it cried. "Show them straight in to me."

CHAPTER IV

THE STORY OF THE BALD-HEADED MAN

WE followed the Indian down the sordid and common passage, ill lighted and worse furnished, until he came to a door upon the right, which he threw open. A blaze of yellow light streamed out upon us, and in the center of the glare there stood a small man with a very high head, a bristle of red hair all around the fringe of it, and a bald, shining scalp, which shot out from among it like a mountain-peak from fir trees. He rubbed his hands together as he stood, and his features were in a perpetual jerk, now smiling, now scowling, but never for an instant in repose. Nature had given him a pendulous lip, and a too visible line of yellow and irregular teeth, which he strove feebly to conceal by constantly passing his hand over the lower part of his face. In spite of his obtrusive baldness, he gave the impression of youth. In point of fact, he had just turned his thirtieth year.

"Your servant, Miss Morstan," he kept repeating in a thin, high voice. "Your servant, gentlemen. Pray step into my little sanctum. A small place, miss, but furnished to my own liking. An oasis of art in this howling desert of South London."

We were all astonished by the appearance of the apartment into which he invited us. In that sorry house it looked as out of place as a diamond of the first water in a setting of brass. The richest and glossiest of curtains and draperies draped the walls, looped back here and there to expose some richly mounted painted or oriental vase. The carpet was of amber and black, so soft and so thick that the foot sunk pleasantly into it, as into a bed of moss. Two great tiger skins thrown athwart it increased the suggestion of Eastern luxury, as did a huge hookah which stood upon a mat in the corner. A lamp in the fashion of a silver dove was hung from an almost invisible golden wire in the center of the room. As it burned, it filled the air with a subtle and aromatic odor.

"Mr. Thaddeus Sholto," said the little man, still jerking and smiling. "That is my name. You are Miss Morstan, of course. And these gentlemen——"

"This is Mr. Sherlock Holmes, and this Doctor Watson."

"A doctor, eh?" cried he, much excited. "Have you your stethoscope? Might I ask you—would you have the kindness? I have grave doubts as to my mitral valve, if you would be so very good. The aortic I may rely upon, but I should value your opinion upon the mitral."

I listened to his heart as requested, but was unable to find anything amiss, save indeed that he was in an ecstacy of fear, for he shivered from head to foot. "It appears to be normal," I said. "You have no cause for uneasiness."

"You will excuse my anxiety, Miss Morstan, he remarked, airily. "I am a great sufferer, and I have long had suspicions as to that valve. I am delighted to hear that they are unwarranted. Had your father, Miss Morstan, refrained from throwing a strain upon his heart, he might have been alive now."

I could have struck the man across the face, so hot was I at this callous and off-hand reference to so delicate a matter. Miss Morstan sat down, and her face grew white to the lips. "I knew in my heart that he was dead," said she.

"I can give you every information," said he, " and what is more, I can do you justice; and I will, too, whatever brother Bartholomew may say. I am so glad to have your friends here, not only as an escort to you, but also as witnesses to what I am about to do and say. The three of us can show a bold front to brother Bartholomew. But let us have no outsiders—no police or officials. We can settle everything satisfactory among ourselves, without any interference. Nothing would annoy brother Bartholomew more than any publicity." He sat down upon a low settee and blinked at us inquiringly with his weak, watery blue eyes.

"For my part," said Holmes, "whatever you may choose to say will go no further."

I nodded to show my agreement.

"That is well! That is well!" said he. "May I offer you a glass of Chianti, Miss Morstan? or of Tokay? I

keep no other wines. Shall I open a flask? No? Well,
then, I trust that you have no objection to tobacco smoke,
to the mild, balsamic odor of the Eastern tobacco. I am
a little nervous, and I find my hookah an invaluable sedative." He applied a taper to the great bowl, and the
smoke bubbled merrily through the rose water. We sat
all three in a semicircle, with our heads advanced, and
our chins upon our hands, while the strange, jerky little
fellow, with high, shining head, puffed uneasily in the
center.

"When I first determined to make this communication
to you," said he. "I might have given you my address,
but I feared that you might disregard my request and
bring unpleasant people with you. I took the liberty,
therefore, of making an appointment in such a way that
my man Williams might be able to see you first. I have
complete confidence in his discretion, and he had orders,
if he were dissatisfied, to proceed no further in the matter. You will excuse these precautions, but I am a man
of somewhat retiring, and, I might even say, refined
tastes, and there is nothing more unæsthetic than a policeman. I have a natural shrinking from all forms of rough
materialism. I seldom come in contact with the rough
crowd. I live, as you see, with some little atmosphere of
elegance around me. I may call myself a patron of the
arts. It is my weakness. The landscape is a genuine
Corot, and, though a connoisseur might perhaps throw a
doubt upon that Salvator Rosa, there cannot be the least
question about the Bouguereau. I am partial to the
modern French school."

"You will excuse me, Mr. Sholto," said Miss Morstan,
"but I am here at your request to learn something which
you desire to tell me. It is very late, and I should desire
the interview to be as short as possible."

"At the best it must take some time," he answered;
"for we shall certainly have to go to Norwood and see

brother Bartholomew. We shall all go and try if we can get the better of brother Bartholomew. He is very angry with me for taking the course which has seemed right to me. I had quite high words with him last night. You cannot imagine what a terrible fellow he is when he is angry."

"If we are to go to Norwood it would perhaps be as well to start at once," I ventured to remark.

He laughed until his ears were quite red. "That would hardly do," he cried. "I don't know what he would say if I brought you in that sudden way. No; I must prepare you by showing you how we all stand to each other. In the first place, I must tell you that there are several points in the story of which I am myself ignorant. I can only lay the facts before you as far as I know them myself."

"My father was, as you may have guessed, Major John Sholto, once of the Indian army. He retired some eleven years ago, and came to live at Pondicherry Lodge in Upper Norwood. He had prospered in India, and brought back with him a considerable sum of money, a large collection of valuable curiosities, and a staff of native servants. With these advantages, he bought himself a house, and lived in great luxury. My twin brother Bartholomew and I were the only children.

"I very well remember the sensation which was caused by the disappearance of Captain Morstan. We read the details in the papers and, knowing that he had been a friend of our father's, we discussed the case freely in his presence. He used to join in our speculations as to what could have happened. Never for an instant did we suspect that he had the whole secret hidden in his own breast —that of all men he alone knew the fate of Arthur Morstan.

"We did know, however, that some mystery—some positive danger—overhung our father. He was very fearful of going out alone, and he always employed two prize fighters to act as porters at Pondicherry Lodge. Williams, who drove you tonight, was one of them. He was once a lightweight champion of England. Our father would never tell us what it was he feared, but he had a most marked aversion to men with wooden legs. On one occasion he actually fired his revolver at a wooden legged man, who proved to be a harmless tradesman canvassing for orders. We had to pay a large sum to hush the matter up. My brother and I used to think this a mere whim of father's, but events have since led us to change our opinion.

"Early in 1882, my father received a letter from India which was a great shock to him. He nearly fainted at the breakfast table when he opened it, and from that day he sickened to his death. What was in the letter we could never discover, but I could see as he held it that it was short and written in a scrawling hand. He had suffered for years from an enlarged spleen, but he now bcame rapidly worse, and toward the end of April we were informed that he was beyond all hope, and that he wished to make a last communication to us.

"When we entered his room he was propped up with pillows and breathing heavily. He besought us to lock the door and to come upon either side of the bed. Then, grasping our hands, he made a remarkable statement to us, in a voice which was broken as much by emotion as by pain. I shall try and give it to you in his own very words.

"'I have only one thing,' he said, 'which weighs upon my mind at this supreme moment. It is my treatment of poor Morstan's orphan. The cursed greed which has been my besetting sin through life has withheld from her the treasure, half at least of which should have been hers. And yet I have made no use of it myself—so blind and foolish a thing is avarice. The mere feeling of possession has been so dear to me that I could not bear to share it with another. See that chaplet tipped with pearls beside the quinine bottle? Even that I could not bear to part with, although I had got it out with the design of sending it to her. You, my sons, will give her a fair share of the Agra treasure. But send her nothing—not even the chaplet—until I am gone. After all, men have been as bad as this and have recovered.

"'I will tell you how Morstan died,' he continued. 'He had suffered for years from a weak heart, but he concealed it from every one. I alone knew it. When in India, he and I, through a remarkable chain of circumstances, came into possession of a considerable treasure. I brought it over to England, and on the night of Morstan's arrival he came straight over here to claim his share. He walked over from the station, and was admitted by my faithful old Lal Chowdar, who is now dead. Morstan and I had a difference of opinion as to the division of the treasure, and we came to heated words. Morstan had sprung out of his chair in a paroxysm of anger, when he suddenly pressed his hand to his side, his face turned a dusky hue, and he fell backward, cutting his head against the corner of the treasure chest. When I stooped over him I found, to my horror, that he was dead.

"'For a long time I sat half distracted, wondering what I should do. My first impulse was, of course, to call for assistance; but I could not but recognize that there was every chance that I would be accused of his murder. His death at the moment of a quarrel, and the gash in his head, would be black against me. Again, an official inquiry could not be made without bringing out some facts about the treasure, which I was particularly anxious to keep secret. He had told me that no soul upon earth knew where he had gone. There seemed to be no necessity why any soul ever should know.

" 'I was still pondering over the matter, when, looking up, I saw my servant, Lal Chowder, in the doorway. He stole in, and bolted the door behind him. "Do not fear, sahib," he said. "No one need know that you have killed him. Let us hide him away, and who is the wiser?" "I did not kill him," said I. Lal Chowdar shook his head, and smiled, "I heard it all, sahib," said he. "I heard you quarrel, and I heard the blow. But my lips are sealed. All are asleep in the house. Let us put him away together." That was enough to decide me. If my own servant could not believe my innocence, how could I hope to make it good before twelve foolish tradesmen in a jury box? Lal Chowdar and I disposed of the body that night, and within a few days the London papers were full of the mysterious disappearance of Captain Morstan. You will see from what I say that I can hardly be blamed in the matter. My fault lies in the fact that we concealed, not only the body, but also the treasure, and that I have clung to Morstan's share as well as to my own. I wish you, therefore, to make restitution. Put your ears down to my mouth. The treasure is hidden in—' at this instant a horrible change came over his expression; his eyes stared wildly, his jaws dropped, and he yelled, in a voice which I can never forget, 'Keep him out! For Christ's sake, keep him out!' We both stared round at the window behind us upon which his gaze was fixed. A face was looking in at us out of the darkness. We could see the whitening of the nose where it was pressed against the glass. It was a bearded, hairy face, with wild, cruel eyes and an expression of concentrated malevolence. My brother and I rushed toward the window, but the man was gone. When we returned to my father, his head had dropped and his pulse had ceased to beat.

"We searched the garden that night, but found no sign of the intruder, save that just under the window a single footmark was visible in the flower bed. But for that one trace, we might have thought that our imaginations had conjured up that wild, fierce face. We soon, however, had another and a more striking proof that there were secret agencies at work all around us. The window of my father's room was found open in the morning, his cupboards and boxes had been rifled, and upon his chest was fixed a torn piece of paper with the words, 'The sign of the four' scrawled across it. What the phrase meant, or who our secret visitor may have been, we never knew. As far as we can judge, none of my father's property had been actually stolen, though everything had been turned out. My brother and I naturally associated this peculiar incident with the fear which haunted my father during his life; but it is still a complete mystery to us."

The little man stopped to relight his hookah, and puffed thoughtfully for a few moments. We had all sat absorbed, listening to his extraordinary narrative. At the short account of her father's death, Miss Morstan had turned deathly white, and for a moment I feared that she was about to faint. She rallied, however, on drinking a glass of water which I quietly poured out for her from a Venetian carafe upon the side table. Sherlock Holmes leaned back in his chair with an abstracted expression and the lids drawn over his glittering eyes. As I glanced at him I could not but think how, on that very day, he had complained bitterly of the commonplaceness of life. Here, at least, was a problem which would tax his sagacity to the utmost. Mr. Thaddeus Sholto looked from one to the other of us with an obvious pride at the effect which his story had produced, and then continued between the puffs of his overgrown pipe:

"My brother and I," said he, "were, as you may imagine, much excited as to the treasure which my father had spoken of. For weeks and for months we dug and delved in every part of the garden, without discovering its whereabouts. It was maddening to think that the hiding place was on his very lips at the moment that he died. We could judge the splendor of the missing riches by the chaplet which he had taken out. Over this chaplet my brother Bartholomew and I had some little discussion. The pearls were evidently of great value, and he was averse to part with them, for, between friends, my brother was himself a little inclined to my father's fault. He thought, too, that if we parted with the chaplet it might give rise to gossip, and finally bring us into trouble. It was all that I could do to persuade him to let me find out Miss Morstan's address and send her a detached pearl at fixed intervals, so that, at least, she might never feel destitute."

"It was a kindly thought," said our companion, earnestly. "It was extremely good of you."

The little man waved his hand deprecatingly. "We were your trustees," he said. "That was the view which I took of it, though brother Bartholomew could not altogether see it in that light. We had plenty of money ourselves. I desired no more. Besides, it would have been such bad taste to have treated a young lady in so scurvy a fashion. 'Le mauvais gout mene au crime.' The French have a very neat way of putting these things. Our difference of opinion on this subject went so far that I thought it best to set up rooms for myself; so I left Pondicherry Lodge, taking the old knit-mutgar and Williams with me. Yesterday, however, I learned that an event of extreme importance had occurred. The treasure has been discovered. I instantly communicated with Miss Morstan, and it only remains for us to drive out to Norwood and demand our share. I explained my views last night to brother Bartholomew; so we shall be expected, if not welcome visitors."

Mr. Thaddeus Sholto ceased, and sat twitching on his luxurious settee. We all remained silent, with our thoughts upon the new development which the mysterious business had taken. Holmes was the first to spring to his feet.

"You have done well, sir, from first to last," said he. "It is possible that we may be able to make you some small return by throwing some light upon that which is still dark to you. But, as Miss Morstan remarked just now, it is fate, and we had best put the matter through without delay."

Our new acquaintance very deliberately coiled up the tube of his hookah, and produced from behind a curtain a very long befrogged top coat with astrakhan collar and cuffs. This he buttoned tightly up, in spite of the extreme closeness of the night, and finished his attire by putting on a rabbit skin cap with hanging lappets which covered the ears, so that no part of him was visible save his mobile and peaky face. "My health is somewhat fragile," he remarked, as he led the way down the passage. "I am compelled to be a valetudinarian."

Our cab was awaiting us outside, and our program was evidently prearranged, for the driver started off at once at a rapid pace. Thaddeus Sholto talked incessantly, in a voice which rose high above the rattle of the wheels.

"Bartholomew is a clever fellow," said he. "How do you think he found out where the treasure was? He had come to the conclusion that it was somewhere indoors; so he worked out all the cubic space of the house, and made measurements everywhere, so that not one inch should be unaccounted for. Among other things, he found that the height of the building was seventy-four feet, but on adding together the heights of all the separate rooms, and making every allowance for the space between, which he ascertained by borings, he could only bring the total to more than seventy feet. There were four feet unaccounted for. These could not be at the top of the building. He knocked a hole, therefore, in the lath and plaster ceiling of the highest room, and there, sure enough, he came upon another little garret above it, which had been sealed up and was known to no one. In the center stood the treasure chest, resting upon two rafters. He lowered it through the hole, and there it lies. He computes the value of the jewels at not less than half a million sterling."

At the mention of this gigantic sum we all stared at one another open-eyed. Miss Morstan, could we secure her rights, would change from a needy governess to the richest heiress in England. Surely it was the place of a loyal friend to rejoice at such news; yet I am ashamed to say that selfishness took me by the soul, and that my heart turned as heavy as lead within me. I stammered out some few halting words of congratulation, and then sat down-cast, with my head drooped, deaf to the babble of our new acquaintance. He was clearly a confirmed hypochon-driac, and I was dreamily conscious that he was pour-ing forth interminable trains of symptoms, and imploring information as to the composition and action of in-numerable quack nostrums, some of which he bore about in a leather case in his pocket. I trust that he may not remember any of the answers which I gave him that night. Holmes declares that he overheard me caution him against the great danger of taking more than two drops of castor oil, while I recommended strychnine in larger doses as a sedative. However that may be, I was cer-tainly relieved when our cab pulled up with a jerk and the coachman sprang down to open the door.

"This, Miss Morstan, is Pondicherry Lodge," said Mr. Thaddeus Sholto, as he handed her out.

CHAPTER V

THE TRAGEDY OF PONDICHERRY LODGE

It was nearly eleven o'clock when we reached this final stage of our night's adventures. We had left the damp fog of the great city behind us, and the night was fairly fine. A warm wind blew from the westward, and heavy clouds moved slowly across the sky, with half a moon peeping occasionally through the rifts. It was clear enough to see for some distance, but Thaddeus Sholto took down one of the side lamps from the carriage to give us a better light upon our way.

Pondicherry Lodge stood in its own grounds, and was girt round with a very high stone wall topped with broken glass. A single narrow, iron-clamped door formed the only means of entrance. On this our guide knocked with a peculiar postman-like rat-tat.

"Who is there?" cried a gruff voice from within.

"It is I, McMurdo. You surely know my knock by this time."

There was a grumbling sound, and a clanking and jarring of keys. The door swung heavily back, and a short, deep-chested man stood in the opening, with the yellow light of the lantern shining upon his protruded face and twinkling, distrustful eyes.

"That you, Mr. Thaddeus? But who are the others? I had no orders about them from the master."

"No, McMurdo? You surprise me! I told my brother last night that I should bring some friends."

"He hain't been out o' his room today, Mr. Thaddeus.

and I have no orders. You know very well that I must stick to regulations. I can let you in; but your friends they must just stop where they are."

This was an unexpected obstacle. Thaddeus Sholto looked about him in a perplexed and helpless manner. "This is too bad of you, McMurdo!" he said. "If I guarantee them, that is enough for you. There is a young lady, too. She cannot wait on the public road at this hour."

"Very sorry, Mr. Thaddeus," said the porter, inexorably. "Folk may be friends o' yours, and yet no friends o' the master's. He pays me well to do my duty, and my duty I'll do. I don't know none o' your friends."

"Oh, yes, you do, McMurdo," cried Sherlock Holmes, genially. "I don't think you can have forgotten me. Don't you remember the amateur who fought three rounds with you at Alison's rooms on the night of your benefit four years back?"

"Not Mr. Sherlock Holmes?" roared the prize fighter. "God's truth! how could I have mistook you. If, instead o' standin' there so quiet, you had just stepped up and given me that cross-hit of yours under the jaw, I'd ha' known you without a question. Ah, you're one that has wasted his gifts, you have. You might have aimed high, if you had joined the fancy."

"You see, Watson, if all else fails me I have still one of the scientific professions open to me," said Holmes, laughing. "Our friend won't keep us out in the cold now, I am sure."

"In you come, sir; in you come—you and your friends," he answered. "Very sorry, Mr. Thaddeus, but orders are very strict. Had to be certain of your friends before I let them in."

Inside a gravel path wound through desolate grounds to a huge clump of a house, square and prosaic, all plunged in shadow save where a moonbeam struck one corner and glimmered in a garret window. The vast size of the building, with its gloom and its deathly silence, struck a chill to the heart. Even Thaddeus Sholto seemed ill at ease, and the lantern quivered and rattled in his hand.

"I cannot understand it," he said. "There must be some mistake. I distinctly told Batholomew that we should be here, and yet there is no light in his window. I do not know what to make of it."

"Does he always guard the premises in this way?" asked Holmes.

"Yes; he has followed my father's custom. He was the favorite son, you know, and I sometimes think that my father may have told him more than he ever told me. That is Bartholomew's window up there where the moonshine strikes. It is quite bright, but there is no light from within, I think."

"None," said Holmes. "But I see the glint of a light in that little window beside the door."

"Ah, that is the housekeeper's room. That is where old Mrs. Bernstone sits. She can tell us all about it. But perhaps you would not mind waiting here for a minute or two, for if we all go in together, and she has no word of our coming, she may be alarmed. But hush! what is that?"

He held up the lantern, and his hand shook until the circles of light flickered and wavered all around us. Miss Morstan seized my wrist, and we all stood with thumping hearts, straining our ears. From the great black house there sounded through the silent night the saddest and most pitiful of sounds—the shrill, broken whimpering of a frightened woman.

"It is Mrs. Bernstone," said Sholto. "She is the only woman in the house. Wait here. I shall be back in a moment." He hurried for the door, and knocked in his peculiar way. We could see a tall old woman admit him and sway with pleasure at the very sight of him.

"Oh, Mr. Thaddeus, sir, I am so glad you have come! I am so glad you have come, Mr. Thaddeus, sir!" We heard her reiterated rejoicings until the door was closed and her voice died away into a muffled monotone.

Our guide had left us with the lantern. Holmes swung it slowly round, and peered keenly at the house and at the great rubbish heaps which cumbered the grounds. Miss Morstan and I stood together, and her hand was in mine. A wondrous subtle thing is love, for here were we two who had never seen each other before that day, between whom no word or even look of affection had ever passed, and yet now in an hour of trouble our hands instinctively sought for each other. I have marveled at it since, but at the time it seemed the most natural thing that I should go out to her so, and, as she has often told me, there was in her also the instinct to turn to me for comfort and protection. So we stood hand in hand, like two children, and there was peace in our hearts for all the dark things that surrounded us.

"What a strange place!" she said, looking round.

"It looks as though all the moles in England had been let loose in it. I have seen something of the sort on the side of a hill near Ballarat, where the prospectors had been at work."

"And for the same cause," said Holmes. "These are the traces of the treasure seekers. You must remember that they were six years looking for it. No wonder that the grounds look like a gravel pit."

At that moment the door of the house burst open, and Thaddeus Sholto came running out, with his hands thrown forward and terror in his eyes.

"There is something amiss with Bartholomew!" he cried. "I am frightened! My nerves cannot stand it." He was, indeed, half blubbering with fear and his twitching, feeble face, peeping out from the great astrakhan collar, had the helpless, appealing expression of a terrified child.

"Come into the house," said Holmes, in his crisp, firm way.

"Yes, do!" pleaded Thaddeus Sholto. "I really do not feel equal to giving directions."

We all followed him into the housekeeper's room, which stood upon the left hand side of the passage. The old woman was pacing up and down with a scared look and restless, picking fingers, but the sight of Miss Morstan appeared to have a soothing effect upon her.

"God bless your sweet, calm face!" she cried, with a hysterical sob. "It does me good to see you. Oh, but I have been sorely tried this day!"

Our companion patted her thin, work-worn hand, and murmured some few words of kindly, womanly comfort which brought the color back into the other's bloodless cheeks.

"Master has locked himself in and will not answer me," she explained. "All day I have waited to hear from him, for he often likes to be alone; but an hour ago I feared that something was amiss, so I went up and peeped through the keyhole. You must go up, Mr. Thaddeus— you must go up and look for yourself. I have seen Mr. Bartholomew Sholto in joy and in sorrow for ten long years, but I never saw him with such a face on him as that."

Sherlock Holmes took the lamp and led the way, for Thaddeus Sholto's teeth were chattering in his head. So shaken was he that I had to pass my hand under his arm as we went up the stairs, for his knees were trembling under him. Twice as we ascended Holmes whipped his lens out of his pocket and carefully examined marks which appeared to me to be mere shapeless smudges of dust upon the cocoanut matting which served as a stair carpet. He walked slowly from step to step, holding the lamp low, and shooting keen glances to right and left.

Miss Morstan had remained behind with the frightened housekeeper.

The third flight of stairs ended in a straight passage of some length, with a great picture in Indian tapestry upon the right of it and three doors upon the left. Holmes advanced along it in the same slow and methodical way, while we kept close at his heels, with our long black shadows streaming backward down the corridor. The third door was that which we were seeking. Holmes knocked without receiving any answer, and then tried to turn the handle and force it open. It was locked on the inside, however, and by a broad and powerful bolt, as we could see when we set our lamp up against it. The key being turned, however, the hole was not entirely closed. Sherlock Holmes bent down to it, and instantly rose again with a sharp intaking of the breath.

"There is something devilish in this, Watson," said he, more moved than I had ever before seen him. "What do you make of it?"

I stooped to the hole, and recoiled in horror. Moonlight was streaming into the room, and it was bright with a vague and shifty radiance. Looking straight at me, and suspended, as it were, in the air, for all beneath was in shadow, there hung a face—the very face of our companion Thaddeus. There was the same high, shining head, the same circular bristle of red hair, the same bloodless countenance. The features were set, however, in a horrible smile, a fixed and unnatural grin, which, in that still and moonlit room, was more jarring to the nerves than any scowl or contortion. So like was the face to that of our little friend that I looked round at him to make sure that he was indeed with us. Then I recalled to mind that he mentioned to us that his brother and he were twins.

"This is terrible!" I said to Holmes. "What is to be done?"

"The door must come down," he answered, and, springing against it, he put all the weight upon the lock. It creaked and groaned, but did not yield. Together we flung ourselves upon it once more, and this time it gave way with a sudden snap, and we found ourselves within Bartholomew Sholto's chamber.

It appeared to have been fitted up as a chemical laboratory. A double line of glass-stoppered bottles was drawn up upon the wall opposite the door, and the table was littered over with Bunsen burners, test tubes, and retorts. In the corners stood carboys of acid in wicker baskets. One of these appeared to leak or to have been broken, for a stream of dark-colored liquid had trickled out from it, and the air was heavy with a peculiarly pungent, tar-like odor. A set of steps stood at one side of the room, in the midst of a litter of lath and plaster, and above them was an opening in the ceiling large enough for a man to pass through. At the foot of the steps a long coil of rope was thrown carelessly together.

By the table, in a wooden armchair, the master of the house was seated all in a heap, with his head sunk upon his left shoulder, and that ghastly, inscrutable smile upon his face. He was stiff and cold, and had clearly been dead many hours. It seemed to me that not only his features but all his limbs were twisted and turned in the most fantastic fashion. By his hand upon the table there lay a peculiar instrument—a brown, close-grained stick, with a stone head like a hammer, rudely lashed on with coarse twine. Beside it was a torn sheet of note paper with some words scrawled upon it. Holmes glanced at it, and then handed it to me.

"You see," he said, with a significant raising of the eyebrows.

In the light of the lantern I read, with a thrill of horror, "The sign of the four."

"In God's name, what does it all mean?"

"It means murder," said he, stooping over the dead man. "Ah, I expected it. Look here!" He pointed to what looked like a long, dark thorn stuck in the skin just above the ear.

"It looks like a thorn," said I.

"It is a thorn. You may pick it out. But be careful, for it is poisoned."

I took it up between my finger and thumb. It came away from the skin so readily that hardly any mark was left behind. One tiny speck of blood showed where the puncture had been.

"This is all an insoluble mystery to me," said I. "It grows darker instead of clearer."

"On the contrary," he answered, "it clears every instant. I only require a few missing links to have an entirely connected case."

We had almost forgotten our companion's presence since we entered the chamber. He was still standing in the doorway, the very picture of terror, wringing his hands and moaning to himself. Suddenly, however, he broke out into a sharp, querulous cry.

"The treasure is gone!" he said. "They have robbed him of the treasure! There is the hole through which we lowered it. I helped him to do it! I was the last person who saw him! I left him here last night and I heard him lock the door as I came downstairs."

"What time was that?"

"It was ten o'clock. And now he is dead, and the police will be called in, and I shall be suspected of having had a hand in it. Oh, yes, I am sure I shall. But you don't think so, gentlemen? Surely you don't think that it was I? Is it likely that I would have brought you here if it were I? Oh, dear! oh, dear! I know that I shall go mad!" He jerked his arms and stamped his feet in a kind of convulsive frenzy.

"You have no reason to fear, Mr. Sholto," said Holmes, kindly, putting his hand upon his shoulder. "Take my advice, and drive down to the station and report the matter to the police. Offer to assist them in every way. We shall wait here until your return."

The little man obeyed in a half-stupefied fashion, and we heard him stumbling down the stairs in the dark.

CHAPTER VI

SHERLOCK HOLMES GIVES A DEMONSTRATION

"Now, Watson," said Holmes, rubbing his hands, "we have half an hour to ourselves. Let us make good use of it. My case is, as I have told you, almost complete; but we must not err on the side of over-confidence. Simple as the case seems now, there may be something deeper underlying it."

"Simple!" I ejaculated.

"Surely," said he, with something of the air of a clinical professor expounding to his class. "Just sit in the corner there, that your foot prints may not complicate matters. Now to work! In the first place, how did these folks come, and how did they go? The door has not been opened since last night. How of the window?" He carried the lamp across to it, muttering his observations aloud the while, but addressing them to himself rather than to me. "Window is snibbed on the inner side. Framework is solid. No hinges at the side. Let us open it. No water pipe near it. Roof quite out of reach. Yet a man has mounted by the window. It rained a little last night. Here is the print of a foot in mold upon the sill. And here is a circular muddy mark, and here again upon the floor, and here again by the table. See here, Watson! This is really a very pretty demonstration.

I looked at the round, well-defined, muddy disks. "This is not a foot mark," said I.

"It is something much more valuable to us. It is the impression of a wooden stump. You see here on the sill is the boot mark, a heavy boot with a broad metal heel, and beside it is the mark of the timber toe."

"It is the wooden-legged man."

"Quite so. But there has been some one else—a very able and efficient ally. Could you scale that wall, doctor?"

I looked out of the open window. The moon still shone brightly on that angle of the house. We were a good sixty feet from the ground, and, look where I would, I could see no foothold, nor as much as a crevice in the brick work.

"It is absolutely impossible," I answered.

"Without aid it is so. But suppose you had a friend up here who lowered you this good stout rope which I see in the corner, securing one end of it to this great hook in the wall. Then, I think, if you were an active man you might climb up, wooden leg and all. You would depart, of course, in the same fashion, and your ally would draw up the rope, untie it from the hook, shut the window, snib it on the inside, and get away in the way that he originally came. As a minor point it may be noted," he continued, fingering the rope, "that our wooden-legged friend, though a fair climber, was not a professional sailor. His hands were far from horny. My lens discloses more than one blood mark, especially toward the end of the rope, from which I gather that he slipped down with such velocity that he took the skin off his hands."

"This is all very well," said I, "but the thing becomes more unintelligible than ever. How about this mysterious ally? How came he into the room?"

"Yes, the ally!" repeated Holmes, pensively. "There are features about this ally. He lifts the case from the regions of the commonplace. I fancy that this ally breaks

fresh ground in the annals of crime in this country—
though parallel cases suggest themselves from India, and,
if my memory serves me, from Senegambia."

"How came he, then?" I reiterated. "The door is
locked, the window is inaccessible. Was it through the
chimney?"

"The grate is much too small," he answered. "I have
already considered that possibility."

"How then?" I persisted.

"You will not apply my precept," he said, shaking his
head. "How often have I said to you that when you
have eliminated the impossible, whatever remains, however improbable, must be the truth? We know that he
did not come through the door, the window or the chimney. We also know that he could not have been concealed in the room, as there is no concealment possible.
Whence, then, did he come?"

"He came through the hole in the roof," I cried.

"Of course he did. He must have done so. If you
will have the kindness to hold the lamp for me, we shall
now extend our researches to the room above—the secret
room in which the treasure was found."

He mounted the steps, and seizing a rafter with either
hand, he swung himself up into the garret. Then, lying
on his face, he reached down for the lamp and held it
while I followed him.

The chamber in which we found ourselves was about
ten feet one way and six the other. The floor was formed
by the rafters, with thin lath and plaster between them,
so that in walking one had to step from beam to beam.
The roof ran up to an apex, and was evidently the inner
shell of the true roof of the house. There was no furniture of any sort, and the accumulated dust of years lay
thick upon the floor.

"Here you are, you see," said Sherlock Holmes, putting
his hand against the sloping wall. "This is a trap door

which leads out on to the roof. I can press it back, and here is the roof itself, sloping at a gentle angle. This, then, is where Number One entered. Let us see if we can find some other traces of his individuality."

He held down the lamp to the floor, and as he did so I saw for the second time that night a startled, surprised look come over his face. For myself, as I followed his gaze, my skin was cold under my clothes. The wall was covered thickly with the prints of a naked foot—clear, well defined, perfectly formed, but scarce half the size of those of an ordinary man.

"Holmes," I said, in a whisper, "a child has done this horrid thing."

He had recovered his self-possession in an instant. "I was staggered for the moment," he said, "but the thing is quite natural. My memory failed me, or I should have been able to foretell it. There is nothing more to be learned here. Let us go down."

"What is your theory, then, as to those foot marks?" I asked, eagerly, when we had regained the lower room once more.

"My dear Watson, try a little analysis yourself," said he, with a touch of impatience. "You know my methods. Apply them; and it will be instructive to compare results."

"I cannot conceive anything which will cover the facts," I answered.

"It will be clear enough to you soon," he said, in an off-hand way. "I think that there is nothing else of importance here, but I will look." He whipped out his lens and a tape measure, and comparing, examining, with his long thin nose only a few inches from the planks, and his beady eyes gleaming and deep set like those of a bird. So swift, silent and furtive were his movements, like those of a trained bloodhound picking out a scent, that I could not but think what a terrible criminal he would have made had he turned his energy and sagacity against the law instead of exerting them in its defense. As he hunted about, he kept muttering to himself, and finally he broke into a loud crow of delight.

"We are certainly in luck," said he. "We ought to have very little trouble now. Number One has had the misfortune to tread in the creosote. You can see the outline of the edge of his small foot here at the right of this evil-smelling mess. The carboy has been cracked, you see, and the stuff has leaked out."

"What then?" I asked.

"Why, we have got him, that's all," said he. "I know a dog that would follow that scent to the world's end. If a pack can track a trailed herring across a shire, how far can a specially trained hound follow so pungent a smell as this? It sounds like a sum in the rule of three. The answer should give us the— But halloo! here are the accredited representatives of the law."

Heavy steps and the clamor of loud voices were audible from below, and the hall door shut with a loud crash.

"Before they come," said Holmes, "just put your hand here on this poor fellow's arm, and here on his leg. What do you feel?"

"The muscles are as hard as a board," I answered.

"Quite so. They are in a state of extreme contraction, far exceeding the usual 'rigor mortis.' Coupled with this distortion of the face, this Hippocratic smile, or 'risus sardonicus,' as the old writers called it, what conclusion would it suggest to your mind?"

"Death from some powerful vegetable alkaloid," I answered; "some strychnine-like substance which would produce tetanus."

"That was the idea which occurred to me the instant I saw the drawn muscles of the face. On getting into the room I at once looked for the means by which the poison had entered the system. As you saw, I discovered a thorn which had been driven or shot with no great force into the scalp. You observe that the part struck was that which would be turned toward the hole in the ceiling if the man were erect in his chair. Now examine this thorn."

I took it up gingerly and held it in the light of the lantern. It was long, sharp, and black, with a glazed look near the point as though some gummy substance had dried upon it. The blunt end had been trimmed and rounded off with a knife.

"Is that an English thorn?"

"No, it certainly is not."

"With all these data you should be able to draw some just inference. But here are the regulars; so the auxiliary forces may beat a retreat."

As he spoke, the steps which had been coming nearer sounded loudly on the passage, and a very stout, portly man in a gray suit strode heavily into the room. He was red-faced, burly and plethoric, with a pair of very small twinkling eyes which looked keenly out from between swollen and puffy pouches. He was closely followed by an inspector in uniform, and by the still palpitating Thaddeus Sholto.

"Here's a business!" he cried, in a muffled, husky voice. "Here's a pretty business! But who are all these? Why, the house seems to be as full as a rabbit warren."

"I think you must recollect me, Mr. Athelney Jones," said Holmes quietly.

"Why, of course I do!" he wheezed. "It's Mr. Sherlock Holmes, the theorist. Remember you? I'll never forget how you lectured us all on causes, and inferences, and effects in the Bishopgate jewel case. It's true you set us on the right track, but you'll own now that it was more by good luck than good guidance."

"It was a piece of very simple reasoning."

"Oh, come, now, come! Never be ashamed to own

up. But what is all this? Bad business! Bad business! Stern facts here—no room for theories. How lucky I happened to be out at Norwood over another case! I was at the station when the message arrived. What d'you think the man died of."

"Oh, this is hardly a case for me to theorize over," said Holmes, dryly.

"No, no. Still, we can't deny that you hit the nail on the head sometimes. Dear me! Door locked, I understand. Jewels worth half a million missing. How was the window?"

"Fastened; but there are steps on the sill."

"Well, well; if it was fastened, the steps could have nothing to do with the matter. That's common sense. Man might have died in a fit; but then the jewels are missing. Ha! I have a theory. These flashes come upon me at times. Just step outside, sergeant, and you, Mr. Sholto. Your friend can remain. What do you think of this, Holmes? Sholto was, on his own confession, with his brother last night. The brother died in a fit, on which Sholto walked off with the treasure. How's that?"

"On which the dead man very considerately got up and locked the door on the inside."

"Hum! There's a flaw there. Let us apply common sense to the matter. This Thaddeus Sholto was with his brother; there was a quarrel; so much we know. The brother is dead and the jewels are gone. So much also we know. No one saw the brother from the time Thaddeus left him. His bed had not been slept in. Thaddeus is evidently in a most disturbed state of mind. His appearance is—well, not attractive. You see that I am weaving my web round Thaddeus. The net begins to close upon him."

"You are not quite in possession of the facts yet," said Holmes. "This splinter of wood, which I have every reason to believe to be poisond, was in the man's scalp where you still see the mark; this card, inscribed as you see it, was on the table; and beside it lay this rather curious stone-headed instrument. How does all this fit into your theory?"

"Confirms it in every respect," said the fat detective, pompously. "House is full of Indian curiosities. Thaddeus brought this up, and if this splinter be poisonous Thaddeus may as well have made murderous use of it as any other man. The card is some hocus-pocus—a blind, like as not. The only question is, How did he depart? Ah, of course, here is a hole in the roof." With great activity, considering his bulk, he sprung up the steps and squeezed through into the garret, and immediately afterward we heard his exulting voice proclaiming that he had found the trap door.

"He can find something," remarked Holmes, shrugging his shoulders. "He has occasional glimmerings of reason. I'l n'y a pas des sots si incommodes que ceux qui ont de l'esprit!"

"You see!" said Athelney Jones, reappearing down the steps again. "Facts are better than mere theories, after all. My view of the case is confirmed. There is a trap door communicating with the roof, and it is partly open."

"It was I who opened it."

"Oh, indeed! You did notice it, then?" He seemed a little crestfallen at the discovery. "Well, whoever noticed it, it shows how our gentleman got away. Inspector!"

"Yes, sir," from the passage.

"Ask Mr. Sholto, to step this way. Mr. Sholto, it is my duty to inform you that anything which you may say will be used against you. I arrest you in the queen's name as being concerned in the death of your brother."

"There, now! Didn't I tell you?" cried the poor little man, throwing out his hands, and looking from one to the other of us.

"Don't trouble yourself about it, Mr. Sholto," said

Holmes. "I think that I can engage to clear you of the charge."

"Don't promise too much, Mr. Theorist—don't promise too much!" snapped the detective. "You may find it a harder matter than you think."

"Not only will I clear him, Mr. Jones, but I will make you a free present of the name and description of one of the two people who were in the room last night. His name, I have every reason to believe, is Jonathan Small. He is a poorly educated man; small, active, with his right leg off, and wearing a wooden stump which is worn away upon the inner side. His left boot has a coarse, square-toed sole, with an iron band round the heel. He is a middle-aged man, much sunburned, and has been a convict. These few indications may be of some assistance to you, coupled with the fact that there is a good deal of skin missing from the palm of his hand. The other man—"

"Ah! the other man?" asked Athelney Jones, in a sneering voice, but impressed none the less, as I could easily see, by the precision of the other's manner.

"Is a rather curious person," said Sherlock Holmes, turning upon his heel. "I hope before very long to be able to introduce you to the pair of them. A word with you, Watson."

He led me out to the head of the stair. "This unexpected occurrence," he said, "has caused us rather to lose sight of the original purpose of our journey."

"I have just been thinking so," I answered. "It is not right that Miss Morstan should remain in this stricken house."

"No. You must escort her home. She lives with Mrs. Cecil Forrester, in Lower Camberwell; so it is not very far. I will wait for you, here, if you will drive out again. Or perhaps you are too tired?"

"By no means. I don't think I could rest until I know

more of this fantastic business. I have seen enough of the rough side of life, but I give you my word that this quick succession of strange surprises tonight has shaken my nerve completely. I should like, however, to see the matter through with you, now that I have got so far."

"Your presence will be of great service to me," he answered. "We shall work the case out independently, and leave this fellow Jones to exult over any mare's nest which he may choose to construct. When you have dropped Miss Morstan I wish you to go to No. 3 Pinchin Lane, down near the water's edge, at Lambeth. The third house on the right hand side is a bird stuffer's; Sherman is the name. You will see a weasel holding a young rabbit in the window. Rouse old Sherman up, and tell him with my compliments, that I want Toby at once. You will bring Toby back in the cab with you."

"A dog, I suppose?"

"Yes, a queer mongrel, with a most amazing power of scent. I would rather have Toby's help than that of the whole detective force of London."

"I shall bring him, then," said I. "It is one now. I ought to be back before three, if I can get a fresh horse."

"And I," said Holmes, "shall see what I can learn from Mrs. Bernstone, and from the Indian servant, who, Mr. Thaddeus tells me, sleeps in the next garret. Then I shall study the great Jones' methods, and listen to his not too delicate sarcasms. 'Wir sind gewohnt, dass die Menschen verhohnen was sie nicht verstehen.' Goethe is always pithy."

CHAPTER VII

THE EPISODE OF THE BARREL

THE police had brought a cab with them, and in this I escorted Miss Morstan back to her home. After the angelic fashion of women, she had borne trouble with a calm face as long as there was some one weaker than herself to support, and I had found her bright and placid by the side of the frightened housekeeper. In the cab, however, she first turned faint, and then burst into a passion of weeping, so sorely had she been tried by the adventures of the night. She has told me since that she thought me cold and distant upon that journey. She little guessed the struggle within my breast, or the effort of self-restraint which held me back. My sympathies and my love went out to her, even as my hand had in the garden. I felt that years of the conventionalities of life could not teach me to know her sweet, brave nature as had this one day of strange experiences. Yet there were two thoughts which sealed the words of affection upon my lips. She was weak and helpless, shaken in mind and nerve. It was to take her at a disadvantage to obtrude love upon her at such a time. Worse still she was rich. If Holmes' researches were successful, she would be an heiress. Was it fair, was it honorable, that a half pay surgeon should take such advantage of an intimacy which chance had brought about? Might she not look upon me as a vulgar fortune-seeker? I could not bear to risk that such a thought should cross her mind. This

Agra treasure intervened like an impassable barrier between us.

It was nearly two o'clock when we reached Mrs. Cecil Forrester's. The servants had retired hours ago, but Mrs. Forrester had been so interested by the strange message which Miss Morstan had received, that she had sat up in the hope of her return. She opened the door herself, a middle-aged, graceful woman, and it gave me joy to see how tenderly her arm stole round the other's waist, and how motherly was the voice in which she greeted her. She was clearly no mere paid dependent, but an honored friend. I was introduced, and Mrs. Forrester earnestly begged me to step in and to tell her our adventures. I explained, however, the importance of my errand, and promised faithfully to call and report any progress which we might make with the case. As we drove away I stole a glance back, and I still seem to see that little group on the step, the two graceful, clinging figures, the half-opened door, the hall light shining through stained glass, the barometer, and the bright stair-rods. It was soothing to catch even the passing glimpse of a tranquil English home in the midst of the wild, dark business which had absorbed us.

And the more I thought of what had happened, the wilder and darker it grew I reviewed the whole extraordinary sequence of events as I rattled on through the silent gas-lighted streets. There was the original problem: that at least was pretty clear now. The death of Captain Morstan, the sending of the pearls, the advertisement, the letter—we had had light upon all those events. They had only led us, however, to a deeper and far more tragic mystery. The Indian treasure, the curious plan found among Morstan's baggage, the strange scene at Major Sholto's death, the rediscovery of the treasure immediately followed by the murder of the discover, the very singular accompaniments to the crime, the footsteps, the remarkable weapons, the words upon the card, corresponding with those upon Captain Morstan's chart—here was indeed a labyrinth in which a man less singularly endowed than my fellow lodger might well despair at ever finding the clew.

Pinchin Lane was a row of shabby two-storied brick houses in the lower quarter of Lambeth. I had to knock for some time at No. 3 before I could make any impression. At last, however, there was the glint of a candle behind the blind, and a face looked out at the upper window.

"Go on, you drunken vagabond!" said the face. "If you kick up any more row I'll open the kennels and let out forty-three dogs at you."

"If you'll let one out it's just what I have come for," said I.

"Go on!" yelled the voice. "So help me gracious, I have a wiper in this bag, an' I'll drop it on your 'ead if you don't hook it!"

"But I want a dog," I cried.

"I won't be argued with!" shouted Mr. Sherman. "Now stand clear; for when I say 'three,' down goes the wiper."

"Mr. Sherlock Holmes—" I began; but the words had a most magical effect, for the window instantly slammed down, and within a minute the door was unbarred and open. Mr. Sherman was a lanky, lean old man, with stooping shoulders, a stringy neck, and blue-tinted glasses.

"A friend of Mr. Sherlock is always welcome," said he. "Step in, sir. Keep clear of the badger; for he bites. Ah, naughty, naughty! would you take a nip at the gentleman?" This to a stoat which thrust its wicked head and red eyes between the bars of its cage. "Don't mind that, sir; it's only a slow-worm. It hain't got no fangs, so I gives it the run o' the room, for it keeps the beetles down. You must not mind my bein' just a little short wi' you at first, for I'm guyed by the children, and there's many a one who just comes down this lane to rouse me up. What was it that Mr. Sherlock Holmes wanted, sir?"

"He wanted a dog of yours."

"Ah! that would be Toby."

"Yes, Toby was the name."

"Toby lives at No. 7, on the left here." He moved slowly forward with his candle among the queer animal family which he had gathered round him. In the uncertain, shadowy light I could see dimly that there were glancing, glimmering eyes peeping down at us from every cranny and corner. Even the rafters above our heads were lined by solemn fowls, who lazily shifted their weight from one leg to the other as our voices disturbed their slumbers.

Toby proved to be an ugly, long-haired, lop-eared creature, half spaniel and half lurcher, brown and white in color, with a very clumsy waddling gait. It accepted, after some hesitation, a lump of sugar which the old naturalist handed to me, and having thus sealed an alliance, it followed me to the cab, and made no difficulties about accompanying me. It had just struck three on the Palace clock when I found myself back once more at Pondicherry Lodge. The Ex-prize fighter, McMurdo, had, I found, been arrested as an accessory, and both he and Mr. Sholto had been marched off to the station. Two constables guarded the narrow gate, but they allowed me to pass with the dog on my mentioning the detective's name.

Holmes was standing on the doorstep, with his hands in his pockets, smoking his pipe.

"Ah, you have him there!" said he. "Good dog, then! Athelney Jones has gone. We have had an immense display of energy since you left. He has arrested not only friend Thaddeus, but the housekeeper, the gatekeeper and the Indian servant. We have the place to ourselves but for a sergeant upstairs. Leave the dog here and come up."

We tied Toby to the hall table, and reascended the stairs. The room was as we had left it, save that a sheet had been draped over the central figure. A weary-looking police sergeant reclined in the corner.

"Lend me your bull's-eye, sergeant," said my companion. "Now tie this bit of card round my neck, so as to hang it in front of me. Thank you. Now I must kick off my boots and stockings. Just you carry them down with you, Watson. I am going to do a little climbing. And dip my handkerchief into the creosote. That will do. Now come up into the garret with me for a moment."

We clambered up through the hole. Holmes turned his light once more upon the footsteps in the dust.

"I wish particularly to notice these foot marks," he said. "Do you observe anything noteworthy about them?"

"They belong," I said, "to a child or a small woman."

"Apart from their size, though. Is there nothing else?"

"They appear to be much as other foot marks."

"Not at all. Look here! This is the print of a right foot in the dust. Now I make one with my naked foot beside it. What is the chief difference?"

"Your toes are all cramped together. The other print has each toe distinctly divided."

"Quite so. That is the point. Bear that in mind. Now, would you kindly step over to that flap-window and smell the edge of the woodwork? I shall stay over here as I have this handkerchief in my hand."

I did as he directed, and was instantly conscious of a strong tarry smell.

"That is where he put his foot in getting out. If you can trace him, I should think that Toby will have no difficulty. Now run downstairs, loose the dog, and look out for Blondin."

By the time that I got out into the grounds, Sherlock Holmes was on the roof, and I could see him like an enormous glowworm crawling very slowly along the ridge. I lost sight of him behind a stack of chimneys, but he presently reappeared, and then vanished once more upon the opposite side. When I made my way round there I found him seated at one of the corner eaves.

"That you, Watson?" he cried.

"Yes."

"This is the place. What is that black thing down there?"

"A water barrel."

"Top on it?"

"Yes."

"No sign of a ladder?"

"No."

"Confound the fellow! It's a most break-neck place. I ought to be able to come down where he could climb up. The water pipe feels pretty firm. Here goes, anyhow."

There was a shuffling of the feet, and the lantern began to come steadily down the side of the wall. Then with a light spring he came on to the barrel, and from there to the earth.

"It was easy to follow him," he said, drawing on his stockings and boots. "Tiles were loosened the whole way along, and in his hurry he had dropped this. It confirms my diagnosis, as you doctors express it."

The object which he held up to me was a small pocket or pouch woven out of colored grasses and with a few tawdry beads strung round it. In shape and size it was not unlike a cigarette case. Inside were half a dozen spines of dark wood, sharp at one end and rounded at the other, like that which had struck Bartholomew Sholto.

"They are hellish things," said he. "Look out that

you don't prick yourself. I'm delighted to have them, for the chances are that they are all he has. There is the less fear of you or me finding one in our skin before long. I would sooner face a Martini bullet myself. Are you game for a six-mile trudge, Watson?"

"Certainly," I answered.

"Your leg will stand it?"

"Oh, yes."

"Here you are, doggy! Good old Toby! Smell it, Toby; smell it!" He pushed the creosote handkerchief under the dog's nose, while the creature stood with its fluff legs separated, and with a most comical cock to its head, like a connoisseur sniffing the bouquet of a famous vintage. Holmes then threw the handkerchief to a distance fastened a stout cord to the mongrel's collar, and led him to the foot of the water barrel. The creature instantly broke into a succession of high, tremulous yelps, and, with his nose on the ground and his tail in the air, pattered off the trail at a pace which strained his leash and kept us at the top of our speed.

The east had been gradually whitening, and we could now see some distance in the cold, gray light. The square, massive house, with its black, empty windows and high, bare walls, towered up, sad and forlorn, behind us. Our coarse led right across the grounds, in and out among the trenches and pits with which they were scarred and intersected. The whole place, with its scattered dirt heaps and ill-grown shrubs, had a blighted, ill-omened look which harmonized with the black tragedy which hung over it.

On reaching the boundary wall Toby ran along, whining eagerly, underneath its shadow, and stopped finally in a corner screened by a young beech. Where the two walls joined, several bricks had been loosened, and the crevices left were worn down and rounded upon the lower side, as though they had frequently been used as a ladder. Holmes clambered up, and, taking the dog from me, he dropped it over upon the other side.

"There's the print of the wooden-leg's hand," he remarked, as I mounted up beside him. "You see the slight smudge of blood upon the white plaster. What a lucky thing it is that we have had no very heavy rain since yesterday! The scent will lie upon the road in spite of their eight-and-twenty hours' start."

I confess that I had my doubts myself when I reflected upon the great traffic which had passed along the London road in the interval. My fears were soon appeased, however. Toby never hesitated or swerved, but waddled on in his peculiar rolling fashion. Clearly, the pungent smell of the creosote rose high above all other contending scents.

"Do not imagine," said Holmes, "that I depend for my success in this case upon the mere chance of one of these fellows having put his foot in the chemical. I have knowledge now which would enable me to trace them in many different ways. This, however, is the readiest, and, since fortune has put it into our hands, I should be culpable if I neglected it. It has, however, prevented the case from becoming the pretty little intellectual problem which it at one time promised to be. There might have been some credit to be gained out of it but for this too palpable clew."

"There is credit, and to spare," said I. "I assure you, Holmes, that I marvel at the means by which you obtain your results in this case, even more than I did in the Jefferson Hope murder. The thing seems to me to be deeper and more inexplicable. How, for example, could you describe with such confidence the wooden-legged man?"

"Pshaw, my dear boy! it was simplicity itself. I don't wish to be theatrical. It is all patent and above board. Two officers who are in command of a convict guard learn an important secret as to buried treasure. A map is drawn for them by an Englishman named Jonathan Small. You remember that we saw the name upon the chart in Captain Morstan's possession. He had signed it in behalf of himself and his associates—the sign of the four, as he somewhat dramatically called it. Aided by this chart, the officers—or one of them—gets the treasure and brings it to England, leaving, we will suppose, some condition under which he received it unfulfilled. Now, then, why did not Jonathan Small get the treasure himself? The answer is obvious. The chart is dated at a time when Morstan was brought into close association with convicts. Jonathan Small did not get the treasure because he and his associates were themselves convicts and could not get away."

"But this is mere speculation," said I.

"It is more than that. It is the only hypothesis which covers the facts. Let us see how it fits in with the sequel. Major Sholto remains at peace for some years, happy in the possession of his treasure. Then he receives a letter from India which gives him a great fright. What was that?"

"A letter to say that the men whom he had wronged had been set free."

"Or had escaped. That is much more likely, for he would have known what their term of imprisonment was. It would not have been a surprise to him. What does he do then? He guards himself against a wooden-legged man—a white man, mark you, for he mistakes a white tradesman for him, and actually fires a pistol at him. Now, only one white man's name is on the chart. The others are Hindoos or Mohammedans. There is no other white man. Therefore we may say with confidence that the wooden-legged man is identical with Jonathan Small. Does the reasoning strike you as being faulty?"

"No; it is clear and concise."

"Well, now, let us put ourselves in the place of Jonathan Small. Let us look at it from his point of view. He comes to England with the double idea of regaining what he would consider to be his rights and of having his revenge upon the man who had wronged him. He found out where Sholto lived, and very possibly he established communications with some one inside the house. There is this butler, Lal Rao, whom we have not seen. Mrs. Bernstone gives him far from a good character. Small could not find out, however, where the treasure was hid, for no one ever knew, save the major and one faithful servant who had died. Suddenly Small learns that the major is on his death-bed. In a frenzy lest the secret of the treasure die with him, he runs the gauntlet of the guards, makes his way to the dying man's window, and is only deterred from entering by the presence of his two sons. Mad with hate, however, against the dead man, he enters the room that night, searches his private papers in the hope of discovering some memorandum relating to the treasure, and finally leaves a memento of his visit in the short inscription upon the card. He had doubtless planned beforehand that should he slay the major he would leave some such record upon the body as a sign that it was not a common murder, but, from the point of view of the four associates, something in the nature of an act of justice. Whimsical and bizarre conceits of this kind are common enough in the annals of crime, and usually afford valuable indications as to the criminal. Do you follow all this?"

"Very clearly."

"Now, what could Jonathan Small do? He could only continue to keep a secret watch upon the efforts made to find the treasure. Possibly he leaves England and only comes back at intervals. Then comes the discovery of the garret, and he is instantly informed of it. We again trace the presence of some confederate in the household.

Jonathan, with his wooden leg, is utterly unable to reach the lofty room of Bartholomew Sholto. He takes with him however, a rather curious associate, who gets over this difficulty, but dips his naked foot into creosote, whence come Toby, and a six-mile limp for a half-pay officer with a damaged Achillis tendo."

"But it was the associate, and not Jonathan, who committed the crime."

"Quite so. And rather to Jonathan's disgust, to judge by the way he stamped about when he got into the room. He bore no grudge against Bartholomew Sholto, and would have preferred if he could have been simply bound and gagged. He did not wish to put his head in a halter. There was no help for it, however; the savage instincts of his companion had broken out, and the poison had done its work; so Jonathan Small left his record, lowered the treasure box to the ground, and followed it himself. That was the train of events as far as I can decipher them. Of course, as to his personal appearance, he must be middle-aged, and must be sunburned after serving his time in such an oven as the Andamans. His height is readily calculated from the length of his stride, and we know that he was bearded. His hairiness was the one point which impressed itself upon Thaddeus Sholto when he saw him at the window. I don't know that there is anything else."

"The associate?"

"Ah, well, there is no great mystery in that. But you will know all about it soon enough. How sweet the morning air is? See how that one little cloud floats like a pink feather from some gigantic flamingo. Now the red rim of the sun pushes itself over the London cloud bank. It shines on a good many folk, but on none, I dare bet, who is on a stranger errand than you and I. How small we feel with our petty ambitions and strivings in the presence of the great elemental forces of nature! Are you well up in your Jean Paul?"

"Fairly so. I worked back to him through Carlyle."

"That was like following the brook to the parent lake. He makes one curious but profound remark. It is that the chief proof of a man's real greatness lies in his perception of his own smallness. It argues, you see, a power of comparison and of appreciation, which is in itself a proof of nobility. There is much food for thought in Richter. You have not a pistol, have you?"

"I have my stick."

"It is just possible that we may need something of the sort if we get to their lair. Jonathan I shall leave to you, but if the other turns nasty I shall shoot him dead." He took out his revolver as he spoke, and, having loaded two of the chambers, he put it back into the right-hand pocket of his jacket.

We had during this time been following the guidance of Toby down the half-rural, villa-lined roads which lead to the metropolis. Now, however, we were beginning to come among continuous streets, where laborers and dockmen were already astir, and slatternly women were taking down shutters and brushing doorsteps. At the square-topped corner public house business was just beginning, and rough-looking men were emerging, rubbing their sleeves across their beards after their morning wet. Strange dogs sauntered up, and stared wonderingly at us as we passed, but our inimitable Toby looked neither to the right nor to the left, but trotted onward with his nose to the ground and an occasional eager whine, which spoke of a hot scent.

We had traversed Streatham, Brixton, Camberwell, and now found ourselves in Kennington Lane, having borne away through the side streets to the east of the Oval. The men whom we pursued seemed to have taken a curiously zigzag road, with the idea probably of escaping observation. They had never kept to the main road if a parallel side street would serve their turn. At the foot of Kennington Lane they had edged away to the left through Bond Street and Miles Street. Where the latter street turns into Knight's Place, Toby ceased to advance, but began to run backward and forward with one ear cocked and the other drooping, the very picture of canine indecision. Then he waddled around in circles, looking up to us from time to time, as if to ask for sympathy in his embarrassment.

"What the deuce is the matter with the dog?" growled Holmes. "They surely would not take a cab, or go off in a balloon."

"Perhaps they stood here for some time," I suggested.

"Ah! it's all right. He's off again," said my companion, in a tone of relief.

He was indeed off; for, after sniffing round again, he suddenly made up his mind, and darted away with an energy and determination such as he had not yet shown. The scent appeared to be much hotter than before, for he had not even to put his nose on the ground, but tugged at his leash, and tried to break into a run. I could see by the gleam in Holmes eyes that he thought we were nearing the end of our journey.

Our course now ran down Nine Elms until we came to Broderick and Nelson's large timber yard, just past the White Eagle tavern. Here the dog, frantic with excitement, turned down through the side gate into the inclosure, where the sawyers were already at work. On the dog raced through sawdust and shavings, down an alley, round a passage, between two woodpiles, and finally, with a triumphant yelp, sprang upon a large barrel, which still stood upon the hand trolley on which it had been brought. With lolling tongue and blinking eyes, Toby stood upon the cask, looking from one to the other of us for some sign of appreciation. The staves of the barrel and the wheels of the trolley were smeared with a dark liquid, and the whole air was heavy with the smell of creosote.

Sherlock Holmes and I looked blankly at each other, and then burst simultaneously into an uncontrollable fit of laughter.

CHAPTER VIII

THE BAKER STREET IRREGULARS

"What now?" I asked. "Toby has lost his character for infallibility."

"He acted according to his lights," said Holmes, lifting him down from the barrel and walking him out of the timber yard. "If you consider how much creosote is carried about London in one day, it is no great wonder that our trail should have been crossed. It is much used now, especially for the seasoning of wood. Poor Toby is not to blame."

"We must get on the main scene again, I suppose."

"Yes. And, fortunately, we have no distance to go. Evidently what puzzled the dog at the corner of Knight's Place was that there were two different trails running in opposite directions. We took the wrong one. It only remains to follow the other."

There was no difficulty about this. On leading Toby to the place where he had committed his fault, he cast about in a wide circle, and finally dashed off in a fresh direction.

"We must take care that he does not now bring us to the place where the creosote barrel came from," I observed.

"I had thought of that. But you notice that he keeps on the pavement, whereas the barrel passed down the roadway. No, we are on the true scent now."

It tended down toward the river-side, running through

Belmont Place and Prince's Street. At the end of Broad Street it ran right down to the water's edge, where there was a small wooden wharf. Toby led us to the very edge of this, and there stood whining, looking out on the dark current beyond.

"We are out of luck," said Holmes. "They have taken a boat here." Several small punts and skiffs were lying about in the water on the edge of the wharf. We took Toby round to each in turn, but though he sniffed earnestly, he made no sign.

Close to the rude landing stage was a small brick house, with a wooden placard slung out through the second window. "Mordecai Smith" was printed across it in large letters, and, underneath, "Boats to hire by the hour or day." A second inscription above the door informed us that a steam launch was kept—a statement which was confirmed by a great pile of coke upon the jetty. Sherlock Holmes looked slowly round, and his face assumed an ominous expression.

"This looks bad," said he. "These fellows are sharper than I expected. They seem to have covered their tracks. There has, I fear, been preconcerted management."

He was approaching the door of the house, when it opened, and a little, curly-headed lad of six came running out, followed by a stoutish, red-faced woman, with a large sponge in her hand.

"You come back and be washed, Jack!" she shouted. "Come back, you young imp; for if your father comes home and finds you like this, he'll let us hear of it!"

"Dear little chap!" said Holmes, strategically. "What a rosy-cheeked young rascal! Now, Jack, is there anything you would like?"

The youth pondered for a moment. "I'd like a shillin'," said he.

"Nothing you would like better?"

"I like two shillin' better," the prodigy answered, after some thought.

"Here you are, then! Catch! A fine child, Mrs. Smith."

"Lor' bless you, sir, he is that, and forward. He gets a'most too much for me to manage, 'specially when my man is away days at a time."

"Away, is he?" said Holmes, in a disappointed voice. "I am sorry for that, for I wanted to speak to Mr. Smith."

"He's been away since yesterday mornin', sir, and, truth to tell, I am beginning to feel frightened about him. But if it was about a boat, sir, maybe I could serve as well."

"I wanted to hire his steam launch."

"Why, bless you, sir, it is in the steam launch that he has gone. That's what puzzles me; for I know there ain't more coals in her than would take her to about Woolwich and back. If he'd been away in the barge I'd ha' thought nothin'; for many a time a job has taken him as far as Gravesend, and then if there was much doin' there he might ha' stayed over. But what good is a steam launch without coals?"

"He might have bought some at a wharf down the river."

"He might, sir, but it weren't his way. Many a time I've heard him call out at the prices they charge for a few odd bags. Besides, I don't like that wooden-legged man, wi' his ugly face and outlandish talk. What did he want always knockin' about here for?"

"A wooden-legged man?" said Holmes, with bland surprise.

"Yes, sir; a brown, monkey-faced chap that's called more'n once for my old man. It was him that roused him up yesternight, and what's more, my man knew he was comin', for he had steam up in the launch. I tell you straight, sir, I don't feel easy in my mind about it."

"But, my dear Mrs. Smith," said Holmes, shrugging his shoulders, "you are frightening yourself about nothing. How could you possibly tell that it was the wooden-legged man who came in the night? I don't quite understand how you could be so sure."

"His voice, sir. I know his voice, which is kind o' thick and foggy. He tapped at the winder—about three it would be. 'Show a leg, matey,' says he; 'time to turn out guard.' My old man woke Jim up—that's my eldest —and away they went, without so much as a word to me. I could hear the wooden leg clackin' on the stones."

"And was this wooden-legged man alone?"

"Couldn't say, I am sure, sir. I didn't hear no one else."

"I am sorry, Mrs. Smith, for I wanted a steam launch, and I have heard good reports of the— Let me see, what is her name?"

"The 'Aurora,' sir."

"Ah! She's not that old green launch with a yellow line, very broad in the beam?"

"No, indeed. She's as trim a little thing as any on the river. She's been fresh painted, black with two red streaks."

"Thanks. I hope that you will hear soon from Mr. Smith. I am going down the river; and if I should see anything of the 'Aurora' I shall let him know that you are uneasy. A black funnel, you say?"

"No, sir. Black with a white band."

"Ah, of course. It was the sides which were black. Good morning, Mrs. Smith. There is a boatman here with a wherry, Watson. We shall take it and cross the river."

"The main thing with people of that sort," said Holmes, as we sat in the sheets of the wherry, "is never to let them think that their information can be of the slightest importance to you. If you do, they will instantly shut up like an oyster. If you listen to them under protest, as it were, you are very likely to get what you want."

"Our course now seems pretty clear," said I.

"What would you do then?"

"I would engage a launch and go down the track of the 'Aurora.'"

"My dear fellow, it would be a colossal task. She may have touched at any wharf on either side of the stream between here and Greenwich. Below the bridge there is a perfect labyrinth of landing places for miles. It would take you days and days to exhaust them, if you set about it alone."

"Employ the police then."

"No. I shall probably call Athelney Jones in at the last moment. He is not a bad fellow, and I should not like to do anything which would injure him professionally. But I have a fancy for working it out myself, now that we have gone so far."

"Could we advertise, then, asking for information from wharfingers?"

"Worse and worse! Our men would know that the chase was hot at their heels, and then would be off out of the country. As it is, they are likely enough to leave, but as long as they think they are perfectly safe they will be in no hurry. Jones' energy will be of use there, for his view of the case is sure to push itself into the daily press, and the runaways will think that every one is off on the wrong scent."

"What are we to do then?" I asked, as we landed near Milbank Penitentiary.

"Take this hansom, drive home, have some breakfast, and get an hour's sleep. It is quite on the cards that we may be afoot tonight again. Stop at a telegraph office, cabby. We will keep Toby, for he may be of use to us yet."

We pulled up at the Great Peter Street Post Office, and Holmes Dispatched his wire. "Whom do you think that is to?" he asked, as we resumed our journey.

"I am sure I don't know."

"You remember the Baker Street division of the detective police force whom I employed in the Jefferson Hope case?"

"Well," said I, laughing.

"This is just the case where they might be invaluable. If they fail, I have other resources; but I shall try them first. That wire was to my dirty little lieutenant, Wiggins, and I expect that he and his gang will be with us before we have finished our breakfast."

It was between eight and nine o'clock now, and I was conscious of a strong reaction after the successive excitement of the night. I was limp and weary, befogged in mind and fatigued in body. I had not the professional enthusiasm which carried my companion on, nor could I look at the matter as a mere abstract intellectual problem. As far as the death of Bartholomew Sholto went, I had heard little good of him, and could feel no intense antipathy to his murderer. The treasure, however, was a different matter. That, or part of it, belonged rightfully to Miss Morstan. While there was a chance of recovering it, I was ready to devote my life to the one object. True, if I found it, it would probably put her forever beyond my reach. Yet it would be a petty and selfish love which would be influenced by such a thought as that. If Holmes could work to find the criminals, I had a tenfold stronger reason to urge me on to find the treasure.

A bath at Baker Street and a complete change freshened me up wonderfully. When I came down to our room I found the breakfast laid and Holmes pouring out the coffee.

"Here it is," said he, laughing, and pointing to an open newspaper. "The energetic Jones and the ubiquitous reporter have fixed it up between them. But you have had enough of the case. Better have your ham and eggs first."

I took the paper from him and read the short notice, which was headed "Mysterious Business at Upper Norwood."

"About twelve o'clock last night," said the *Standard*, "Mr. Bartholomew Sholto, of Pondicherry Lodge, Upper Norwood, was found dead in his room under circumstances which point to foul play. As far as we can learn, no traces of violence were found upon Mr. Sholto's person, but a valuable collection of Indian gems, which the deceased gentleman had inherited from his father, has been carried off. The discovery was first made by Sherlock Holmes and Dr. Watson, who had called at the house with Mr. Thaddeus Sholto, brother of the deceased. By a singular piece of good fortune, Mr. Athelney Jones, the well-known member of the detective police force, happened to be at the Norwood Police Station, and was on the ground within half an hour of the first alarm. His trained and experienced faculties were at once directed toward the detection of the criminals, with the gratifying result that the brother, Thaddeus Sholto, has already been arrested, together with the housekeeper, Mrs. Bernstone, an Indian butler named Lal Rao, and a porter or gatekeeper, named McMurdo. It is quite certain that the thief or thieves were well acquainted with the house, for Mr. Jones' well-known technical knowledge and his powers of minute observation have enabled him to prove conclusively that the miscreants could not have entered by the door or by the window, but must have made their way across the roof of the building, and so through a trap door into a room which communicated with that in which the body was found. This fact, which has been very clearly made out, proves conclusively that it was no mere haphazard burglary. The prompt and energetic action of the officers of the law shows the great advantage of the presence on such occasions of a single vigorous and masterful mind. We cannot but think that it supplies an argument to those who would wish to see our detectives more decentralized, and so brought into closer and more effective touch with the cases which it is their duty to investigate."

"Isn't it gorgeous?" said Holmes, grinning over his coffee cup. "What do you think of it?"

"I think that we have had a close shave ourselves of being arrested for the crime."

"So do I. I wouldn't answer for our safety now, if he should happen to have another of his attacks of energy."

At this moment there was a loud ring at the bell, and I could hear Mrs. Hudson, our landlady, raising her voice in a wail of expostulation and dismay.

"By Heaven, Holmes," I said, half rising. "I believe they are really after us."

"No, it's not quite so bad as that. It is the unofficial force—the Baker Street irregulars."

As he spoke, there came a swift pattering of naked feet upon the stairs, a clatter of high voices, and in rushed a dozen dirty and ragged little street Arabs. There was some show of discipline among them, despite their tumultuous entry, for they instantly drew up in line and stood facing us with expectant faces. One of their number, taller and older than the others, stood forward with an air of lounging superiority which was very funny in such a disreputable little scarecrow.

"Got your message, sir," said he, "and brought 'em on sharp. Three bob and a tanner for tickets."

"Here you are," said Holmes, producing some silver. "In future they can report to you, Wiggins, and you to me. I cannot have the house invaded in this way. However, it is just as well that you should all hear the instructions. I want to find the whereabouts of a steam launch called the 'Aurora,' owner, Mordecai Smith, black with two red streaks, funnel black with a white band. She is down the river somewhere. I want one boy to be at Mordecai Smith's landing stage, opposite Milbank, to say if the boat comes back. You must divide it out among yourselves, and do both banks thoroughly. Let me know the moment you have news. Is that all clear?"

"Yes, guv'nor," said Wiggins.

"The old scale of pay, and a guinea to the boy who finds the boat. Here's a day in advance. Now off you go!" He handed them a shilling each, and away they buzzed down the stairs, and I saw them a moment later streaming down the street.

"If the launch is above water they will find her," said Holmes, as he rose from the table and lighted his pipe. "They can go everywhere, see everything, overhear every one. I expect to hear before evening that they have spotted her. In the meanwhile, we can do nothing but await results. We cannot pick up the broken trail until we find either the 'Aurora' or Mr. Mordecai Smith."

"Toby could eat these scraps, I dare say. Are you going to bed, Holmes?"

"No; I am not tired. I have a curious constitution. I never remember feeling tired by work, though idleness exhausts me completely. I am going to smoke, and to think over this queer business to which my fair client has introduced us. If ever man had an easy task, this of ours ought to be. Wooden-legged men are not so common, but the other man must, I should think, be absolutely unique."

"That other man again!"

"I have no wish to make a mystery of him—to you, anyway. But you must have formed your own opinion. Now, do consider the data. Diminutive foot marks, toes never fettered by boots, naked feet, stone-headed wooden mace, great agility, small, poisoned darts. What do you make of all this?"

"A savage!" I exclaimed. "Perhaps one of those Indians who were the associates of Jonathan Small."

"Hardly that," said he. "When first I saw signs of strange weapons I was inclined to think so, but the remarkable characters of the foot marks caused me to reconsider my views. Some of the inhabitants of the Indian Peninsula are small men, but none could have left such marks as that. The Hindoo proper has long and thin feet. The sandal-wearing Mohammedan has the great toe well separated from the others, because the thong is commonly passed between. These little darts, too, could only be shot in one way. They were from a blow pipe. Now, then, where are we to find our savage?"

"South America," I hazarded.

He stretched his hand up, and took down a bulky volume from the shelf. "This is the first volume of a gazeteer which is now being published. It may be looked upon as the very latest authority. What have we here? 'Andaman Islands, situated three hundred and forty miles to the north of Sumatra in the Bay of Bengal.' Hum! hum! What's all this? 'Moist climate, coral reefs, sharks, Port Blair, convict barracks, Rutland Island, cottonwood—' Ah, here we are. 'The aborigines of the Andaman Island may perhaps claim the distinction of being the smallest race upon this earth, though some anthropologists prefer the Bushmen of Africa, the Digger Indians of America, and the Terra del Fuegians. The average height is rather below four feet, although many full-grown adults may be found who are very much smaller than this. They are a fierce, morose, and intractable people, though capable of forming most devoted friendships when their confidence has once been gained.' Mark that, Watson. Now, then, listen to this. 'They are naturally hideous, having large, misshapen heads, small, fierce eyes, and distorted features. Their feet and hands, however, are remarkably small. So intractable and fierce are they that all the efforts of the British officials have failed to win them over in any degree. They have always been a terror to shipwrecked crews, braining the survivors with their stone-headed clubs, or shooting them with their poisoned arrows. These massacres are invariably concluded by a cannibal feast.' Nice, amiable people, Watson! If this fellow had been left to his own unaided devices this affair might have taken an even more ghastly turn. I fancy that, even as it is, Jonathan Small would give a good deal not to have employed him."

"But how came he to have so singular a companion?"

"Ah, that is more than I can tell. Since, however, we had already determined that Small had come from the Andamans, it is not so very wonderful that this islander should be with him. No doubt we shall know all about it in time. Look here, Watson; you look regularly done. Lie down there on the sofa, and see if I can put you to sleep."

He took up his violin from the corner, and as I stretched myself out he began to play some low, dreamy, melodious air—his own, no doubt, for he had a remarkable gift for improvisation. I have a vague remembrance of his gaunt limbs, his earnest face, and the rise and fall of his bow. Then I seemed to be floating peacefully away upon a soft sea of sound, until I found myself in dreamland, with the sweet face of Mary Morstan looking down upon me.

CHAPTER IX

A BREAK IN THE CHAIN

It was late in the afternoon before I awoke, strengthened and refreshed. Sherlock Holmes still sat exactly as I had left him, save that he had laid aside his violin and was deep in a book. He looked across at me as I stirred, and I noticed that his face was dark and troubled.

"You have slept soundly," he said. "I feared that our talk would wake you."

"I heard nothing," I answered. "Have you had fresh news, then?"

"Unfortunately, no. I confess that I am surprised and disappointed. I expected something definite by this time. Wiggins has just been up to report. He says that no trace can be found of the launch. It is a provoking check, for every hour is of importance."

"Can I do anything? I am perfectly fresh now, and quite ready for another night's outing."

"No; we can do nothing. We can only wait. If we go ourselves, the message might come in our absence, and delay be caused. You can do what you will, but I must remain on guard."

"Then I shall run over to Camberwell and call upon Mrs. Cecil Forrester. She asked me to yesterday."

"On Mrs. Cecil Forrester?" asked Holmes, with the twinkle of a smile in his eye.

"Well, of course, on Miss Morstan, too. They were anxious to hear what happened."

"I would not tell them too much," said Holmes. "Women are never to be entirely trusted—not the best of them."

I did not pause to argue over this atrocious sentiment. "I shall be back in an hour or two," I remarked.

"All right! Good luck! But, I say, if you are crossing the river you may as well return Toby, for I don't think it at all likely that we shall have any use for him now."

I took our mongrel accordingly, and left him, together with a half sovereign, at the old naturalist's in Pinchin Lane. At Camberwell I found Miss Morstan a little weary after her night's adventures, but very eager to hear the news. Mrs. Forrester, too, was full of curiosity. I told them all that we had done, suppressing, however, the more dreadful parts of the tragedy. Thus, although I spoke of Mr. Sholto's death, I said nothing of the exact manner and method of it. With all my omissions, however, there was enough to startle and amaze them.

"It is a romance!" cried Mrs. Forrester. "An injured lady, half a million in treasure, a black cannibal, and a wooden-legged ruffian. They take the place of the conventional dragon or wicked earl."

"And two knight-errants to the rescue," added Miss Morstan, with a bright glance at me.

"Why, Mary, your fortune depends upon the issue of this search. I don't think that you are nearly excited enough. Just imagine what it must be to be so rich and to have the world at your feet."

It sent a thrill of joy to my heart to notice that she showed no sign of elation at the prospect. On the contrary, she gave a toss of her proud head, as though the matter were one in which she took small interest.

"It is for Mr. Thaddeus Sholto that I am anxious," she said. "Nothing else is of any consequence; but I think that he has behaved most kindly and honorably throughout. It is our duty to clear him of this dreadful and unfounded charge."

It was evening before I left Camberwell, and quite dark by the time I reached home. My companion's book and pipe lay by his chair, but he had disappeared. I looked about in the hope of seeing a note, but there was none.

"I suppose that Mr. Sherlock Holmes has gone out," I said to Mrs. Hudson, as she came up to lower the blinds.

"No, sir. He has gone to his room, sir. Do you know, sir," sinking her voice into an impressive whisper, "I am afraid for his health!"

"Why so, Mrs. Hudson?"

"Well, he's that strange, sir. After you was gone he walked, and he walked, up and down, and up and down, until I was weary of the sound of his footstep. Then I heard him talking to himself and muttering, and every time the bell rang out he came on the stair head, with, 'What is that, Mrs. Hudson?' And now he has slammed off to his room, but I can hear him walking away the same as ever. I hope he's not going to be ill, sir. I ventured to say something to him about cooling medicine, but he turned on me, sir, with such a look that I don't know how I ever got out of the room."

"I don't think that you have any cause to be uneasy, Mrs. Hudson," I answered. "I have seen him like this before. He has some small matter upon his mind which makes him restless." I tried to speak lightly to our worthy landlady, but I was myself somewhat uneasy when through the long night I still, from time to time, heard the dull sound of his tread, and knew how his keen spirit was chafing against this involuntary inaction.

At breakfast time he looked worn and haggard, with a little fleck of feverish color upon either cheek.

"You are knocking yourself up, old man," I remarked. "I heard you marching about in the night."

"No, I could not sleep," he answered. "This infernal problem is consuming me. It is too much to be balked by so petty an obstacle, when all else had been overcome. I know the men, the launch, everything; and yet I can get no news. I have set other agencies at work, and used every means at my disposal. The whole river has been searched on either side, but there is no news, nor has Mrs. Smith heard of her husband. I shall come to the conclusion soon that they have scuttled the craft. But there are objections to that."

"No, I think that may be dismissed. I had inquiries made and there is a launch of that description."

"Could it have gone up the river?"

"I have considered that possibility, too, and there is a search party who will work up as far as Richmond. If no news comes today, I shall start off myself tomorrow, and go for the men rather than the boat. But surely, surely, we shall hear something."

We did not, however. Not a word came to us, either from Wiggins or from the other agencies. There were articles in most of the papers upon the Norwood tragedy. They all appeared to be rather hostile to the unfortunate Thaddeus Sholto. No fresh details were to be found, however, in any of them, save that an inquest was to be held upon the following day. I walked over to Camberwell in the evening to report our ill success to the ladies, and on my return I found Holmes dejected and somewhat morose. He would hardly reply to my questions, and busied himself all evening in an abstruse chemical analysis which involved much heating of retorts and distilling of vapors, ending at last in a smell which fairly drove me out of the apartment. Up to the small hours of the morning I could hear the clinking of his test tubes, which told me that he was still engaged in his malodorous experiment.

In the early dawn I woke with a start, and was surprised to find him standing by my bedside, clad in a rude sailor dress, with a pea jacket, and a coarse red scarf round his neck.

"I am off down the river, Watson," said he. "I have been turning it over in my mind, and I can see only one way out of it. It is worth trying, at all events."

"Surely I can come with you, then?" said I.

"No; you can be much more useful if you will remain here as my representative. I am loath to go, for it is quite on the cards that some message may come during the day, though Wiggins was despondent about it last night. I want you to open all notes and telegrams, and to act on your own judgment if any news should come. Can I rely upon you?"

"Most certainly."

"I am afraid that you will not be able to wire to me, for I can hardly tell yet where I may find myself. If I am in luck, however, I may not be gone so very long. I shall have news of some sort or other before I get back."

I heard nothing of him by breakfast time. On opening the *Standard*, however, I found that there was a fresh allusion to the business. "With reference to the Upper Norwood tragedy," it remarked, "we have reason to believe that the matter promises to be even more complex and mysterious than was originally supposed. Fresh evidence has shown that it is quite impossible that Mr. Thaddeus Sholto could have been in any way concerned in the matter. He and the housekeeper, Mrs. Bernstone, were both released yesterday evening. It is believed, however, that the police have a clew to the real culprits, and that it is being prosecuted by Mr. Athelney Jones, of Scotland Yard, with all his well-known energy and sagacity. Further arrests may be expected at any moment."

"That is satisfactory so far as it goes," thought I. "Friend Sholto is safe, at any rate. I wonder what the fresh clew may be; though it seems to be a stereotyped form whenever the police have made a blunder."

I tossed the paper down upon the table, but at that moment my eye caught an advertisement in the agony column. It ran in this way:

"Lost.—Whereas, Mordecai Smith, boatman, and his son, Jim, left Smith's Wharf at or about three o'clock last Tuesday morning, in the steam launch 'Aurora,' black with two red stripes; funnel black with a white band; the sum of five pounds will be paid to any one who can give information to Mrs. Smith, at Smith's Wharf, or at 222 *b* Baker Street, as to the whereabouts of the said Mordecai Smith and the launch 'Aurora.'"

This was clearly Holmes' doing. The Baker Street address was enough to prove that. It struck me as rather ingenious, because it might be read by the fugitives without their seeing in it more than the natural anxiety of a wife for her missing husband.

It was a long day. Every time that a knock came to the door, or a sharp step passed in the street, I imagined that it was either Holmes returning or an answer to his advertisement. I tried to read, but my thoughts would wander off to our strange quest and to the ill-assorted and villainous pair whom we were pursuing. Could there be, I wonder, some radical flaw in my companion's reasoning? Might he be suffering from some huge self-deception? Was it not possible that his nimble and speculative mind had built up this wild theory upon faulty premises? I had never known him to be wrong; and yet the keenest reasoner may occasionally be deceived. He was likely, I thought, to fall into error through the over-refinement of his logic—his preference for a subtle and bizarre explanation when a plainer and more commonplace one lay ready to his hand. Yet, on the other hand, I had myself seen the evidence, and I had heard the reasons for my deductions. When I looked back on the

long chain of curious circumstances, many of them trivial
in themselves, but all tending in the same direction, I
could not disguise from myself that even if Holmes' explanation were incorrect the true theory must be equally
outre and startling.

At three o'clock in the afternoon there was a loud peal
at the bell, an authoritative voice in the hall, and, to my
surprise, no less a person than Mr. Athelney Jones was
shown up to me. Very different was he, however,
from the brusque and masterful professor of common-
sense who had taken over the case so confidently at Upper Norwood. His expression was downcast, and his
bearing meek and even apologetic.

"Good day, sir; good day," said he. "Mr. Sherlock
Holmes is out, I understand."

"Yes; and I cannot be sure when he will be back. But
perhaps you would care to wait. Take that chair and try
one of these cigars."

"Thank you; I don't mind if I do," said he, mopping
his face with a red bandana handkerchief.

"And a whisky and soda?"

"Well, half a glass. It is very hot for the time of
year and I have a good deal to worry and try me. You
know my theory about this Norwood case?"'

"I remember that you expressed one."

"Well, I have been obliged to reconsider it. I had
my net drawn tightly round Mr. Sholto, sir, when pop!
he went through a hole in the middle of it. He was
able to prove an alibi which could not be shaken. From
the time that he left his brother's room he was never
out of sight of some one or other. So it could not be he
who climbed over the roofs and through trap doors. It's
a very dark case and my professional credit is at stake.
I should be very glad of a little assistance."

"We all need help sometimes," said I.

"Your friend, Mr. Sherlock Holmes, is a wonderful

man, sir," said he, in a husky and confidential voice. "He's a man who is not to be beat. I have known that young man to go into a good many cases, but I never saw the case yet that he could not throw light upon. He is irregular in his methods, and a little quick, perhaps, in jumping at theories, but, on the whole, I think he would have made a most promising officer, and I don't care who knows it. I have had a wire from him this morning, by which I understand that he has got some clew to this Sholto business. Here is his message.'"

He took the telegram out of his pocket, and handed it to me. It was dated from Poplar at twelve o'clock. "Go to Baker Street at once," it said. "If I have not returned, wait for me. I am close on the track of the Sholto gang. You can come with us tonight if you want to be in at the finish."

"This sounds well. He has evidently picked up the scent again," said I.

"Ah, then he has been at fault, too," exclaimed Jones, with evident satisfaction. "Even the best of us are thrown off sometimes. Of course this may prove to be a false alarm; but it is my duty as an officer of the law to allow no chance to slip. But there is some one at the door. Perhaps this is he."

A heavy step was heard ascending the stairs, with a great wheezing and rattling as from a man who was sorely put to it for breath. Once or twice he stopped, as though the climb were too much for him, but at last he made his way to our door and entered. His appearance corresponded to the sounds which we had heard. He was an aged man, clad in seafaring garb, with an old pea jacket buttoned up to his throat. His back was bowed, his knees were shaky, and his breathing was painfully asthmatic. As he leaned upon a thick oaken cudgel his shoulders heaved in the effort to draw the air into his lungs. He had a colored scarf about his chin, and I could see little of his face save a pair of keen dark eyes, overhung by bushy white brows, and long gray side whiskers. Altogether he gave me the impression of a respectable master mariner who had fallen into years and poverty.

"What is it, my man?" I asked.

He looked about him in the slow, methodical fashion of old age.

"Is Mr. Sherlock Holmes here?" said he.

"No; but I am acting for him. You can tell me any message you have for him."

"It was to him himself I was to tell it," said he.

"But I tell you that I am acting for him. Was it about Mordecai Smith's boat?"

"Yes. I know well where it is. An' I knows where the men he is after are. An' I knows where the treasure is. I knows all about it."

"Then tell me, and I shall let him know."

"It was to him I was to tell it," he repeated, with the petulant obstinacy of a very old man.

"Well, you must wait for him."

"No, no; I ain't goin' to lose a whole day to please no one. If Mr. Holmes ain't here, then Mr. Holmes must find it all out for himself. I don't care about the look of either of you, and I won't tell a word."

He shuffled toward the door, but Athelney Jones got in front of him.

"Wait a bit, my friend," said he. "You have important information, and you must not walk off. We shall keep you, whether you like it or not, until our friend returns."

The old man made a little run toward the door, but, as Athelney Jones put his broad back up against it, he recognized the uselessness of resistance.

"Pretty sort o' treatment this!" he cried, stamping his stick. "I come here to see a gentleman, and you two, who

I never saw in my life, seize me and treat me in this fashion!"

"You will be none the worse," I said. "We shall recompense you for the loss of your time. Sit over here on the sofa, and you will not have long to wait."

He came across sullenly enough, and seated himself with his face resting on his hands. Jones and I resumed our cigars and our talk. Suddenly, however, Holmes' voice broke in upon us.

"I think that you might offer me a cigar, too," he said.

We both started in our chairs. There was Holmes sitting close to us with an air of quiet amusement.

"Holmes!" I exclaimed. "You here? But where is the old man?"

"Here is the old man," said he, holding out a heap of white hair. "Here he is—wig, whiskers, eyebrows and all. I thought my disguise was pretty good, but I hardly expected that it would stand that test."

"Ah, you rogue!" cried Jones, highly delighted. "You would have made an actor, and a rare one. You had the proper workhouse cough, and those weak legs of yours are worth ten pounds a week. I thought I knew the glint of your eye, though. You didn't get away from us so easily, you see."

"I have been working in that get-up all day," said he, lighting his cigar. "You see, a good many of the criminal classes begin to know me—especially since our friend here took to publishing some of my cases; so I can only go on the warpath under some simple disguise like this. You got my wire?"

"Yes; that was what brought me here."

"How has your case prospered?"

"It has all come to nothing. I had to release two of my prisoners, and there is no evidence against the other two."

"'Never mind. We shall give you two others in place

of them. But you must put yourself under my orders. You are welcome to all the official credit, but you must act on the lines that I point out. Is that agreed?"

"Entirely, if you will help me to the men."

"Well, then, in the first place I shall want a fast police boat—a steam launch—to be at the Westminster Stairs at seven o'clock."

"That is easily managed. There is always one about there; but I can step across the road and telephone, to make sure."

"Then I shall want two staunch men, in case of resistance."

"There will be two or three in the boat. What else?"

"When we secure the men we shall get the treasure. I think that it would be a pleasure to my friend here to take the box round to the young lady to whom half of it rightfully belongs. Let her be the first to open it. Eh, Watson?"

"It would be a great pleasure to me."

"Rather an irregular proceeding," said Jones, shaking his head. "However, the whole thing is irregular, and I suppose we must wink at it. The treasure must afterward be handed over to the authorities until after the official investigation."

"Certainly. That is easily managed. One other point. I should much like to have the details about this matter from the lips of Jonathan Small himself. You know I like to work the detail of my cases out. There is no objection to my having an unofficial interview with him, either here in my rooms or elsewhere, as long as he is efficiently guarded?"

"Well, you are master of the situation. I have had no proof yet of the existence of this Jonathan Small. However, if you catch him I don't see how I can refuse you an interview with him."

"That is understood, then?"

"Perfectly. Is there anything else?"

"Only that I insist upon your dining with us. It will be ready in half an hour. I have oysters and a brace of grouse, with something a little choice in white wine. Watson, you have never yet recognized my merits as a housekeeper."

CHAPTER X

THE END OF THE ISLANDER

OUR meal was a merry one. Holmes could talk exceedingly well when he chose, and that night he did choose. He appeared to be in a state of nervous exaltation. I have never seen him so brilliant. He spoke on a quick succession of subjects—on miracle plays, on medieval pottery, on Stradivarius violins, on the Buddhism of Ceylon, and on the warships of the future—handling each as though he had made a special study of it. His bright humor marked the reaction from his black depression of the preceding days. Athelney Jones proved to be a sociable soul in his hours of relaxation, and faced his dinner with the air of a bon vivant. For myself, I felt elated at the thought that we were nearing the end of our task, and I caught something of Holmes' gayety. None of us alluded during the dinner to the cause which had brought us together.

When the cloth was cleared, Holmes glanced at his watch, and filled up three glasses with port. "One bumper," said he, "to the success of our little expedition. And now it is high time we were off. Have you a pistol, Watson?"

"I have my old service revolver in my desk."

"You had best take it then. It is well to be prepared. I see that the cab is at the door. I ordered it for half-past six."

It was a little past seven before we reached the Westminster wharf, and found our launch awaiting us. Holmes eyed it critically.

"Is there anything to mark it as a police boat?"

"Yes—that green lamp at the side."

"Then take it off."

The small change was made; we stepped on board, and the ropes were cast off. Jones, Holmes, and I sat in the stern. There was one man at the rudder, one to tend the engine, and two burly police inspectors forward.

"Where to?" asked Jones.

"To the Tower. Tell them to stop opposite to Jacobson's Yard."

Our craft was evidently a very fast one. We shot past the long lines of loaded barges as though they were stationary. Holmes smiled with satisfaction as we overhauled a river steamer and left her behind us.

"We ought to be able to catch anything on the river," he said.

"Well, hardly that. But there are not many launches to beat us."

"We shall have to catch the 'Aurora,' and she has a name for being a clipper. I will tell you how the land lies, Watson. You recollect how annoyed I was at being balked by so small a thing?"

"Yes."

"Well, I gave my mind a thorough rest by plunging into a chemical analysis. One of our greatest statesmen has said that a change of work is the best rest. So it is. When I had succeeded in dissolving the hydrocarbon which I was at work at, I came back to our problem of the Sholtos, and thought the whole matter out again. My boys had been up the river and down the river without result. The launch was not at any landing stage or wharf, nor had it returned. Yet it could hardly have been scuttled to hide their traces—though that always remained as a possible hypothesis if all else failed. I knew that this man Small had a certain degree of low cunning, but I did not think him capable of anything in the nature of delicate finesse. That is usually a product of higher education. I then reflected that since he had certainly been in London sometime—as we had evidence that he maintained a continual watch over Pondicherry Lodge—he could hardly leave at a moment's notice, but would need some little time, if it were only a day, to arrange his affairs. That was the balance of probability, at any rate."

"It seemed to me to be a little weak," said I. "It is more probable that he had arranged his affairs before ever he set out upon his expedition."

"No, I hardly think so. This lair of his would be too valuable a retreat in case of need for him to give it up until he was sure that he could do without it. But a second consideration struck me: Jonathan Small must have felt that the peculiar appearance of his companion, however much he may have top-coated him, would give rise to gossip, and possibly be associated with this Norwood tragedy. He was quite sharp enough to see that. They had started from their headquarters under cover of darkness, and he would wish to get back before it was broad light. Now it was past three o'clock, according to Mrs. Smith, when they got the boat. It would be quite bright, and people would be about in an hour or so. Therefore, I argued, they did not go very far. They paid Smith well to hold his tongue, reserved his launch for the final escape, and hurried to their lodgings with the treasure box. In a couple of nights, when they had time to see what view the papers took, and whether there was any suspicion, they would make their way under the cover of darkness to some ship at Gravesend or in the Downs, where no doubt they had already arranged for passages to America or the Colonies."

"But the launch? They could not have taken that to their lodgings."

"Quite so. I argued that the launch must be no great way off, in spite of its invisibility. I then put myself in the place of Small, and looked at it as a man of his capacity would. He would probably consider that to send back the launch or to keep it at a wharf would make pursuit easy if the police did happen to get on his track. How, then, could he conceal the launch and yet have her at hand when wanted? I wondered what I should do myself if I were in his shoes. I could only think of one way of doing it. I might hand the launch over to some boat builder or repairer, with the directions to make a trifling change in her. She would then be removed to his shed or yard, and so be effectually concealed, while at the same time I could have her at a few hours' notice."

"That seems simple enough."

"It is just these very simple things which are extremely liable to be overlooked. However, I determined to act on the idea. I started at once in this harmless seaman's rig and inquired at all the yards down the river. I drew blank at fifteen, but at the sixteenth—Jacobson's—I learned that the 'Aurora' had been handed over to them two days ago by a wooden-legged man, with some trivial directions as to her rudder. 'There ain't naught amiss with her rudder,' said the foreman. 'There she lies, with the red streaks.' At that moment who should come down but Mordecai Smith, the missing owner. He was rather the worse for liquor. I should not, of course, have known him, but he bellowed out his name and the name of his launch. 'I want her tonight at eight o'clock,' said he—'eight o'clock sharp, mind, for I have two gentlemen who won't be kept waiting.' They had evidently paid him well, for he was very flush of money, chucking shillings about to the men. I followed him some distance, but he subsided into an ale house; so I went back into the yard, and, happening to pick up one of my boys on the way, I stationed him as a sentry over the launch. He is to stand at the water's edge and wave his handkerchief to us when they start. We shall be lying off in the stream, and it will be a strange thing if we do not take men, treasure and all."

"You have planned it all very neatly, whether they are the right men or not," said Jones; "but if the affair were in my hands, I should have had a body of police in Jacobson's Yard, and arrested them when they came down."

"Which would have been never. This man Small is a pretty shrewd fellow. He would send a scout on ahead, and if anything made him suspicious, he would lie snug for another week."

"But you might have stuck to Mordecai Smith, and so been led to their hiding place," said I.

"In that case I should have wasted my day. I think that it is a hundred to one against Smith knowing where they live. As long as he has liquor and good pay, why should he ask questions? They send him messages what to do. No, I thought over every possible course, and this is the best."

While this conversation had been proceeding, we had been shooting the long series of bridges which span the Thames. As we passed the city the last rays of the sun were gliding the cross upon the summit of St. Paul's. It was twilight before we reached the Tower.

"This is Jacobson's Yard," said Holmes, pointing to a bristle of masts and rigging on the Surrey side. "Cruise gently up and down here under cover of this string of lighters." He took a pair of night glasses from his pocket and gazed some time at the shore. "I see my sentry at his post," he remarked, "but no sign of a handkerchief."

"Suppose we go down stream a short way and lie in wait for them," said Jones, eagerly. We were all eager by this time, even the policeman and stokers, who had a very vague idea of what was going forward.

"We have no right to take anything for granted," Holmes answered. "It is certainly ten to one that they go down stream, but we cannot be certain. From this point we can see the entrance to the yard, and they can hardly see us. It will be a clear night and plenty of light. We must stay where we are. See how the folk swarm over yonder in the gas light."

"They are coming from work in the yard."

"Dirty-looking rascals, but I suppose every one has some little immortal spark concealed about him. You would not think it, to look at them. There is no à priori probability about it. A strange enigma is man!"

"Some one calls him a soul concealed in an animal," I suggested.

"Winwood Reade is good upon the subject," said Holmes. "He remarks that, while the individual man is an insoluble puzzle, in the aggregate he becomes a mathematical certainty. You can, for example, never fortell what any one man will do, but you can say with precision what an average number will be up to. Individuals vary, but percentages remain constant. So says the statistician. But do I see a handkerchief? Surely there is a white flutter over yonder."

"Yes; it is your boy," I cried. "I can see him plainly."

"And there is the 'Aurora,'" exclaimed Holmes, "and going like the devil! Full speed ahead, engineer. Make after that launch with the yellow light. By Heavens, I shall never forgive myself if she proves to have the heels of us!"

She had slipped unseen through the yard entrance, and passed behind two or three small craft, so that she had fairly got her speed up before we saw her. Now she was flying down the stream, near in to the shore, going at a tremendous rate. Jones looked gravely at her and shook his head.

"She is very fast," he said. "I doubt if we shall catch her."

"We must catch her!" cried Holmes, between his teeth. "Heap it on, stokers! Make her do all she can! If we burn the boat we must have them!"

We were fairly after her now. The furnaces roared, and the powerful engines whizzed and clanked like a great metallic heart. Her sharp, steep prow cut through the still river water and sent two rolling waves to right and to left of us. With every throb of the engines she sprang and quivered like a living thing. One great yellow lantern in our bows threw a long, flickering funnel of light in front of us. Right ahead a dark blur upon the water showed where the "Aurora" lay, and the swirl of white foam behind her spoke of the pace at which she was going. We flashed past barges, steamers, merchant vessels, in and out, behind this one and round the other. Voices hailed us out of the darkness, but still the "Aurora" thundered on, and still we followed close upon her track.

"Pile it on, men; pile it on!" cried Holmes looking down into the engine room, while the fierce glow from below beat upon his eager, aquiline face. "Get every pound of steam you can."

"I think we gain a little," said Jones, with his eyes on the "Aurora."

"I am sure of it," said I. "We shall be up with her in a very few minutes."

At that moment, however, as our evil fate would have it, a tug with three barges in tow blundered in between us. It was only by putting our helm hard down that we avoided a collision, and before we could round them and recover our way the "Aurora" had gained a good two hundred yards. She was still, however, well in view, and the murky, uncertain twilight was settling into a clear starlight night. Our boilers were strained to their utmost, and the frail shell vibrated and creaked with the fierce energy which was driving us along. We had shot through the Pool, past the West India Docks, down the long Deptford Reach, and up again after rounding the Isle of Dogs. The dull blur in front of us resolved itself now clearly enough into the dainty "Aurora.'" Jones turned our searchlight upon her, so that we could plainly see the figures upon her deck. One man sat by the stern, with something black between his knees, over which he stooped. Beside him lay a dark mass which looked like a Newfoundland dog. The boy held the tiller, while against the red glare of the furnace I could see old Smith, stripped to the waist and shoveling coal for dear life. They may have had some doubt at first as to whether we were really pursuing them, but now, as we followed every winding and turning which they took, there could no longer be any question about it. At Greenwich we were about three hundred paces behind them. At Blackwell we could not have been more than two hundred and fifty. I have coursed many creatures in many countries during my checkered career, but never did sport give me such a wild thrill as this mad, flying man-hunt down the Thames. Steadily we drew in upon them yard by yard. In the silence of the night we could hear the panting and clanking of their machinery. The man in the stern still crouched upon the deck, and his arms were moving as though he were busy, while every now and then he would look up and measure with a glance the distance which still separated us. Nearer we came and nearer. Jones yelled to them to stop. We were not more than four boats' lengths behind them, both boats flying at a tremendous pace. It was a clear reach of the river, with Barking Level upon one side and the melancholy Plumstead Marshes upon the other. At our hail the man in the stern sprang up from the deck and shook his two clinched fists at us, cursing the while in a high, cracked voice. He was a good-sized, powerful man, and, as he stood poising himself with legs astride, I could see that from the thigh downward there was but a wooden stump upon the right side. At the sound of his strident, angry cries there was a movement in the huddled bundle upon the deck. It straightened itself into a little black man— the smallest I have ever seen—with a great, misshapen head and a shock of tangled, disheveled hair. Holmes had already drawn his revolver, and I whipped out mine at the sight of this savage, distorted creature. He was wrapped in some sort of dark ulster or blanket, which left only his face exposed; but that face was enough to give a man a sleepless night. Never have I seen features so deeply marked with all bestiality and cruelty. His small eyes glowed and burned with a somber light, and his thick lips were writhed back from his teeth, which grinned and chattered at us with a half-animal fury.

"Fire if he raises his hand," said Holmes, quietly. We were within a boat's-length by this time, and almost within touch of our quarry. I can see the two of them now as they stood, the white man with his legs far apart, shrieking out curses, and the unhallowed dwarf, with his hideous face, and his strong, yellow teeth gnashing at us in the light of our lantern.

It was well that we had so clear a view of him. Even as we looked he plucked out from under his covering a short, round piece of wood, like a school ruler, and clapped it to his lips. Our pistols rang out together. He whirled round, threw up his arms, and with a kind of choking cough fell sideways into the stream. I caught one glimpse of his venomous, menacing eyes amid the white swirl of the waters. At the same moment the wooden-legged man threw himself upon the rudder and put it hard down, so that his boat made straight in for

the southern bank, while we shot past her stern, only
clearing her by a few feet. We were round after her
in an instant, but she was already nearly at the bank. It
was a wild and desolate place, where the moon glimmered
upon a wide expanse of marsh land with pools of stag-
nant water and beds of decaying vegetation. The launch
with a dull thud ran up upon the mud bank, with her bow
in the air and her stern flush with the water. The fugi-
tive sprang out, but his stump instantly sank its whole
length into the sodden soil. In vain he struggled and
writhed. Not one step could he possibly take either forward or backward. He yelled in impotent rage, and
kicked frantically into the mud with his other foot, but
his struggles only bored his wooden pin the deeper into
the sticky bank. When we brought our launch alongside
he was so firmly anchored that it was only by throwing
the end of a rope over his shoulders that we were able
to haul him out, and to drag him, like some evil fish, over
our side. The two Smiths, father and son, sat sullenly in
their launch, but came aboard meekly enough when com-
manded. The "Aurora" herself we hauled off and made
fast to our stern. A solid iron chest of Indian workmanship stood upon the deck. This, there could be no question, was the same that had contained the ill-omened treasure of the Sholtos. There was no key, but it was of considerable weight, so we transferred it carefully to our own
little cabin. As we steamed slowly up-stream again, we
flashed our search light in every direction, but there was
no sign of the islander. Somewhere in the dark ooze at
the bottom of the Thames lie the bones of that strange
visitor to our shores.

"See here," said Holmes, pointing to the wooden hatch-
way. "We were hardly quick enough with our pistols."
There, sure enough, just behind where we had been
standing, stuck one of those murderous darts which we
knew so well. It must have whizzed between us at the

instant that we fired. Holmes smiled at it, but I confess
that it turned me sick to think of the horrible death which
had passed so close to us that night.

CHAPTER XI

THE GREAT AGRA TREASURE

OUR captive sat in the cabin opposite the iron box
which he had done so much and waited so long to gain.
He was a sunburned, reckless-eyed fellow, with a net-
work of lines and wrinkles all over his mahogany features, which told of a hard, open-air life. There was a
singular prominence about his bearded chin which marked
a man who was not to be easily turned from his purpose.
His age may have been fifty or thereabouts, for his black,
curly hair was thickly shot with gray. His face, in repose, was not an unpleasing one, though his heavy brows
and aggressive chin gave him, as I had lately seen, a terrible expression when moved to anger. He sat now with
his handcuffed hands upon his lap, and his head sunk
upon his breast, while he looked with his keen, twinkling
eyes at the box which had been the cause of his ill-do-
ings. It seemed to me that there was more sorrow than
anger in his rigid and contained countenance. Once he
looked up with a gleam of something like humor in his
eyes.

"Well, Jonathan Small," said Holmes, lighting a cigar,
"I am sorry that it has come to this."

"And so am I, sir," he answered, frankly. "I don't believe that I can swing over the job. I give you my word
on the Book that I never raised hand against Mr. Sholto.
It was that little hell-hound, Tonga, who shot one of his
cursed darts into him. I had no part in it, sir. I was as
grieved as if it had been my blood relation. I welted the

little devil with the slack end of the rope for it, but it was done, and I could not undo it again."

"Have a cigar," said Holmes; "and you had better take a pull out of my flask, for you are very wet. How could you expect so small and weak a man as this black fellow to overpower Mr. Sholto and hold him while you were climbing the rope?"

"You seem to know as much about it as if you were there, sir. The truth is that I hoped to find the room clear. I knew the habits of the house pretty well, and it was the time when Mr. Sholto usually went down to his supper. I shall make no secret of the business. The best defense that I can make is just the simple truth. Now, if it had been the old major, I would have swung for him with a light heart. I would have thought no more of knifing him than of smoking this cigar. But it's cursed hard that I should be lagged over this young Sholto, with whom I had no quarrel whatever."

"You are under the charge of Mr. Athelney Jones, of Scotland Yard. He is going to bring you up to my rooms, and I shall ask you for a true account of the matter. You must make a clean breast of it, for if you do I hope that I may be of use to you. I think I can prove that the poison acts so quickly that the man was dead before you ever reached the room."

"That he was, sir. I never got such a turn in my life as when I saw him grinning at me with his head on his shoulder as I climbed through the window. It fairly shook me, sir. I'd have half killed Tonga for it, if he had not scrambled off. That was how he came to leave his club, and some of his darts, too, as he tells me, which, I dare say, helped to put you on our track; though how you kept on it is more than I can tell. I don't feel no malice against you for it. But it does seem a queer thing," he added, with a bitter smile, "that I, who have a fair claim to nigh upon half a million of money, should spend the first half of my life building a breakwater in the Andamans, and am likely to spend the other half digging drains at Dartmoor. It was an evil day for me when first I clapped eyes upon the merchant Achmet, and had to do with the Agra treasure, which never brought anything but a curse upon the man who owned it. To him it brought murder; to Major Sholto it brought fear and guilt; to me it has meant slavery for life."

At this moment Athelney Jones thrust his broad face and heavy shoulders into the tiny cabin. "Quite a family party," he remarked. "I think I shall have a pull at that flask, Holmes. Well, I think we all may congratulate each other. Pity we didn't take the other alive; but there was no choice. I say, Holmes, you must confess that you cut it rather fine. It was all we could do to overhaul her."

"All is well that ends well," said Holmes. "But I certainly did not know that the 'Aurora' was such a clipper."

"Smith says she is one of the fastest launches on the river, and that if he had had another man to help him with the engines we should never have caught her. He swears he knew nothing of this Norwood business."

"Neither he did," cried our prisoner; "not a word. I chose his launch, because I heard that she was a flyer. We told him nothing, but we paid him well, and he was to get something handsome if we reached our vessel, the 'Esmeralda,' at Gravesend, outward bound for the Brazils."

"Well, if he has done no wrong, we shall see that no wrong comes to him. If we are pretty quick in catching our men, we are not so quick in condemning them." It was amusing to notice how the consequential Jones was already beginning to give himself airs on the strength of the capture. From the slight smile which played over Sherlock Holmes' face, I could see that the speech had not been lost upon him.

"We will be at Vauxhall Bridge presently," said Jones, "and shall land you, Doctor Watson, with the treasure box. I need hardly tell you that I am taking a very grave responsibility upon myself in doing this. It is most irregular; but, of course, an agreement is an agreement. I must, however, as a matter of duty, send an inspector with you, since you have so valuable a charge. You will drive, no doubt?"

"Yes, I shall drive."

"It is a pity there is no key, that we may make an inventory first. You will have to break it open. Where is the key, my man?"

"At the bottom of the river," said Small, shortly.

"Hum! There was no use your giving this unnecessary trouble. We have had work enough already through you. However, doctor, I need not warn you to be careful. Bring the box back with you to the Baker Street rooms. You will find us there, on our way to the station."

They landed me at Vauxhall, with my heavy iron box, and with a bluff, genial inspector as my companion. A quarter of an hour's drive brought us to Mrs. Cecil Forrester's. The servant seemed surprised at so late a visitor. Mrs. Cecil Forrester was out for the evening, she explained, and likely to be very late. Miss Morstan, however, was in the drawing room; so to the drawing room I went, box in hand, leaving the obliging inspector in the cab.

She was seated by the open window, dressed in some sort of white, diaphanous material, with a little touch of scarlet in the neck and waist. The soft light of a shaded lamp fell upon her as she leaned back in the basket chair, playing over her sweet, grave face, and tinting with a dull, metallic sparkle the rich coils of her luxuriant hair; one white arm and hand drooped over the side of the chair, and her whole pose and figure spoke of an absorbing melancholy. At the sound of my footfall she sprang to her feet, however, and a bright flush of surprise and of pleasure colored her pale cheeks.

"I heard a cab drive up," she said. "I thought that Mrs. Forrester had come back very early, but I never dreamed that it might be you. What news have you brought me?"

"I have brought something better than news,," said I, putting down the box upon the table, and speaking jovially and boisterously, though my heart was heavy within me. "I have brought you something which is worth all the news in the world. I have brought you a fortune."

She glanced at the iron box. "Is that the treasure, then?" she asked, coolly enough.

"Yes, this is the great Agra treasure. Half of it is yours and half is Thaddeus Sholto's. You will have a couple of hundred thousand each. Think of that! An annuity of ten thousand pounds. There will be few richer young ladies in England. Is it not glorious?"

I think that I must have been rather overacting my delight, and that she detected a hollow ring in my congratulations, for I saw her eyebrows rise a little, and she glanced at me curiously.

"If I have it," said she, "I owe it to you."

"No, no," I answered; "not to me, but to my friend Sherlock Holmes. With all the will in the world, I could never have followed up a clew which has taxed even his analytical genius. As it was, we very nearly lost it at the last moment."

"Pray sit down and tell me all about it, Doctor Watson," said she.

I narrated briefly what had occurred since I had seen her last—Holmes' new method of search, the discovery of the "Aurora," the appearance of Athelney Jones, our expedition in the evening, and the wild chase down the Thames. She listened, with parted lips and shining eyes, to my recital of our adventures. When I spoke of the dart which had so narowly missed us, she turned so white that I feared she was about to faint.

"It is nothing," she said, as I hastened to pour her out some water. "I am all right again. It was a shock to me to hear that I had placed my friends in such horrible peril."

"That is all over," I answered. "It was nothing. I will tell you no more gloomy details. Let us turn to something brighter. There is the treasure. What could be brighter than that? I got leave to bring it with me, thinking that it would interest you to be the first to see it."

"It would be of the greatest interest to me," she said. There was no eagerness in her voice, however. It struck her, doubtless, that it might seem ungracious upon her part to be indifferent to a prize which had cost so much to win.

"What a pretty box!" she said, stooping over it. "This is Indian work, I suppose?"

"Yes; it is Benares metal work."

"And so heavy!" she exclaimed, trying to raise it. "The box alone must be of some value. Where is the key?"

"Small threw it into the Thames," I answered. "I must borrow Mrs. Forrester's poker." There was, in the front, a thick and broad hasp, wrought in the image of a sitting Buddha. Under this I thrust the end of the poker and twisted it outward as a lever. The hasp sprung open with a loud snap. With trembling fingers I flung back the lid. We both stood gazing in astonishment. The box was empty!

No wonder that it was heavy. The iron work was two-thirds of an inch thick all around. It was massive, well made, and solid, like a chest constructed to carry things of great price, but not one shred or crumb of metal or jewelry lay within it. It was absolutely and completely empty.

"The treasure is lost," said Miss Morstan, calmly.

As I listened to the words and realized what they meant, a great shadow seemed to pass from my soul. I did not know how this Agra treasure had weighed me down until now that it was finally removed. It was selfish, no doubt, disloyal, wrong, but I could realize nothing save that the golden barrier was gone from between us.

"Thank God!" I ejaculated from my very heart.

She looked at me with a quick, questioning smile. "Why do you say that?" she asked.

"Because you are within my reach again," I said, taking her hand. She did not withdraw it. "Because I love you, Mary, as truly as ever a man loved a woman. Because this treasure, these riches, sealed my lips. Now that they are gone, I can tell you how I love you. That is why I said, 'Thank God.'"

"Then I say, 'Thank God,' too," she whispered, as I drew her to my side. Whoever had lost a treasure, I knew that night that I had gained one.

CHAPTER XII

THE STRANGE STORY OF JONATHAN SMALL

A very patient man was the inspector in the cab, for it was a weary time before I rejoined him. His face clouded over when I showed him the empty box.

"There goes the reward!" said he, gloomily. "Where there is no money there is no pay. This night's work would have been worth a tenner each to Sam Brown and me, if the treasure had been there."

"Mr. Thaddeus Sholto is a rich man," I said. "He will see that you are rewarded, treasure or no treasure."

The inspector shook his head despondently, however.

"It's a bad job," he repeated; "and so Mr. Athelney Jones will think."

His forecast proved to be correct, for the detective looked blank enough when I got to Baker Street and showed him the empty box. They had only just arrived, Holmes, the prisoner, and he, for they had changed their plans so far as to report themselves at a station upon the way. My companion lounged in his armchair with his usual listless expression, while Small sat stolidly opposite to him with his wooden leg cocked over his sound one. As I exhibited the empty box he leaned back in his chair and laughed aloud.

"This is your doing, Small," said Athelney Jones, angrily.

"Yes, I have put it away where you shall never lay hand upon it," he cried, exultantly. "It is my treasure; and if I can't have the loot, I'll take darned good care that no one else does. I tell you that no living man has any right to it, unless it is three men who are in the Andaman convict barracks and myself. I know now that I cannot have the use of it and I know that they cannot. I have acted all through for them as much as for myself. It's been the sign of four with us always. Well, I know that they would have had me do just what I have done, and throw the treasure into the Thames rather than let it go to kith or kin of Sholto or of Morstan. It was not to make them rich that we did for Achmet. You'll find the treasure where the key is, and where little Tonga is. When I saw that your launch must catch us, I put the loot in a safe place. There are no rupees for you this journey."

"You are deceiving us, Small," said Athelney Jones, sternly. "If you had wished to throw the treasure into the Thames, it would have been easier for you to have thrown box and all."

"Easier for me to throw, and easier for you to recover,"

he answered, with a shrewd, sidelong look. "The man that was clever enough to hunt me down is clever enough to pick an iron box from the bottom of a river. Now that they are scattered over five miles or so, it may be a harder job. It went to my heart to do it, though. I was half mad when you came up with us. However, there's no good grieving over it. I've had ups in my life, and I've had downs, but I've learned not to cry over spilled milk."

"This is a very serious matter, Small," said the detective. "If you had helped justice, instead of thwarting it in this way, you would have had a better chance at your trial."

"Justice?" snarled the ex-convict. "A pretty justice! Whose loot is this, if it is not ours? Where is the justice that I should give it up to those who had never earned it? Look how I have earned it. Twenty long years in that fever-ridden swamp, all day at work under the mangrove tree, all night chained up in the filthy convict huts, bitten by mosquitoes, racked with ague, bullied by every cursed black-faced policemen who loved to take it out of a white man. That was how I earned the Agra treasure; and you talk to me of justice because I cannot bear to feel that I have paid this price only that another may enjoy it! I would rather swing a score of times, or have one of Tonga's darts in my hide, than live in a convict's cell and feel that another man is at his ease in a palace with the money that should be mine!" Small had dropped his mask of stoicism, and all this came out in a wild whirl of words, while his eyes blazed, and the handcuffs clanked together with the impassioned movement of his hands. I could understand, as I saw the fury and the passion of the man, that it was no groundless or unnatural terror which had possessed Major Sholto when he first learned that the injured convict was upon his track.

"You forget that we know nothing of all this," said

Holmes, quietly. "We have not heard your story, and we cannot tell how far justice may originally have been on your side."

"Well, sir, you have been very fair-spoken to me, though I can see that I have you to thank that I have these bracelets upon my wrists. Still, I bear no grudge for that. It is all fair and aboveboard. If you want to hear my story, I have no wish to hold it back. What I say to you is God's truth, every word of it. Thank you; you can put the glass beside me here, and I'll put my lips to it if I am dry.

"I am a Worcestershire man myself—born near Pershore. I dare say you would find a heap of Smalls living there now if you were to look. I have often thought of taking a look round there, but the truth is that I was never much of a credit to the family, and I doubt if they would be so very glad to see me. They were all steady, chapel-going folk, small farmers, well known and respected over the country side, while I was always a bit of a rover. At last, however, when I was about eighteen, I gave them no more trouble, for I got into a mess over a girl, and could only get out of it by taking the queen's shilling and joining the Third Buffs, which was just starting for India.

"I wasn't destined to do much soldiering, however. I had just got past the goose-step, and learned to handle my musket, when I was fool enough to go swimming in the Ganges. Luckily for me, my company sergeant, John Holder, was in the water at the same time, and he was one of the finest swimmers in the service. A crocodile took me, just as I was half-way across, and nipped off my right leg, as clean as a surgeon could have done it, just above the knee. What with the shock and loss of blood, I fainted, and should have been drowned if Holder had not caught hold of me and paddled for the bank. I was five months in hospital over it, and when at last I was able to limp out of it, with this timber toe strapped to my stump, I found myself invalided out of the army and unfitted for any active occupation.

"I was, as you can imagine, pretty down on my luck at this time, for I was a useless cripple, though not yet in my twentieth year. However, my misfortune soon proved to be a blessing in disguise. A man named Abel-white, who had come out there as an indigo planter, wanted an overseer to look after his coolies and keep them up to their work. He happened to be a friend of our colonel's who had taken an interest in me since the accident. To make a long story short, the colonel recommended me strongly for the post, and, as the work was mostly to be done on horseback, my leg was no great obstacle, for I had enough knee to keep a good grip on the saddle. What I had to do was to ride over the plantation, to keep an eye on the men as they worked, and to report the idlers. The pay was fair, I had comfortable quarters, and altogether I was content to spend the remainder of my life in indigo planting. Mr. Abelwhite was a kind man, and he would often drop into my little shanty and smoke a pipe with me, for white folk out there feel their hearts warm to each other as they never do here at home."

"Well, I was never in luck's way long. Suddenly, without a note of warning, the great mutiny broke upon us. One month India lay as still and peaceful, to all appearance, as Surrey or Kent; the next there were two hundred thousand black devils let loose, and the country was a perfect hell. Of course, you know all about it, gentlemen, a deal more than I do, very like, since reading is not in my line. I only know what I saw with my own eyes. Our plantation was at a place called Muttra, near the border of the Northwest Provinces. Night after night the whole sky was alight with the burning bungalows, and day after day we had small companies of

Europeans passing through our estate, with their wives
and children, on their way to Agra, where were the nearest troops. Mr. Abelwhite was an obstinate man. He
had it in his head that the affair had been exaggerated,
and that it would blow over as suddenly as it had sprung
up. There he sat on his veranda, drinking whiskey pegs
and smoking cheroots, while the country was in a blaze
about him. Of course, we stuck by him, I and Dawson, who, with his wife, used to do the bookwork and the
managing. Well, one fine day the crash came. I had
been away on a distant plantation and was riding slowly
home in the evening, when my eye fell upon something all
huddled together at the bottom of a steep nullah. I rode
down to see what it was, and the cold struck through my
heart when I found it was Dawson's wife, all cut into
ribbons, and half eaten by jackals and native dogs. A
little further up the road Dawson himself was lying on
his face, quite dead, with an empty revolver in his hand,
and four Sepoys lying across one another in front of him.
I reined up my horse, wondering which way I should turn,
but at that moment I saw thick smoke curling up from
Abelwhite's bungalow and the flames beginning to burst
through the roof. I knew then that I could do my employer no good, but would only throw my own life away
if I meddled in the matter. From where I stood I could
see hundreds of the black fiends, with their red coats still
on their backs, dancing and howling round the burning
house. Some of them pointed at me, and a couple of
bullets sung past my head; so I broke away across the
paddy-fields, and found myself late at night, safe within
the walls at Agra.

"As it proved, however, there was no great safety
there, either. The whole country was up like a swarm
of bees. Wherever the English could collect in little
bands they held just the ground that their guns com-
manded. Everywhere else they were helpless fugitives.

It was a fight of the millions against the hundreds; and the cruelest part of it was that these men that we fought against, foot, horse and gunners, were our own picked troops, whom we had taught and trained, handling our own weapons, and blowing our own bugle calls. At Agra there were the Third Bengal Fusiliers, some Sikhs, two troops of horse, and a battery of artillery. A volunteer corps of clerks and merchants had been formed, and this I joined, wooden leg and all. We went out to meet the rebels at Shahgunge early in July, and we beat them back for a time, but our powder gave out, and we had to fall back upon the city. Nothing but the worst news came to us from every side—which is not to be wondered at, for if you look at the map you will see that we were right in the heart of it. Lucknow is rather better than a hundred miles to the east, and Cawnpore about as far to the south. From every point on the compass there was nothing but torture, and murder, and outrage.

"The city of Agra is a great place, swarming with fanatics and fierce devil-worshipers of all sorts. Our handful of men were lost among the narrow, winding streets. Our leader moved across the river, therefore, and took up his position in the old fort of Agra. I don't know if any of you gentlemen have ever read or heard anything of that old fort. It is a very queer place—the queerest that ever I was in, and I have been in some rum corners, too. First of all, it is enormous in size. I should think that the inclosure must be acres and acres. There is a modern part, which took all our garrison, women, children, stores and everything else, with plenty of room over. But the modern part is nothing like the size of the old quarter, where nobody goes, and which is given over to the scorpions and the centipedes. It is all full of great, deserted halls, and winding passages, and long corridors twisting in and out, so that it is easy enough for folks to get lost in it. For this reason, it was seldom that any one went into it, though now and again a party with torches might go exploring.

"The river washes along the front of the old fort, and so protects it, but on the sides and behind there are many doors, and these had to be guarded, of course, in the old quarters as well as in that which was actually held by our troops. We were short-handed, with hardly men enough to man the angles of the building and to serve the guns. It was impossible for us, therefore, to station a strong guard at every one of the innumerable gates. What we did was to organize a central guard house in the middle of the fort, and to leave each gate under the charge of one white man and two or three natives. I was selected to take charge during certain hours of the night of a small, isolated door upon the southwest side of the building. Two Sikh troopers were placed under my command, and I was instructed if anything went wrong to fire my musket when I might rely upon help coming at once from the central guard. As the guard was a good two hundred paces away, however, and as the space between was cut up into a labyrinth of passages and corridors, I had great doubts as to whether they could arrive in time to be of any use in case of an actual attack.

"Well, I was pretty proud at having this small command given me, since I was a raw recruit, and a game-legged one at that. For two nights I kept the watch with my Punjaubees. They were tall, fierce-looking chaps, Mohammed Singh and Abdullah Khan by name, both old fighting men who had borne arms against us at Chilianwallah. They could talk English pretty well, but I could get little out of them. They preferred to stand together and jabber all night in their queer Sikh lingo. For myself, I used to stand outside the gateway, looking down on the broad, winding river and on the twinkling lights of the great city. The beating of drums, the rattle of tom-toms, and the yells and howls of the rebels, drunk with opium and with bang, were enough to remind us all night of our dangerous neighbors across the stream. Every two hours the officers of the night used to come round to all the posts, to make sure that all was well.

The third night of my watch was dark and dirty, with a small, driving rain. It was dreary work standing in the gateway hour after hour in such weather. I tried again and again to make my Sikhs talk, but without much success. At two in the morning the rounds passed, and broke for a moment the weariness of the night. Finding that my companions would not be led into conversation, I took out my pipe, and laid down my musket to strike a match. In an instant the two Sikhs were upon me. One of them snatched my fire-lock up and leveled it at my head, while the other held a great knife at my throat and swore between his teeth that he would plunge it into me if I moved a step.

"My first thought was that these fellows were in league with the rebels, and that this was the beginning of an assault. If our door were in the hands of the Sepoys, the place must fall and the women and children be treated as they were in Cawnpore. Maybe you gentlemen think that I am just making out a case for myself, but I give you my word that when I thought of that, though I felt the point of the knife at my throat, I opened my mouth with the intention of giving a scream, if it was my last one, which might alarm the main guard. The man who held me seemed to know my thoughts; for even as I braced myself to it, he whispered, 'Don't make a noise. The fort is safe enough. There are no rebel dogs on this side of the river.' There was the ring of truth in what he said, and I knew that if I raised my voice I was a dead man. I could read it in the fellow's brown eyes. I waited, therefore, in silence, to see what it was they wanted from me.

"'Listen to me, sahib,' said the taller and fiercer of

the pair, the one whom they called Abdullah Khan. 'You must either be with us now or you must be silenced forever. The thing is too great a one for us to hesitate. Either you are heart and soul with us, on your oath on the cross of the Christians, or your body this night shall be thrown into the ditch, and we shall pass over to our brothers in the rebel army. There is no middle way. Which is it to be, death or life? We can only give you three minutes to decide, for the time is passing, and all must be done before the rounds come again.'

" 'How can I decide?' said I. 'You have not told me what you want of me. But I tell you now, that if it is anything against the safety of the fort, I will have no truck with it; so you can drive home your knife, and welcome.'

" 'It is nothing against the fort,' said he. 'We only ask you to do that which your countrymen come to this land for. We ask you to be rich. If you will be one of us this night, we will swear to you upon the naked knife, and by the threefold oath which no Sihk was ever known to break, that you shall have your fair share of the loot. A quarter of the treasure shall be yours. We can say no fairer.'

" 'But what is the treasure, then?' I asked. 'I am as ready to be rich as you can be, if you will but show me how it can be done.'

" 'You swear, then,' said he, 'by the bones of your father, by the honor of your mother, by the cross of your faith, to raise no hand and speak no word against us, either now or afterward?"

" 'I will swear it,' I answered, 'provided that the fort is not endangered.'

" 'Then my comrades and I will swear that you shall have a quarter of the treasure, which shall be equally divided among the four of us.'

" 'There are but three,' said I.

" 'No; Dost Akbar must have his share. We can tell

the tale to you while we await them. Do you stand at the gate, Mohammed Singh, and give notice of their coming. The thing stands thus, sahib, and I tell it to you because I know that an oath is binding upon a Feringhee, and that we may trust you. Had you been a lying Hindoo, though you had sworn by all the gods in their false temples, your blood would have been upon the knife and your body in the ditch. But the Sikh knows the Englishman, and the Englishman knows the Sikh. Hearken, then, to what I have to say.

"'There is a rajah in the northern provinces who has much wealth, though his lands are small. Much has come to him from his father, and more still he has set by himself, for he is of a low nature and hoards his gold rather than spend it. When the trouble broke out he would be friends both with the lion and the tiger—with the Sepoy and with the Company's Raj. Soon, however, it seemed to him that the white men's day was come, for through all the land he could hear of nothing but of their death and their overthrow. Yet, being a careful man, he made such plans that, come what might, half at least of his treasure should be left to him. That which was in gold and silver he kept by him in the vaults of his palace, but the most precious stones and the choicest pearl that he had he put in an iron box, and sent it by a trusty servant who, under the guise of a merchant, should take it to the fort at Agra, there to lie until the land is at peace. Thus, if the rebels won he would have his money, but if the Company conquer, his jewels would be saved to him. Having thus divided his hoard, he threw himself into the cause of the Sepoys, since they were strong upon his borders. By his doing this, mark you sahib, his property becomes the due of those who have been true to their salt.

"'This pretended merchant, who travels under the name of Achmet, is now in the city of Agra, and desires to gain his way into the fort. He has with him, as traveling companion, my foster brother, Dost Akbar, who knows his secret. Dost Akbar has promised this night to lead him to a side postern of the fort, and has chosen this one for his purpose. Here he will come presently and here he will find Mohammed Singh and myself awaiting him. The place is lonely, and none shall know of his coming. The world shall know of the merchant Achmet no more, but the great treasure of the rajah shall be divided among us. What say you to it, sahib?'

"In Worcestershire the life of a man seems a great and a sacred thing; but it is very different when there is fire and blood all round you and you have been used to meeting death at every turn. Whether Achmet the merchant lived or died was a thing as light as air to me, but at the talk about the treasure my heart turned to it, and I, thought of what I might do in the old country with it, and how my folk would stare when they saw their ne'er-do-well coming back with his pockets full of gold moidores. I had, therefore, already made up my mind. Abdullah Khan, however, thinking that I hesitated, pressed the matter more closely.

" 'Consider, sahib,' said he, 'that if this man is taken by the commandant he will be hung or shot, and his jewels taken by the government, so that no man will be a rupee the better for them. Now, since we do the taking of him, why should we not do the rest as well? The jewels will be as well with us as in the Company's coffers. There will be enough to make every one of us rich men and great chiefs. No one can know about the matter, for here we are cut off from all men. What could be better for the purpose? Say again, then, sahib, whether you are with us, or if we must look upon you as an enemy.'

" 'I am with you, heart and soul,' said I.

" 'It is well,' he answered, handing me back my fire-lock. 'You see that we trust you, for your word, like ours, is not to be broken. We have now only to wait for my brother and the merchant.'

"'Does your brother know, then, of what you will do?" I asked.

"'The plan is his. He has devised it. We will go to the gate and share the watch with Mohammed Singh."

"The rain was still falling steadily, for it was just the begining of the wet season. Brown, heavy clouds were drifting across the sky, and it was hard to see more than a stone-cast. A deep moat lay in front of our door, but the water was in places nearly dried up, and it could easily be crossed. It was strange to me to be standing there with those two wild Punjaubees waiting for the man who was coming to his death.

"Suddenly my eye caught the glint of a shaded lantern at the other side of the moat. It vanished among the mould heaps, and then appeared again coming slowly in our direction.

"'Here they are!' I exclaimed.

"'You will challenge him, sahib, as usual,' whispered Abdullah. 'Give him no cause for fear. Send us in with him, and we shall do the rest while you stay on guard. Have the lantern ready to uncover, that he may be sure that it is indeed the man.'

"The light had flickered onward, now stopping and now advancing, until I could see two dark figures upon the other side of the moat. I let them scramble down the sloping bank, splash through the mire, and climb half-way up to the gate, before I challenged them.

"'Who goes there?' said I, in a subdued voice.

"'Friends,' came the answer. I uncovered my lantern and threw a flood of light upon them. The first was an enormous Sikh, with a black beard which swept nearly down to his cummerbund. Outside of a show I have never seen so tall a man. The other was a little, fat, round fellow, with a great yellow turban, and a bundle

in his hand, done up in a shawl. He seemed to be all in
a quiver with fear, for his hands twitched as if he had the
ague, and his head kept turning to left and right with
two bright little twinkling eyes, like a mouse when he
ventures out from his hole. It gave me the chills to
think of killing him, but I thought of the treasure, and
my heart set as hard as a flint within me. When he saw
my white face he gave a little chirrup of joy and came
running up toward me.

"'Your protection, sahib,' he panted; 'your protection
for the unhappy merchant Achmet. I have traveled
across Rajpootna that I might seek the shelter of the
fort at Agra. I have been robbed, and beaten, and abused
because I have been the friend of the Company. It is a
blessed night this when I am once more in safety—I and
my poor possessions.'

"'What have you in the bundle?' I asked.

"'An iron box,' he answered, 'which contains one or
two little family matters which are of no value to others,
but which I should be sorry to lose. Yet I am not a
beggar; and I shall reward you, young sahib, and your
governor also, if he will give me the shelter I ask.'

"I could not trust myself to speak longer with the
man. The more I looked at his fat, frightened face, the
harder did it seem that we should slay him in cold blood.
It was best to get it over.

"'Take him to the main guard,' said I. The two Sikhs
closed in upon him on each side, and the giant walked
behind, while they marched in through the dark gateway.
Never was a man so compassed round with death. I remained at the gateway with the lantern.

"I could hear the measured tramp of their footsteps
sounding through the lonely corridors. Suddenly it
ceased, and I heard voices, and a scuffle, with the sound of
blows. A moment later there came, to my horror, a rush
of footsteps coming in my direction, with the loud breath-

ing of a running man. I turned my lantern down the long, straight passage, and there was the fat man, running like the wind, with a smear of blood across his face, and close at his heels, bounding like a tiger, the great, black-bearded Sikh, with a knife flashing in his hand. I have never seen a man run so fast as that little merchant. He was gaining on the Sikh, and I could see that if he once passed me and got to the open air, he would save himself yet. My heart softened to him, but again the thought of his treasure turned me hard and bitter. I cast my fire-lock between his legs as he raced past, and he rolled twice over like a shot rabbit. Ere he could stagger to his feet the Sikh was upon him, and buried his knife twice in his side. The man never uttered moan nor moved muscle, but lay where he had fallen. I think, myself, that he may have broken his neck with the fall. You see, gentlemen, that I am keeping my promise. I am telling you every word of this business just exactly as it happened, whether it is in my favor or not."

He stopped and held out his manacled hands for the whisky and water which Holmes had brewed for him. For myself, I confess that I had now conceived the utmost horror of the man, not only for this cold-blooded business in which he had been concerned, but even more for the somewhat flippant and careless way in which he narrated it. Whatever punishment was in store for him I felt that he might expect no sympathy from me. Sherlock Holmes and Jones sat with their hands upon their knees, deeply interested in the story, but with the same disgust written upon their faces. He may have observed it, for there was a touch of defiance in his voice and manner as he proceeded:

"It was all very bad, no doubt," said he. "I should like to know how many fellows in my shoes would have refused a share of this loot when they knew that they would have their throats cut for their pains. Besides, it was my life or his when once he was in the fort. If he had got out, the whole business would have come to light, and I should have been court-martialed and shot as likely as not; for people were not very lenient at a time like that."

"Go on with your story," said Holmes, shortly.

"Well, we carried him in, Abdullah, Akbar and I. A fine weight he was, too, for all that he was so short. Mohammed Singh was left to guard the door. We took him to a place where the Sikhs had already prepared. It was some distance off, where a winding passage leads to a great empty hall, the brick walls of which were all crumbling to pieces. The earth floor had sunk in at one place, making a natural grave, so we left Achmet the merchant there, having first covered him over with loose bricks. This done, we all went back to the treasure.

"It lay where he had dropped it when he was first attacked. The box was the same which now lies open upon your table. A key was hung by a silken cord to that carved handle upon the top. We opened it, and the light of the lantern gleamed upon a collection of gems such as I have read of and thought about when I was a little lad at Pershore. It was blinding to look upon them. When we had feasted our eyes we took them all out and made a list of them. There were one hundred and forty-three diamonds of the first water, including one which has been called, I believe, 'the great Mogul' and is said to be the second largest stone in existence. Then there were ninety-seven very fine emeralds, and one hundred and seventy rubies, some of which, however, were small. There were forty carbuncles, two hundred and ten sapphires, sixty-one agates, and a great quantity of beryls, onyxes, cat's-eyes, turquoises, and other stones, the very names of which I did not know at the time, though I have become more familiar with them since. Beside this, there were nearly three hundred very fine pearls, twelve of which were set in a gold chaplet. By the way, these last had been taken out of the chest and were not there when I recovered it.

"After we had counted our treasures we put them back into the chest and carried them to the gateway to show them to Mohammed Singh. Then we solemnly renewed our oath to stand by each other and be true to our secret. We agreed to conceal our loot in a safe place until the country should be at peace again, and then to divide it equally among ourselves. There was no use dividing it at present, for if gems of such value were found upon us, it would cause suspicion, and there was no privacy in the fort nor any place where we could keep them. We carried the box, therefore, into the same hall where we had buried the body, and there, under certain bricks, in the best preserved wall, we made a hollow and put our treasure. We made careful note of the place, and next day I drew four plans, one for each of us, and put the sign of the four of us at the bottom, for we had sworn that we should each always act for all, so that none might take advantage. That is an oath that I can put my hand to my heart and swear that I have never broken.

"Well, there is no use my telling you, gentlemen, what came of the Indian mutiny. After Wilson took Delhi, and Sir Colins relieved Lucknow, the back of the business was broken. Fresh troops came pouring in, and Nana Sahib made himself scarce over the frontier. A flying column under Colonel Greathead came round to Agra and cleared the Pandies away from it. Peace seemed to be settling upon the country, and we four were beginning to hope that the time was at hand when we might safely go off with our shares of the plunder. In a moment, however, our hopes were shattered, by our being arrested as the murderers of Asmet.

"It came about in this way. When the rajah put his jewels into the hands of Achmet, he did it because he

knew that he was a trusty. They are suspicious folk in
the East, however; so what does this rajah do but take
a second even more trusty servant, and set him to
play the spy upon the first? This second man was
ordered never to let Achmet out of his sight, and he followed him like his shadow. He went after him that
night, and saw him pass through the doorway. Of
course, he thought he had taken refuge in the fort, and
applied for admission there himself next day, but could
find no trace of Achmet. This seemed to him so strange
that he spoke about it to a sergeant of guides. A thorough search was quickly made, and the body was discovered. Thus, at the very moment that we thought
all was safe, we were all four seized and brought to trial
on a charge of murder—three of us because we held the
gate that night, and the fourth because he was known to
have been in company of the murdered man. Not a
word about the jewels came out at the trial, for the
rajah had been deposed and driven out of India; so no
one had any particular interest in them. The murder,
however, was clearly made out, and it was certain that we
must all have been concerned it it. The three Sikhs got
penal servitude for life, and I was condemned to death,
though my sentence was afterward commuted into the
same as the others.

"It was rather a queer position that we found ourselves
in then. There we were all four tied by the leg, with
precious little chance of ever getting out again, while we
each held a secret which might have put each of us in a
palace if we could only have made use of it. It was enough
to make a man eat his heart out to have to stand the kick
and the cuff of every petty jack-in-office, to have rice to
eat and water to drink, when that gorgeous fortune was
ready for him outside, just waiting to be picked up. It
might have driven me mad; but I was always a pretty
stubborn one, so I just held on and bided my time.

"At last it seemed to me to have come. I was changed from Agra to Madras, and from there to Blair Island, in the Andamans. There are very few white convicts at this settlement, and, as I had behaved well from the first, I soon found myself a privileged person. I was given a hut in Hope Town, which is a small place on the slopes of Mount Harriet, and I was left pretty much to myself. It is a dreary, fever-stricken place, and all beyond our little clearings was infested with wild cannibal natives, who were ready enough to blow a poisoned dart at us if they saw a chance. They were digging, and ditching, and yam planting, and a dozen other things to be done, so we were busy enough all day; though in the evening we had a little time to ourselves. Among other things, I learned to dispense drugs for the surgeon, and picked up a smattering of his knowledge. All the time I was on the look-out for a chance of escape; but it is hundreds of miles from any other land, and there is little or no wind in those seas; so it was a terribly difficult job to get away.

"The surgeon, Doctor Somerton, was a fast, sporting young chap, and the other young officers would meet in his rooms of an evening and play cards. The surgery, where I used to make up my drugs, was next to his sitting room, with a small window between us. Often, if I felt lonesome, I used to turn out the lamp in the surgery, and then, standing there, I could hear their talk and watch their play. I am fond of a hand at cards myself and it was almost as good as having one to watch the others. There were Major Sholto, Captain Morstan, and Lieutenant Bromley Brown, who were in command of the native troops, and there were the surgeon himself, and two or three prison officials, crafty old hands who played a nice, sly, safe game. A very snug little party they use to make.

"Well, there was one thing which very soon struck me, and that was that the soldiers used always to lose and the civilians to win. Mind, I don't say that there was anything unfair, but so it was. These prison chaps had done little else than play cards ever since they had been at the Andamans, and they knew each other's game to a point, while the others just played to pass the time and threw their cards down anyhow. Night after night the soldiers got up poorer men, and the poorer they got the more keen they were to play. Major Sholto was the hardest hit. He used to pay in notes and gold at first, but soon it came to notes of hand, and for big sums. He sometimes would win for a few deals, just to give him heart, and then the luck would set in against him worse than ever. All day he would wander about as black as thunder, and he took to drinking a deal more than was good for him.

"One night he lost even more heavily than usual. I was sitting in my hut when he and Captain Morstan came stumbling along on the way to their quarters. They were bosom friends, those two, and never far apart. The major was raving about his losses.

" 'It's all up, Morstan,' he was saying, as they passed my hut. 'I shall have to send in my papers. I am a ruined man.'

" 'Nonsense, old chap!' said the other, slapping him upon the shoulder. 'I've had a nasty facer myself, but—' That was all I could hear, but it was enough to set me thinking.

"A couple of days later Major Sholto was strolling on the beach; so I took the chance of speaking to him.

" 'I wish to have your advice, major,' said I.

" 'Well, Small, what is it?' he said, taking his cheroot from his lips.

" 'I wanted to ask you, sir,' said I, 'who is the proper person to whom hidden treasure should be handed over. I know where half a million worth lies, and, as I cannot use it myself, I thought perhaps the best thing that I could do would be to hand it over to the proper authorities, and then, perhaps, they would get my sentence shortened for me.'

" 'Half a million, Small?' he gasped, looking hard at me to see if I was in earnest.

" 'Quite that, sir—in jewels and pearls. It lies there ready for any one. And the queer thing about it is that the real owner is outlawed and cannot hold property, so that it belongs to the first comer.'

" 'To government, Small,' he stammered; 'to government.' But he said it in a halting fashion, and I knew in my heart that I had got him.

" 'You think, then, sir, that I should give the information to the governor-general?' said I, quietly.

" 'Well, well, you must not do anything rash, or that you might repent. Let me hear all about it, Small. Give me the facts.'

"I told him the whole story, with small changes, so that he could not identify the place. When I had finished he stood stock-still and full of thought. I could see by the twitch of his lip that there was a struggle going on within him.

" 'This is a very important matter, Small,' he said, at last. 'You must not say a word to any one about it, and I shall see you again soon.'

"Two nights later he and his friend, Captain Morstan, came to my hut in the dead of the night with a lantern.

" 'I want you just to let Captain Morstan hear that story from your own lips, Small,' said he.

"I repeated it as I had told it before.

" 'It rings true, eh?' said he. 'It's good enough to act upon?'

"Captain Morstan nodded.

" 'Look here, Small,' said the major. 'We have been talking it over, my friend here and I, and we have come to the conclusion that this secret of yours is hardly a government matter after all, but is a private concern of your own, which, of course, you have the power of disposing of as you think best. Now, the question is, what price would you ask for it? We might be inclined to take it up, and at least look into it, if we could agree as to terms.' He tried to speak in a cool, careless way, but his eyes were shining with excitement and greed.

"'Why, as to that, gentlemen,' I answered, trying also to be cool, but feeling as excited as he did, 'there is only one bargain which a man in my position can make. I shall want you to help me to my freedom, and to help my three companions to theirs. We shall then take you into partnership, and give you a fifth share to divide between you.'"

"'Hum!' said he. 'A fifth share! That is not very tempting.'

"'It would come to fifty thousand apiece,' said I.

"'But how can we gain your freedom? You know very well that you ask an impossibility.'

"'Nothing of the sort,' I answered. 'I have thought it all out to the last detail. The only bar to our escape is that we can get no boat fit for the voyage, and no provisions to last us for so long a time. There are plenty of little yachts and yawls at Calcutta or Madras which would serve our turn well. Do you bring one over. We shall engage to get aboard her by night, and if you will drop us on any part of the Indian coast, you will have done your part of the bargain.'

"'If there was only one,' he said.

"'None or all,' I answered. 'We have sworn it. The four of us must always act together.'

"'You see, Morstan,' said he, 'Small is a man of his word. He does not flinch from his friends. I think we may very well trust him.'

"'It's a dirty business,' the other answered. 'Yet, as

you say, the money would save our commissions handsomely.'

" 'Well, Small,' said the major, 'we must, I suppose, try and meet you. We must first, of course, test the truth of your story. Tell me where the box is hid, and I shall get leave of absence and go back to India in the monthly relief boat to inquire into the affair.'

" 'Not so fast,' said I, growing colder as he got hold. 'I must have the consent of my three comrades. I tell you that it is four or none with us.'

" 'Nonsense!' he broke in. 'What have three black fellows to do with our agreement?'

" 'Black or blue,' said I, 'they are in with me, and we all go together.'

"Well, the matter ended by a second meeting, at which Mohammed Singh, Abdullah Khan and Dost Akbar were all present. We talked the matter over again and at last we came to an arrangement. We were to provide both the officers with charts of the part of the Agra fort, and mark the place in the wall where the treasure was hid. Major Sholto was to go to India to test our story. If he found the box he was to leave it there, to send out a small yacht provisioned for a voyage, which was to lie off Rutland Island, and to which we were to make our way, and finally to return to his duties. Captain Morstan was then to apply for leave of absence, to meet us at Agra, and there we were to have a final division of the treasure, he taking the major's share as well as his own. All this we sealed by the most solemn oaths that the mind could think or the lips utter. I sat up all night with paper and ink, and by the morning I had the two charts all ready, signed with the sign of four—that is, of Abdullah, Akbar, Mohammeded and myself.

"Well, gentlemen, I weary you with my long story, and I know my friend, Mr. Jones, is impatient to get me safely stowed in chokey. I'll make it as short as I can.

The villain Sholto went off to India, but he never came back again. Captain Morstan showed me his name among a list of passengers in one of the mail boats very shortly afterward. His uncle had died, leaving him a fortune, and he had left the army, yet he could stoop to treat five men as he had treated us. Morstan went over to Agra shortly afterward, and found, as we expected, that the treasure was indeed gone. The scoundrel had stolen it all, without carrying out one of the conditions on which we had sold him the secret. From that day I lived only for vengeance. I thought of it by day and I nursed it by night. It became an overpowering, absorbing passion with me. I cared nothing for the law—nothing for the gallows. To escape, to track down Sholto, to have my hand upon his throat—that was my one thought. Even the Agra treasure had come to be a smaller thing in my mind than the slaying of Sholto.

"Well, I have set my mind on many things in this life, and never one which I did not carry out. But it was weary years before my time came. I have told you that I had picked up something of medicine. One day, when Doctor Somerton was down with a fever, a little Andaman Islander was picked up by a convict gang in the woods. He was sick to death and had gone to a lonely place to die. I took him in hand, though he was as venomous as a young snake, and after a couple of months I got him all right and able to walk. He took a kind of fancy to me then, and would hardly go back to his woods, but was always hanging about my hut. I learned a little of his lingo from him, and this made him all the fonder of me.

"Tonga—for that was his name—was a fine boatman, and owned a big, roomy canoe of his own. When I found that he was devoted to me and would do anything to serve me, I saw my chance of escape. I talked it over with him. He was to bring his boat round on a certain night to an old wharf which was never guarded, and there he was to pick me up. I gave him directions to have several gourds of water and a lot of yams, cocoanuts and sweet potatoes.

"He was stanch and true, was little Tonga. No man ever had a more faithful mate. At the night named he had his boat at the wharf. As it chanced, however, there was one of the convict guard down there—a vile Pathan who had never missed a chance of insulting and injuring me. I had always vowed vengeance, and now I had my chance. It was as if fate had placed him in my way that I might pay my debt before I left the island. He stood on the bank with his back to me and his carbine on his shoulder. I looked about for a stone to beat out his brains with, but none could I see. Then a queer thought came into my head and showed me where I could lay my hand on a weapon. I sat down in the darkness and unstrapped my wooden leg. With three long hops I was on him. He put his carbine to his shoulder, but I struck him full and knocked the whole front of his skull in. You can see the split in the wood now where I hit him. We both went down together, for I could not keep my balance, but when I got up, I found him still lying quiet enough. I made for the boat, and in an hour we were well out at sea. Tonga had brought all his earthly possessions with him, his arms and his gods. Among other things, he had a long bamboo spear, and some Andaman cocoanut matting, with which I made a sort of a sail. For ten days we were beating about, trusting to luck, and on the eleventh we were picked up by a trader which was going from Singapore to Jiddah with a cargo of Malay pilgrims. They were a rum crowd, and Tonga and I soon managed to settle down among them. They had one very good quality; they let you alone and asked no questions.

"Well, if I were to tell you all the adventures that my little chum and I went through, you would not thank me, for I would have you here until the sun was shining. Here and there we drifted about the world, something always turning up to keep us from London. All the time, however, I never lost sight of my purpose. I would dream of Sholto at night. A hundred times I have killed him in my sleep. At last, however, some three or four years ago, we found ourselves in England. I had no great difficulty in finding where Sholto lived, and I set to work to discover whether he had realized the treasure or if he still had it. I made friends with some one who could help me—I name no names, for I don't want to get any one else in a hole—and I soon found that he still had the jewels. Then I tried to get at him in many ways; but he was pretty sly, and had always two prize fighters, besides his sons and his khitmutgar, on guard over him.

"One day, however, I got word that he was dying. I hurried at once to the garden, mad that he should slip out of my clutches like that, and looking through the window, I saw him lying in his bed, with his sons on each side of him. I'd have come through and taken my chance with the three of them, only, even as I looked at him, his jaw dropped, and I knew that he was gone. I got into his room that same night, though, and I searched his papers to see if there was any record of where he had hidden our jewels. There was not a line, however; so I came away, bitter and savage as a man could be. Before I left I bethought me that if I ever met my Sikh friends again it would be a satisfaction to know that I had left some mark of our hatred; so I scrawled down the sign of the four of us, as it had been on the chart, and pinned it on his bosom. It was too much that he should be taken to the grave without some token from the men whom he had robbed and befooled.

"We earned a living at this time by my exhibiting poor Tonga at fairs and other such places as the black cannibal. He would eat raw meat and dance his war dance;

so we always had a hatful of pennies after a day's work. I still heard all the news from Pondicherry Lodge, and for some years there was no news to hear, except that they were hunting for the treasure. At last, however, came what we had waited for so long. The treasure had been found. It was up at the top of the house, in Mr. Bartholomew Sholto's chemical laboratory. I came at once and had a look at the place, but I could not see how, with my wooden leg, I was to make my way up to it. I learned, however, about a trap door in the roof, and also about Mr. Sholto's supper hour. It seemed to me that I could manage the thing easily through Tonga. I brought him out with me with a long rope wound round his waist. He could climb like a cat, and he soon made his way through the roof, but, as ill-luck would have it, Bartholomew Sholto was still in the room, to his cost. Tonga thought he had done something very clever in killing him, for when I came up by the rope I found him strutting about as proud as a peacock. Very much surprised was he when I made at him with the rope's end and cursed him for a little bloodthirsty imp. I took the treasure box and let it down, and then slid down myself, having first left the sign of the four upon the table, to show that the jewels had come back at last to those who had most right to them. Tonga then pulled up the rope, closed the window, and made off the way he had come.

"I don't know that I have anything else to tell you. I had heard a waterman speak of the speed of Smith's launch, the 'Aurora,' so I thought she would be a handy craft for our escape. I engaged with old Smith, and was to give him a big sum if he got us safe to our ship. He knew, no doubt, that there was some screw loose, but he was not in our secret. All this is the truth, and if I tell it to you, gentlemen, it is not to amuse you—for you have not done me a very good turn—but it is because I believe the best defense I can make is just to hold back nothing, but let all the world know how badly I have myself been served by Major Sholto, and how innocent I am of the death of his son."

"A very remarkable account," said Sherlock Holmes. "A fitting wind-up to an extremely interesting case. There is nothing at all new to me in the latter part of your narrative, except that you brought your own rope. That I did not know. By the way, I had hoped that Tonga had lost all his darts; yet he managed to shoot one at us in the boat."

"He had lost them all, sir, except the one which was in his blow pipe at the time."

"Ah, of course," said Holmes, "I had not thought of that."

"Is there any other point which you would like to ask about?" asked the convict, affably.

"I think not, thank you," my companion answered.

"Well, Holmes," said Athelney Jones, you are a man to be humored, and we all know that you are a connoisseur of crime, but duty is duty, and I have gone rather far in doing what you and your friend asked me. I shall feel more at ease when we have our story-teller here safe under lock and key. The cab still waits, and there are two inspectors downstairs. I am much obliged to you both for your assistance. Of course you will be wanted at the trial. Good night to you."

"Good night, gentlemen both," said Jonathan Small.

"You first, Small," remarked the wary Jones as they left the room. "I'll take particular care that you don't club me with your wooden leg, whatever you may have done to the gentleman at the Andaman Isles."

"Well, and there is the end of our little drama," I remarked, after we had sat some time smoking in silence. "I fear that it may be the last investigation in which I shall have the chance of studying your methods. Miss

Morstan has done me the honor to accept me as a husband in prospective."

He gave a most dismal groan. "I feared as much," said he; "I really cannot congratulate you."

I was a little hurt. "Have you any reason to be dissatisfied with my choice?"

"Not at all. I think she is one of the most charming young ladies I ever met, and might have been most useful in such work as we have been doing. She has a decided genius that way; witness the way in which she preserved that Agra plan from all the other papers of her father. But love is an emotional thing, and whatever is emotional is opposed to that true cold reason which I place above all things. I should never marry myself, lest I bias my judgment."

"I trust," said I, laughing, "that my judgment may survive the ordeal. But you look weary."

"Yes, the reaction is already upon me. I shall be as limp as a rag for a week."

"Strange," said I, "how terms of what in another man I should call laziness alternate with fits of splendid energy and vigor."

"Yes," he answered, "there are in me the makings of a very fine loafer, and also of a pretty spry sort of fellow. I often think of those lines of old Goethe—

" 'Schade dass die Natur nur einen Mensch aus dir schuf,

Denn zum wurdigen Mann war und zum Schelmen der Stoff.'

By the way, apropos of this Norwood business, you see that they had, as I surmised, a confederate in this house, who could be none other than Lal Rao, the butler; so Jones actually has the undivided honor of having caught one fish in his great haul."

"The division seems rather unfair," I remarked. "You have done all the work in this business. I get a wife out of it, Jones gets the credit. Pray, what remains for you?"

"For me," said Sherlock Holmes, "there still remains the cocaine bottle." And he stretched his long white hand up for it.

A SCANDAL IN BOHEMIA

I

To Sherlock Holmes she is always the woman. I have seldom heard him mention her under any other name. In his eyes she eclipses and predominates the whole of her sex. It was not that he felt any emotion akin to love for Irene Adler. All emotions, and that one particularly, were abhorrent to his cold, precise but admirably balanced mind. He was, I take it, the most perfect reasoning and observing machine that the world has seen; but as a lover, he would have placed himself in a false position. He never spoke of the softer passions, save with a gibe and a sneer. They were admirable things for the observer—excellent for drawing the veil from men's motives and actions. But for the trained reasoner to admit such intrusions into his own delicate and finely adjusted temperament was to introduce a distracting factor which might throw a doubt upon all his mental results. Grit in a sensitive instrument, or a crack in one of his own high-power lenses, would not be more disturbing than a strong emotion in a nature such as his. And yet there was but one woman to him, and that woman was the late Irene Adler, of dubious and questionable memory.

I had seen little of Holmes lately. My marriage had drifted us away from each other. My own complete happiness and the home-centered interests which rise up around the man who first finds himself master of his own establishment, were sufficient to absorb all my attention; while Holmes, who loathed every form of society with his whole Bohemian soul, remained in our lodging in Baker Street, buried among his old books, and alternating from week to week between cocaine and ambition, the drowsiness of the drug, and the fierce energy of his own keen nature. He was still, as ever, deeply attracted by the study of crime, and occupied his immense faculties and extraordinary powers of observation in following out those clews, and clearing up those mysteries, which had been abandoned as hopeless by the official police. From time to time I heard some vague account of his doings; of his summons to Odessa in the case of the Trepoff murder, of his clearing up the singular tragedy of the Atkinson brothers at Trincomalee, and finally of the mission which he had accomplished so delicately and successfully for the reigning family of Holland. Beyond these signs of his activity, however, which I merely shared with all the readers of the daily press, I knew little of my former friend and companion.

One night—it was on the 20th of March, 1888—I was returning from a journey to a patient (for I had now returned to civil practise), when my way led me through Baker Street. As I passed the well-remembered door, which must always be associated in my mind with my wooing, and with the dark incidents of the Study in Scarlet, I was seized with a keen desire to see Holmes again, and to know how he was employing his extraordinary powers. His rooms were brilliantly lighted, and even as I looked up, I saw his tall spare figure pass twice in a dark silhouette against the blind. He was pacing the room swiftly, eagerly, with his head sunk upon his chest, and his hands clasped behind him. To me, who knew his every mood and habit, his attitude and manner told their own story. He was at work again. He had risen out of his drug-created dreams, and was hot upon the scent of some new problem. I rang the bell, and was shown up to the chamber which had formerly been in part my own.

His manner was not effusive. It seldom was; but he was glad, I think, to see me. With hardly a word spoken, but with a kindly eye, he waved me to an armchair, threw across his case of cigars, and indicated a spirit case and a gasogene in the corner. Then he stood before the fire, and looked me over in his singular introspective fashion.

"Wedlock suits you," he remarked. "I think, Watson, that you have put on seven and a half pounds since I saw you."

"Seven," I answered.

"Indeed, I should have thought a little more. Just a trifle more, I fancy, Watson. And in practise again, I observe. You did not tell me that you intended to go into harness."

"Then how do you know?"

"I see it, I deduce it. How do I know that you have been getting yourself very wet lately, and that you have a most clumsy and careless servant girl?"

"My dear Holmes," said I, "this is too much. You certainly would have been burned had you lived a few centuries ago. It is true that I had a country walk on Thursday and came home in a dreadful mess; but as I have changed my clothes, I can't imagine how you deduce it. As to Mary Jane, she is incorrigible, and my wife has given her notice; but there again I fail to see how you work it out."

He chuckled to himself and rubbed his long, nervous hands together.

"It is simplicity itself," said he; "my eyes tell me that on the inside of your left shoe, just where the fire light strikes it, the leather is scored by six almost parallel cuts. Obviously they have been caused by some one who has very carelessly scraped round the edges of the sole in order to remove crusted mud from it. Hence, you see, my double deduction that you had been out in vile weather, and that you had a particularly malignant boot-slicking specimen of the London slavey. As to your practise, if a gentleman walks into my rooms, smelling of iodoform, with a black mark of nitrate of silver upon his right forefinger, and a bulge on the side of his top hat to show where he has secreted his stethoscope, I must be dull indeed if I do not pronounce him to be an active member of the medical profession."

I could not help laughing at the ease with which he explained his process of deduction. "When I hear you give your reasons," I remarked, "the thing always appears to me so ridiculously simple that I could easily do it myself, though at each successive instance of your reasoning I am baffled, until you explain your process. And yet, I believe that my eyes are as good as yours."

"Quite so," he answered, lighting a cigarette, and throwing himself down into an armchair. "You see, but you do not observe. The distinction is clear. For example, you have frequently seen the steps which lead up from the hall to this room."

"Frequently."

"How often?"

"Well, some hundreds of times."

"Then how many are there?"

"How many? I don't know."

"Quite so! You have not observed. And yet you have seen. That is just my point. Now, I know there are seventeen steps, because I have both seen and observed. By the way, since you are interested in these little problems, and since you are good enough to chronicle one or two of my trifling experiences, you may be interested in this." He threw over a sheet of thick pink-tinted note paper which had been lying open upon the table. "It came by the last post," said he. "Read it aloud."

The note was undated, and without either signature or address.

"There will call upon you tonight, at a quarter to eight o'clock," it said, "a gentleman who desires to consult you upon a matter of the very deepest moment. Your recent services to one of the royal houses of Europe have shown that you are one who may safely be trusted with matters which are of an importance which can hardly be exaggerated. This account of you we have from all quarters received. Be in your chamber, then, at that hour, and do not take it amiss if your visitor wears a mask."

"This is indeed a mystery," I remarked. "What do you imagine that it means?"

"I have no data yet. It is a capital mistake to theorize before one has data. Insensibly one begins to twist facts to suit theories, instead of theories to suit facts. But the note itself—what do you deduce from it?"

I carefully examined the writing, and the paper upon which it was written.

"The man who wrote it was presumably well to do," I remarked, endeavoring to imitate my companion's processes. "Such paper could not be bought under half a crown a packet. It is peculiarly strong and stiff."

"Peculiar—that is the very word," said Holmes. "It is not an English paper at all. Hold it up to the light."

I did so, and saw a large E with a small g, a P and a large G with a small t woven into the texture of the paper.

"What do you make of that?" asked Holmes.

"The name of the maker, no doubt; or his monogram, rather."

"Not at all. The G with the small t stands for 'Gesellschaft,' which is the German for 'Company.' It is a customary contraction like our 'Co.' P, of course, stands for 'Papier.' Now for the Eg. Let us glance at our 'Continental Gazetteer.'" He took down a heavy brown volume from his shelves. "Eglow, Eglonitz—here we are, Egria. It is in a German-speaking country—in Bohemia, not far from Carlsbad. 'Remarkable as being the scene of the death of Wallenstein, and for its numerous glass factories and paper mills.' Ha! ha! my boy, what do you make of that?" His eyes sparkled, and he sent up a great blue triumphant cloud from his cigarette.

"The paper was made in Bohemia," I said.

"Precisely. And the man who wrote the note is a German. Do you note the peculiar construction of the sentence—'This account of you we have from all quarters received?' A Frenchman or Russian could not have written that. It is the German who is so uncourteous to his verbs. It only remains, therefore, to discover what is wanted by this German who writes upon Bohemian paper, and prefers wearing a mask to showing his face. And here he comes, if I am not mistaken, to resolve all our doubts."

As he spoke there was the sharp sound of horses' hoofs and grating wheels against the curb followed by a sharp pull at the bell. Holmes whistled.

"A pair, by the sound," said he. "Yes," he continued, glancing out of the window. "A nice little brougham and a pair of beauties. A hundred and fifty guineas apiece. There's money in this case, Watson, if there is nothing else."

"I think I had better go, Holmes."

"Not a bit, doctor. Stay where you are. I am lost without my Boswell. And this promises to be interesting. It would be a pity to miss it."

"But your client—"

"Never mind him. I may want your help, and so may he. Here he comes. Sit down in that armchair, doctor, and give us your best attention."

A slow and heavy step, which had been heard upon the stairs and in the passage, paused immediately outside the door. Then there was a loud and authoritative tap.

ture of desperation, he tore the mask from his face and hurled it upon the ground.

"You are right," he cried, "I am the king. Why should I attempt to conceal it?"

"Why, indeed?" murmured Holmes. "Your majesty had not spoken before I was aware that I was addressing Wilhelm Gottsreich Sigismond von Ormstein, Grand Duke of Cassel-Felstein, and hereditary King of Bohemia."

"But you understand," said our strange visitor, sitting down once more and passing his hand over his high, white forehead, "you can understand that I am not accustomed to doing such business in my own person. Yet the matter was so delicate that I could not confide it to an agent without putting myself in his power. I have come incognito from Prague for the purpose of consulting you."

"Then, pray consult," said Holmes, shutting his eyes once more.

"The facts are briefly these: Some five years ago, during a lengthy visit to Warsaw, I made the acquaintance of the well-known adventuress Irene Adler. The name is no doubt familiar to you."

"Kindly look her up in my index, doctor," murmured Holmes, without opening his eyes. For many years he had adopted a system for docketing all paragraphs concerning men and things, so that it was difficult to name a subject or a person on which he could not at once furnish information. In this case I found her biography sandwiched in between that of a Hebrew rabbi and that of a staff commander who had written a monogram upon the deep sea fishes.

"Let me see!" said Holmes. "Hum! Born in New Jersey in the year 1858. Contralto—hum! La Scala—hum! Prima-donna Imperial Opera of Warsaw—yes! Retired from operatic stage—ha! Living in London—

quite so! Your majesty, as I understand, became entangled with this young person, wrote her some compromising letters and is now desirous of getting those letters back."

"Precisely so. But how—"

"Was there a secret marriage?"

"None."

"No legal papers or certificates?"

"None."

"Then I fail to follow your majesty. If this young person should produce her letters for blackmailing or other purposes, how is she to prove their authenticity?"

"There is the writing."

"Pooh, pooh! Forgery."

"My private note paper."

"Stolen."

"My own seal."

"Imitated."

"My photograph."

"Bought."

"We were both in the photograph."

"Oh, dear! That is very bad. Your majesty has indeed committed an indiscretion."

"I was mad—insane."

"You have compromised yourself seriously."

"I was only crown prince then. I was young. I am but thirty now."

"It must be recovered."

"We have tried and tried."

"Your majesty must pay. It must be bought."

"She will not sell."

"Stolen, then."

"Five attempts have been made. Twice burglars in my pay ransacked her house. Once we diverted her luggage when she traveled. Twice she has been waylaid. There has been no result."

"No sign of it?"

"Absolutely none."

Holmes laughed. "It is quite a pretty little problem," said he.

"But a very serious one to me," returned the king, reproachfully.

"Very, indeed. And what does she propose to do with the photograph?"

"To ruin me."

"But how?"

"I am about to be married."

"So I have heard."

"To Clothilde Lothman von Saxe-Meiningen, second daughter of the King of Scandinavia. You may know the strict principles of her family. She is herself the very soul of delicacy. A shadow of a doubt as to my conduct would bring the matter to an end."

"And Irene Adler?"

"Threatens to send them the photograph. And she will do it. I know that she will do it. You do not know her, but she has a soul of steel. She has the face of the most beautiful of women and the mind of the most resolute of men. Rather than I should marry another woman, there are no lengths to which she would not go—none."

"You are sure that she has not sent it yet?"

"I am sure."

"And why?"

"Because she has said that she would send it on the day when the betrothal was publicly proclaimed. That will be next Monday."

"Oh, then we have three days yet," said Holmes, with a yawn. "That is very fortunate, as I have one or two matters of importance to look into just at present. Your majesty will, of course, stay in London for the present?"

"Certainly. You will find me at the Langham, under the name of the Count von Kramm."

"Then I shall drop you a line to let you know how we progress."

"Pray do so; I shall be all anxiety."

"Then, as to money?"

"You have carte blanche."

"Absolutely?"

"I tell you that I would give one of the provinces of my kingdom to have that photograph."

"And for present expenses?"

The king took a heavy chamois leather bag from under his cloak, and laid it on the table.

"There are three hundred pounds in gold and seven hundred in notes," he said.

Holmes scribbled a receipt upon a sheet of his notebook, and handed it to him.

"And mademoiselle's address?" he said.

"Is Briony Lodge, Serpentine Avenue, St. John's Wood."

Holmes took a note of it. "One other question," said he, thoughtfully. "Was the photograph a cabinet?"

"It was."

"Then, good night, your majesty, and I trust that we shall soon have some good news for you. And good night, Watson," he added, as the wheels of the royal brougham rolled down the street. "If you will be good enough to call tomorrow afternoon, at three o'clock, I should like to chat this little matter over with you."

II

At three o'clock precisely I was at Baker Street, but Holmes had not yet returned. The landlady informed me that he had left the house shortly after eight o'clock in the morning. I sat down beside the fire, however, with the intention of awaiting him, however long he might be.

I was already deeply interested in his inquiry, for, though it was surrounded by none of the grim and strange features which were associated with the two crimes which I have already recorded, still the nature of the case and the exalted station of his client gave it a character of its own. Indeed, apart from the nature of the investigation, which my friend had on hand, there was something in his masterly grasp of a situation, and his keen, incisive reasoning, which made it a pleasure to me to study his system of work, and to follow the quick, subtle methods by which he disentangled the most inextricable mysteries. So accustomed was I to his invariable success that the very possibility of his failing had ceased to enter into my head.

It was close upon four before the door opened, and a drunken-looking groom, ill-kempt and side-whiskered, with an inflamed face and disreputable clothes, walked into the room. Accustomed as I was to my friend's amazing powers in the use of disguises, I had to look three times before I was certain that it was indeed he. With a nod he vanished into the bedroom, whence he emerged in five minutes tweed-suited and respectable, as of old. Putting his hand into his pockets, he stretched out his legs in front of the fire, and laughed heartily for some minutes.

"Well, really!" he cried, and then he choked, and laughed again until he was obliged to lie back, limp and helpless, in the chair.

"What is it?"

"It's quite too funny. I am sure you could never guess how I employed my morning, or what I ended by doing."

"I can't imagine. I suppose that you have been watching the habits and, perhaps, the house of Miss Irene Adler."

"Quite so, but the sequel was rather unusual. I will tell you, however. I left the house a little after eight o'clock this morning in the character of a groom out of work.

There is a wonderful sympathy and freemasonry among horse men. Be one of them, and you will know all that there is to know. I soon found Briony Lodge. It is a bijou villa, with a garden at the back, but built out in front right up to the road, two stories. Chubb lock to the door. Large sitting room on the right side, well furnished, with long windows almost to the floor, and those preposterous English window fasteners which a child could open. Behind there was nothing remarkable, save that the passage window could be reached from the top of the coach house. I walked round it and examined it closely from every point of view, but without noting anything else of interest.

"I then lounged down the street, and found, as I expected, that there was a mews in a lane which runs down by one wall of the garden. I lent the hostlers a hand in rubbing down their horses, and I received in exchange twopence, a glass of half-and-half, two fills of shag tobacco, and as much information as I could desire about Miss Adler, to say nothing of half a dozen other people in the neighborhood, in whom I was not in the least interested, but whose biographies I was compelled to listen to."

"And what of Irene Adler?" I said.

"Oh, she has turned all the men's heads down in that part. She is the daintiest thing under a bonnet on this planet. So says the Serpentine Mews, to a man. She lives quietly, sings at concerts, drives out at five every day, and returns at seven sharp for dinner. Seldom goes out at other times, except when she sings. Has only one male visitor, but a good deal of him. He is dark, handsome and dashing; never calls less than once a day and often twice. He is a Mr. Godfrey Norton of the Inner Temple. See the advantages of a cabman as a confidant. They had driven him home a dozen times from Serpentine Mews, and knew all about him. When I had listened to all they

had to tell, I began to walk up and down near Briony
Lodge once more, and to think over my plan of campaign.

"This Godfrey Norton was evidently an important
factor in the matter. He was a lawyer. That sounded
ominous. What was the relation between them and what
the object of his repeated visits. Was she his client, his
friend, or his mistress? If the former, she had probably
transferred the photograph to his keeping. If the latter,
it was less likely. On the issue of this question depended
whether I should contniue my work at Briony Lodge, or
turn my attention to the gentleman's chambers in the
Temple. It was a delicate point, and it widened the field
of my inquiry. I fear that I bore you with these details, but I have to let you see my little difficulties, if
you are to understand the situation."

"I am following you closely," I answered.

"I was still balancing the matter in my mind, when
a hansom cab drove up to Briony Lodge and a gentleman sprang out. He was a remarkably handsome man,
dark, aquiline and mustached—evidently the man of
whom I had heard. He appeared to be in a great hurry,
shouted to the cabman to wait, and brushed past the maid
who opened the door, with the air of a man who was thoroughly at home.

"He was in the house about half an hour, and I could
catch glimpses of him in the windows of the sitting room,
pacing up and down, talking excitedly and waving his
arms. Of her I could see nothing. Presently he
emerged, looking even more flurried than before. As he
stepped up to the cab, he pulled a gold watch from his
pocket and looked at it earnestly. 'Drive like the devil!'
he shouted, 'first to Gross & Hankey's in Regent Street,
and then to the Church of St. Monica in the Edgeware
Road. Half a guinea if you do it in twenty minutes!'

"Away they went, and I was just wondering whether
I should not do well to fellow them, when up the lane

came a neat little landau, the coachman with his coat only half buttoned, and his tie under his ear, while all the tags of his harness were sticking out of the buckles. It hadn't pulled up before she shot out of the hall door and into it. I only caught a glimpse of her at the moment, but she was a lovely woman, with a face that a man might die for.

"'The Church of St. Monica, John,' she cried; 'and half a sovereign if you reach it in twenty minutes.'

"This was quite too good to lose, Watson. I was just balancing whether I should run for it, or whether I should perch behind her landau, when a cab came through the street. The driver looked twice at such a shabby fare; but I jumped in before he could object. 'The Church of St. Monica,' said I, 'and half a sovereign if you reach it in twenty minutes.' It was twenty-five minutes to twelve, and of course it was clear enough what was in the wind.

"My cabby drove fast. I don't think I ever drove faster, but the others were there before us. The cab and landau with their steaming horses were in front of the door when I arrived. I paid the man and hurried into the church. There was not a soul there save the two whom I had followed, and the surpliced clergyman, who seemed to be expostulating with them. They were all three standing in a knot in front of the altar. I lounged up the side aisle like any other idler who has dropped into a church. Suddenly, to my surprise, the three at the altar faced round to me, and Godfrey Norton came running as hard as he could toward me.

"'Thank God!' he cried. 'You'll do. Come! Come!'

"'What then?' I asked.

"'Come, man, come; only three minutes, or it won't be legal.'

"I was half dragged up to the altar, and, before I knew where I was, I found myself mumbling responses which were whispered in my ear, and vouching for things of which I knew nothing, and generally assisting in the secure tying up of Irene Adler, spinster, to Godfrey Norton, bachelor. It was all done in an instant, and there was the gentleman thanking me on the one side and the lady on the other, while the clergyman beamed on me in front. It was the most preposterous position in which I ever found myself in my life, and it was the thought of it that started me laughing just now. It seems that there had been some informality about their license; that the clergyman absolutely refused to marry them without a witness of some sort and that my lucky appearance saved the bridegroom from having to sally out into the streets in search of a best man. The bride gave me a sovereign, and I mean to wear it on my watch chain in memory of the occasion."

"This is a very unexpected turn of affairs," said I; "and what then?"

"Well, I found my plans very seriously menaced. It looked as if the pair might take an immediate departure, and so necessitate very prompt and energetic measures on my part. At the church door, however, they separated, he driving back to the Temple, and she to her own house. 'I shall drive out in the park at five as usual,' she said, as she left him. I heard no more. They drove away in different directions, and I went off to make my own arrangements."

"Which are?"

"Some cold beef and a glass of beer," he answered, ringing the bell. "I have been too busy to think of food, and I am likely to be busier still this evening. By the way, doctor, I shall want your co-operation."

"I shall be delighted."

"You don't mind breaking the law?"

"Not in the least."

"Nor running a chance of arrest?"

"Not in a good cause."

"Oh, the cause is excellent!"

"Then I am your man."

"I was sure that I might rely on you."

"But what is it you wish?"

"When Mrs. Turner has brought in the tray I will make it clear to you. Now," he said, as he turned hungrily on the simple fare that our landlady had provided, "I must discuss it while I eat, for I have not much time. It is nearly five now. In two hours we must be on the scene of action. Miss Irene, or Madame, rather, returns from her drive at seven. We must be at Briony Lodge to meet her."

"And what then?"

"You must leave that to me. I have already arranged what is to occur. There is only one point on which I must insist. You must not interfere, come what may. You understand?"

"I am to be neutral?"

"To do nothing whatever. There will probably be some small unpleasantness. Do not join in it. It will end in my being conveyed into the house. Four or five minutes afterward the sitting room window will open. You will station yourself close to that open window."

"Yes."

"You are to watch me, for I will be visible to you."

"Yes."

"And when I raise my hand—so—you will throw into the room what I give you to throw, and will, at the same time, raise the cry of fire. You quite follow me?"

"Entirely."

"It is nothing very formidable," he said, taking a long, cigar-shaped roll from his pocket. It is an ordinary plumber's smoke rocket, fitted with a cap at either end, to make it self-lighting. Your task is confined to that. When you raise your cry of fire, it will be taken up by quite a number of people. You may then walk to the end

of the street and I will rejoin you in ten minutes. I hope
I have made myself clear?"

"I am to remain neutral, to get near the window, to
watch you, and, at the signal, to throw in this object, then
to raise the cry of fire, and to await you at the corner of
the street."

"Precisely."

"Then you may entirely rely on me."

"That is excellent. I think, perhaps, it is almost time
that I prepared for the new role I have to play."

He disappeared into his bedroom and returned in a few
minutes in the character of an amiable and simple-minded
Nonconformist clergyman. His broad, black hat, his
baggy trousers, his white tie, his sympathetic smile, and
general look of peering and benevolent curiosity were such
as Mr. John Hare alone could have equaled. It was not
merely that Holmes changed his costume. His expression,
his manner, his very soul seemed to vary with every fresh
part that he assumed. The stage lost a fine actor, even
as science lost an acute reasoner, when he became a specialist in crime.

It was a quarter past six when we left Baker Street,
and it still wanted ten minutes to the hour when we found
ourselves in Serpentine Avenue. It was already dusk,
and lamps were just being lighted as we paced up and
down in front of Briony Lodge, waiting for the coming
of its occupant. The house was just such as I had pic-
tured it from Sherlock Holmes' succinct description, but
the locality appeared to be less private than I expected.
On the contrary, for a small street in a quiet neighborhood, it was remarkably animated. There was a group
of shabbily dressed men smocking and laughing in a corner, a scissors grinder with his wheel, two guardsmen
who were flirting with a nurse girl, and several well-
dressed young men who were lounging up and down with
cigars in their mouths.

"You see," remarked Holmes, as we paced to and fro in front of the house, "this marriage rather simplifies matters. The photograph becomes a double-edged weapon now. The chances are that she would be as averse to its being seen by Mr. Godfrey Norton as our client is to its coming to the eyes of his princess. Now the question is—where are we to find the photograph?"

"Where, indeed?"

"It is most unlikely that she carries it about with her. It is cabinet size. Too large for easy concealment about a woman's dress. She knows that the king is capable of having her waylaid and searched. Two attempts of the sort have already been made. We may take it, that she does not carry it about with her."

"Where, then?"

"Her banker or her lawyer. There is that double possibility. But I am inclined to think neither. Women are naturally secretive, and they like to do their own secreting. Why should she hand it over to any one else? She could trust her own guardianship, but she could not tell what indirect or political influence might be brought to bear upon a business man. Besides, remember that she had resolved to use it within a few days. It must be where she can lay her hands upon it. It must be in her own house."

"But it has twice been burglarized."

"Pshaw! They did not know how to look."

"But how will you look?"

"I will not look."

"What then?"

"I will get her to show me."

"But she will refuse."

"She will not be able to. But I hear the rumble of wheels. It is her carriage. Now carry out my orders to the letter."

As he spoke, the gleam of the side lights of a carriage

came round the curve of the avenue. It was a smart little
landau which rattled up to the door of Briony Lodge. As
it pulled up one of the loafing men at the corner dashed
forward to open the door in the hope of earning a copper,
but was elbowed away by another loafer who had rushed
up with the same intention. A fierce quarrel broke out
which was increased by the two guardsmen, who took
sides with one of the loungers, and by the scissors-grinder,
who was equally hot upon the other side. A blow was
struck, and in an instant the lady, who had stepped from
her carriage, was the center of a little knot of struggling
men who struck savagely at each other with their fists and
sticks. Holmes dashed into the crowd to protect the
lady, but, just as he reached her, he gave a cry and
dropped to the ground, with the blood running freely
down his face. At his fall the guardsmen took to their
heels in one direction and the loungers in the other, while
a number of better dressed people who had watched the
scuffle without taking part in it crowded in to help the
lady and to attend to the injured man. Irene Adler, as
I will still call her, had hurried up the steps; but she stood
at the top, with her superb figure outlined against the
lights of the hall, looking back into the street."

"Is the poor gentleman much hurt?" she asked.

"He is dead," cried several voices.

"No, no, there's life in him," shouted another. "But
he'll be gone before you can get him to the hospital."

"He's a brave fellow," said a woman. "They would
have had the lady's purse and watch if it hadn't been for
him. They were a gang, and a rough one, too. Ah! he's
breathing now."

"He can't lie in the street. May we bring him in,
marm?"

"Surely. Bring him into the sitting room. There is a
comfortable sofa. This way, please." Slowly and
solemnly he was borne into Briony Lodge, and laid out

in the principal room, while I still observed the proceedings from my post by the window. The lamps had been lighted, but the blinds had not been drawn, so that I could see Holmes as he lay upon the couch. I do not know whether he was seized with compunction at that moment for the part he was playing, but I know that I never felt more heartily ashamed of myself in my life when I saw the beautiful creature against whom I was conspiring, or the grace and kindliness with which she waited upon the injured man. And yet it would be the blackest treachery to Holmes to draw back now from the part which he had intrusted to me. I hardened my heart, and took the smoke rocket from under my ulster. After all, I thought, we are not injuring her. We are but preventing her from injuring another.

Holmes had sat upon the couch, and I saw him motion like a man who is in need of air. A maid rushed across and threw open the window. At the same instance I saw him raise his hand, and at the signal I tossed my rocket into the room with a cry of "Fire!" The word was no sooner out of my mouth than the whole crowd of spectators, well dressed and ill—gentlemen hostlers and servant maids—joined in a general shriek of "Fire!" Thick clouds of smoke curled through the room and out at the open window. I caught a glimpse of rushing figures, and a moment later the voice of Holmes from within assuring them that it was a false alarm. Slipping through the shouting crowd, I made my way to the corner of the street, and in ten minutes was rejoiced to find my friend's arm in mine, and to get away from the scene of uproar. He walked swiftly and in silence for some few minutes, until we had turned down one of the quiet streets which led toward the Edgeware Road.

"You did it very nicely, doctor," he remarked. "Nothing could have been better. It is all right."

"You have the photograph?"

"I know where it is."

"And how did you find out?"

"She showed me, as I told you that she would."

"I am still in the dark."

"I do not wish to make a mystery," said he, laughing. "The matter was perfectly simple. You, of course, saw that every one in the street was an accomplice. They were all engaged for the evening."

"I guessed as much."

"Then, when the row broke out, I had a little moist red paint in the palm of my hand. I rushed forward, fell down, clapped my hand to my face, and became a piteous spectacle. It is an old trick."

"That also I could fathom."

"Then they carried me in. She was bound to have me in. What else could she do? And into her sitting room, which was the very room which I suspected. It lay between that and her bedroom, and I determined to see which. They laid me on a couch, I motioned for air, they were compelled to open the window and you had your chance."

"How did that help you."

"It was all-important. When a woman thinks that her house is on fire, her instinct is at once to rush to the thing which she values most. It is a perfectly overpowering impulse, and I have more than once taken advantage of it. In the case of the Darlington Substitution Scandal it was of use to me, and also in the Arnsworth Castle business. A married woman grabs at her baby—an unmarried one reaches for her jewel box. Now it was clear to me that our lady today had nothing in the house more precious to her than what we are in quest of. She would rush to secure it. The alarm of fire was admirably done. The smoke and shouting were enough to shake nerves of steel. She responded beautifully. The photograph is in a recess behind a sliding panel just above the right bell pull. She was there in an instant, and I caught a glimpse of it as she half drew it out. When I cried out that it was a false alarm, she replaced it, glanced at the rocket, rushed from the room, and I have not seen her since. I rose, and, making my excuses, escaped from the house. I hesitated whether to attempt to secure the photograph at once; but the coachman had come in, and as he was watching me narrowly, it seemed safer to wait. A little over-precipitance may ruin all."

"And now?" I asked.

"Our quest is practically finished. I shall call with the king tomorrow, and with you, if you care to come with us. We will be shown into the sitting room to wait for the lady, but it is probable that when she comes she may find neither us nor the photograph. It might be a satisfaction to his majesty to regain it with his own hands."

"And when will you call?"

"At eight in the morning. She will not be up, so that we shall have a clear field. Besides, we must be prompt, for this marriage may mean a complete change in her life and habits. I must wire to the king without delay."

We had reached Baker Street, and had stopped at the door. He was searching his pockets for the key, when some one passing said:

"Good night, Mister Sherlock Holmes."

There were several people on the pavement at the time, but the greeting appeared to come from a slim youth in an ulster who had hurried by.

"I've heard that voice before," said Holmes, staring down the dimly lighted street. "Now, I wonder who the deuce that could have been?"

III

I SLEPT at Baker Street that night, and we were engaged upon our toast and coffee in the morning, when the King of Bohemia rushed into the room.

"You have really got it?" he cried, grasping Sherlock Holmes by either shoulder, and looking eagerly into his face.

"Not yet."

"But you have hopes?"

"I have hopes."

"Then come. I am all impatience to be gone."

"We must have a cab."

"No, my brougham is waiting."

"Then that will simplify matters." We descended, and started off once more for Briony Lodge.

"Irene Adler is married," remarked Holmes.

"Married! When?"

"Yesterday."

"But to whom?"

"To an English lawyer named Norton."

"But she could not love him."

"I am in hopes that she does."

"And why in hopes?"

"Because it would spare your majesty all fears of future annoyance. If the lady loves her husband, she does not love your majesty. If she does not love your majesty, there is no reason why she should interfere with your majesty's plan."

"It is true. And yet— Well, I wish she had been of my own station. What a queen she would have made!"

He relapsed into a moody silence, which was not broken until we drew up in Serpentine Avenue.

The door of Briony Lodge was open and an elderly woman stood upon the steps. She watched us with a sardonic eye as we stepped from the brougham.

"Mr. Sherlock Holmes, I believe?" said she.

"I am Mr. Holmes," answered my companion, looking at her with a questioning and rather startled gaze.

"Indeed! My mistress told me that you were likely to call. She left this morning, with her husband, by the 5:15 train for Charing Cross, for the Continent."

"What!" Sherlock Holmes staggered back white with chagrin and surprise.

"Do you mean that she has left England?"

"Never to return."

"And the papers?" asked the king, hoarsely. "All is lost!"

"We shall see." He pushed past the servant, and rushed into the drawing room, followed by the king and myself. The furniture was scattered about in every direction, with dismantled shelves, and open drawers, as if the lady had hurriedly ransacked them before her flight. Holmes rushed at the bell-pull, tore back a small sliding shutter, and plunging in his hand, pulled out a photograph and a letter. The photograph was of Irene Adler herself in evening dress; the letter was superscribed to "Sherlock Holmes, Esq. To be left till called for." My friend tore it open, and we all three read it together. It was dated at midnight of the preceding night, and ran in this way:

"MY DEAR MR. SHERLOCK HOLMES—You really did it very well. You took me in completely. Until after the alarm of the fire, I had not a suspicion. But then, when I found how I had betrayed myself, I began to think. I had been warned against you months ago. I had been told that if the king employed an agent, it would certainly be you. And your address had been given me. Yet, with all this, you made me reveal what you wanted to know. Even after I became suspicious, I found it hard to think evil of such a dear, kind old clergyman. But, you know, I have been trained as an actress myself. Male costume is nothing new to me. I often take advantage of the freedom it gives. I sent John, the coachman, to watch you, ran upstairs, got into my walking clothes, as I call them, and came down just as you departed.

"Well, I followed you to the door, and so made sure that I was really an object of interest to the celebrated Mr. Sherlock Holmes. Then I, rather imprudently, wished you good night, and started for the Temple to see my husband.

"We both thought the best resource was flight, when pursued by so formidable an antagonist; so you will find the nest empty when you call tomorrow. As to the photograph, your client may rest in peace. I love and am loved by a better man than he. The king may do what he will without hindrance from one whom he has cruelly wronged. I keep it only to safeguard myself and preserve a weapon which will always secure me from any steps which he might take in the future. I leave a photograph which he might care to possess; and I remain, dear Mr. Sherlock Holmes, very truly yours,

"IRENE NORTON, *nee* ADLER."

"What a woman—oh, what a woman!" cried the King of Bohemia, when we had all three read this epistle. "Did I not tell you how quick and resolute she was? Would she not have made an admirable queen? Is it not a pity that she was not on my level?"

"From what I have seen of the lady, she seems indeed to be on a very different level to your majesty," said Holmes, coldly. "I am sorry that I have not been able to bring your majesty's business to a more successful conclusion."

"On the contrary, my dear sir," cried the king, "nothing could be more successful. I know that her word is inviolate. The photograph is now as safe as if it were in the fire."

"I am glad to hear your majesty say so."

"I am immensely indebted to you. Pray tell me in what way I can reward you. This ring—" He slipped an emerald snake ring from his finger, and held it out upon the palm of his hand.

"Your majesty has something which I should value even more highly," said Holmes.

"You have but to name it."

"This photograph!"

The king stared at him in amazement.

"Irene's photograph!" he cried. "Certainly, if you wish it."

"I thank your majesty. Then there is no more to be done in the matter. I have the honor to wish you a very good morning." He bowed, and turning away without observing the hand which the king had stretched out to him, he set off in my company for his chambers.

And that was how a great scandal threatened to affect the kingdom of Bohemia, and how the best plans of Mr. Sherlock Holmes were beaten by a woman's wit. He used to make merry over the cleverness of women, but I have not heard him do it of late. And when he speaks of Irene Adler, or when he refers to her photograph, it is always under the honorable title of "The Woman."

THE RING OF THOTH

Mr. John Vansittart Smith, F.R.S., of 147-A Gower Street, was a man whose energy of purpose and cleverness of thought might have placed him in the very first rank of scientific observers. He was the victim, however, of a universal ambition which prompted him to aim at distinction in many subjects rather than pre-eminence in one. In his early days he had shown an aptitude for zoology and for botany which caused his friends to look upon him as a second Darwin, but when a professorship was almost within his reach, he had suddenly discontinued his studies and turned his whole attion to chemistry. Here his researches upon the spectra of the metals had won him his fellowship in the Royal Society; but again he played the coquette with his subject, and after a year's absence from the laboratory he joined the Oriental Society and delivered a paper on the Hieroglyphic and Demotic inscriptions of El Kab, thus giving a crowning example both of the versatility and of the inconstancy of his talents.

The most fickle of wooers, however, is apt to be caught at last, and so it was with John Vansittart Smith. The more he burrowed his way in Egyptology the more impressed he became by the vast field which it opened to the inquirer, and by the extreme importance of a subject which promised to throw a light upon the first germs of human civilization and the origin of the great part of our arts and sciences. So struck was Mr. Smith that he straightway married an Egyptological young lady who

had written upon the sixth dynasty, and having thus se-
cured a sound basis of operations, he set himself to collect materials for a work which should unite the research
of Lepsius and the ingenuity of Champollion. The prepa-
rations for this magnum opus entailed many hurried visits
to the magnificent Egyptian collections of the Louvre,
upon the last of which, no longer ago than the middle of
last October, he became involved in a most strange and
noteworthy adventure.

The trains had been slow and the Channel had been
rough, so that the student arrived in Paris in a somewhat
befogged and feverish condition. On reaching the Hotel
de France, in the Rue Lafitte, he had thrown himself upon
a sofa for a couple of hours, but finding that he was unable to sleep, he determined, in spite of his fatigue, to
make his way to the Louvre, settle the point which he
had come to decide and take the evening train back to
Dieppe. Having come to this conclusion, he donned his
great coat, for it was a raw, rainy day, and made his way
across the Boulevard des Italiens and down the Avenue
de l'Opera. Once in the Louvre he was on familiar
ground, and he speedily made his way to the collection
of papyri which it was his intention to consult.

The warmest admirers of John Vansittart Smith could
hardly claim for him that he was a handsome man. His
high-beaked nose and prominent chin had something of
the same acute and incisive character which distinguished
his intellect. He held his head in a bird-like fashion, and
bird-like, too, was the pecking motion with which, in conversation, he threw out his objections and retorts. As he
stood, with the high collar of his great coat raised to his
ears, he might have seen from the reflection in the glass
case before him that his appearance was a singular one.
Yet it came upon him as a sudden jar when an English
voice behind him exclaimed in very audible tones, "What
a queer-looking mortal!"

The student had a large amount of petty vanity in his composition which manifested itself by an ostentatious and overdone disregard of all personal considerations. He straightened his lips and looked rigidly at the roll of the papyrus, while his heart filled with bitterness against the whole race of traveling Britons.

"Yes," said another voice, "he really is an extraordinary fellow."

"Do you know," said the first speaker, "one could almost believe that by the continual contemplation of mummies the chap has become half a mummy himself?"

"He has certainly an Egyptian cast of countenance," said the other.

John Vansittart Smith spun round upon his heel with the intention of shaming his countrymen by a corrosive remark or two. To his surprise and relief, the two young fellows who had been conversing had their shoulders turned toward him, and were gazing at one of the Louvre attendants who was polishing some brass work at the other side of the room.

"Carter will be waiting for us at the Palais Royal," said one tourist to the other, glancing at his watch, and they clattered away, leaving the student to his labors.

"I wonder what these chatterers call an Egyptian cast of countenance," thought John Vansittart Smith, and he moved his position slightly in order to catch a glimpse of the man's face. He started as his eyes fell upon it. It was indeed the very face with which his studies had made him familiar. The regular statuesque features, broad brow, well-rounded chin and dusky complexion were the exact counterpart of the innumerable statues, mummy cases and pictures which adorned the walls of the apartment. The thing was beyond all coincidence. The man must be an Egyptian. The national angularity of the shoulders and narrowness of the hips were alone sufficient to identify him.

John Vansittart Smith shuffled toward the attendant with some intention of addressing him. He was not light of touch in conversation, and found it difficult to strike the happy means between the brusqueness of the superior and the geniality of the equal. As he came nearer, the man presented his side face to him, but kept his gaze still bent upon his work. Vansittart Smith, fixing his eyes upon the fellow's skin, was conscious of a sudden impression that there was something inhuman and preternatural about its appearance. Over the temple and cheek bone it was as glazed and as shiny as varnished parchment. There was no suggestion of pores. One could not fancy a drop of moisture upon that arid surface. From brow to chin, however, it was cross-hatched by a million delicate wrinkles which shot and interlaced as though Nature in some Maori mood had tried how wild and intricate a pattern she could devise.

"Ou est la collection de Memphis?" asked the student, with the awkward air of a man who is devising a question merely for the purpose of opening a conversation.

"C'est la," replied the man, brusquely, nodding his head at the other side of the room.

"Vous etes un Egyptien, n'est-ce pas?" asked the Englishman.

The attendant looked up and turned his strange, dark eyes upon his questioner. They were vitreous, with a misty, dry shininess, such as Smith had never seen in a human head before. As he gazed into them he saw some strong emotion gather in their depths, which rose and deepened until it broke into a look of something akin both to horror and to hatred.

"Non, monsieur; je suis Francais." The man turned abruptly and bent low over his polishing. The student gazed at him for a moment in astonishment, and then turning to a chair in a retired corner behind one of the doors he proceeded to make notes of his researches

among the papyri. His thoughts, however, refused to
return into their natural groove. They would run upon
the enigmatical attendant with the sphinx-like face and the
parchment skin.

"Where have I seen such eyes?" said Vansittart Smith
to himself. "There is something saurian about them,
something reptilian. There's the membrana nictitans of
the snakes," he mused, bethinking himself of his zoologi-
cal studies. "It gives a shiny effect. But there was
something more here. There was a sense of power, of
wisdom—so I read them—and of weariness, utter weariness and ineffable despair. It may be all imagination, but
I never had so strong an impression. By Jove, I must
have another look at them!" He rose and paced round
the Egyptian rooms, but the man who had excited his
curiosity had disappeared.

The student sat down again in his quiet corner and continued to work at his notes. He had gained the information which he required from the papyri; and it only remained to write it down while it was still fresh in his
memory. For a time his pencil traveled rapidly over the
paper, but soon the lines became less level, the words more
blurred, and finally the pencil tinkled down upon the floor
and the head of the student dropped heavily forward upon
his chest. Tired out by his journey, he slept so soundly
in his lonely post behind the door that neither the clanking civil guard, nor the footsteps of sightseers, nor even
the loud, hoarse bell which gives the signal for closing,
were sufficient to arouse him.

Twilight deepened into darkness, the bustle from the
Rue de Rivoli waxed and then waned, distant Notre Dame
clanged out the hour of midnight, and still the dark and
lonely figure sat silently in the shadow. It was not until
close upon one in the morning that, with a sudden gasp
and an intaking of the breath, Vansittart Smith returned
to consciousness. For a moment it flashed upon him that

he had dropped asleep in his study chair at home. The moon was shining fitfully through the unshuttered window, however, and, as his eye ran along the cases, he remembered clearly where he was and how he came there. The student was not a nervous man. He possessed that love of a novel situation which is peculiar to his race. Stretching out his cramped limbs, he looked at his watch and burst into a chuckle as he observed the hour. The episode would make an admirable anecdote to be introduced into his next paper as a relief to the graver and heavier speculations. He was a little cold, but wide awake and much refreshed. It was no wonder that the guardians had overlooked him, for the door threw its heavy black shadow right across him.

The complete silence was impressive. Neither outside nor inside was there a creak or a murmur. He was alone with the dead men of a dead civilization. What though the outer city reeked of the garish nineteenth century? In all this chamber there was scarce an article, from the shriveled ear of wheat to the pigment box of the painter, which had not held its own against four thousand years. Here were the flotsam and jetsam washed up by the great ocean of time from that far-off empire. From stately Thebes, from lordly Luxor, from the great temples of Heliopolis, from a hundred rifled tombs, these relics had been brought. The student glanced round at the long-silent figures who flickered vaguely up through the gloom, at the busy toilers who were now so restful, and he fell into a reverent and thoughtful mood. An unwonted sense of his own youth and insignificance came over him. Leaning back in his chair, he gazed dreamily down the long vista of rooms, all silvery with the moonshine, which extended through the whole wing of the widespread building. His eyes fell upon the yellow glare of a distant lamp.

John Vansittart Smith sat up on his chair with his

nerves all on edge. The light was advancing slowly toward him, pausing from time to time, and then coming jerkily forward. The bearer moved noiselessly. In the utter silence there was no suspicion of the pat of a footfall. An idea of robbers entered the Englishman's head. He snuggled up further into the corner. The light was two rooms off. Now it was in the next chamber and still there was no sound. With something approaching to a thrill of fear, the student observed a face, floating in the air as it were, behind the flare of the lamp. The figure was wrapped in shadow, but the light fell full upon the strange, eager face. There was no mistaking the metallic, glistening eyes and the cadaverous skin. It was the attendant with whom he had conversed.

Vansittart Smith's first impulse was to come forward and address him. A few words of explanation would set the matter clear, and lead doubtless to his being conducted to some side door from which he might make his way to his hotel. As the man entered the chamber, however, there was something so stealthy in his movements, and so furtive in his expression, that the Englishman altered his intention. This was clearly no ordinary official walking the rounds. The fellow wore felt-soled slippers, stepped with a rising chest, and glanced quickly from left to right, while his hurried, gasping breathing thrilled the flame of his lamp. Vansittart Smith crouched silently back into the corner and watched him keenly, convinced that his errand was one of secret and probably sinister import.

There was no hesitation in the other's movements. He stepped lightly and swiftly across to one of the great cases and, drawing a key from his pocket, he unlocked it. From the upper shelf he pulled down a mummy, which he bore away with him and laid it with much care and solicitude upon the ground. By it he placed his lamp, and then squatting down beside it in Eastern fashion, he began with long, quivering fingers to undo the cere-cloths and bandages which girt it round. As the crackling rolls of linen peeled off one after the other, a strong aromatic odor filled the chamber and fragments of scented wood and of spices spattered down upon the marble floor.

It was clear to John Vansittart Smith that this mummy had never been unswathed before. The operation interested him keenly. He thrilled all over with curiosity, and his bird-like head protruded further and further from behind the door. When, however, the last roll had been removed from the four-thousand-year-old head, it was all that he could do to stifle an outcry of amazement. First, a cascade of long, black, glossy tresses poured over the workman's hands and arms. A second turn of the bandage revealed a low white forehead, with a pair of delicately arched eyebrows. A third uncovered a pair of bright, deeply fringed eyes and a straight, well-cut nose, while a fourth and last showed a sweet, full, sensitive mouth, and a beautifully curved chin. The whole face was one of extraordinary loveliness, save for the one blemish that in the center of the forehead there was a single irregular, coffee-colored splotch. It was a triumph of the embalmer's art. Vansittart Smith's eyes grew larger and larger as he gazed upon it, and he chirruped in his throat with satisfaction.

Its effect upon the Egyptologist was as nothing, compared with that which it produced upon the strange attendant. He threw his hands up into the air, burst into a harsh clatter of words, and then, hurling himself down upon the ground beside the mummy, he threw his arms round her, and kissed her repeatedly upon the lips and brow. "Ma petite!" he groaned in French. "Ma pauvre petite!" His voice broke with emotion, and his innumerable wrinkles quivered and writhed, but the student observed in the lamp light that his shining eyes were still as dry and tearless as two beads of steel. For some minutes he lay, with a twitching face, crooning and moaning over the beautiful head. Then he broke into a sudden smile, said some words in an unknown tongue, and sprang to his feet with the vigorous air of one who has braced himself for an effort.

In the center of the room there was a large circular case which contained, as the student had frequently remarked, a magnificent collection of early Egyptian rings and precious stones. To this the attendant strode and, unlocking it, he threw it open. On the ledge at the side he placed his lamp and beside it a small earthenware jar which he had drawn from his pocket. He then took a handful of rings from the case and with a most serious and anxious face he proceeded to smear each in turn with some liquid substance from the earthen pot, holding them to the light as he did so. He was clearly disappointed with the first lot, for he threw them petulantly back into the case and drew out some more. One of these, a massive ring with a large crystal set in it, he seized and eagerly tested with the contents of the jar. Instantly he uttered a cry of joy, and threw out his arms in a wild gesture which upset the pot and sent the liquid streaming across the floor to the very feet of the Englishman. The attendant drew a red handkerchief from his bosom and mopping up the mess, he followed it into the corner, where in a moment he found himself face to face with his observer.

"Excuse me," said John Vansittart Smith, with all imaginable politeness; "I have been unfortunate enough to fall asleep behind this door."

"And you have been watching me?" the other asked in English, with a most venomous look on his corpse-like face.

The student was a man of veracity. "I confess," said he, "that I have noticed your movements and that they have aroused my curiosity and interest in the highest degree."

The man drew a long, flamboyant-bladed knife from his bosom. "You have had a very narrow escape," he said; "had I seen you ten minutes ago, I should have driven this through your heart. As it is, if you touch me or interfere with me in any way, you are a dead man."

"I have no wish to interfere with you," the student answered. "My presence here is entirely accidental. All I ask is that you will have the extreme kindness to show me out through some side door." He spoke with great suavity, for the man was still pressing the tip of his dagger against the palm of his left hand, as though to assure himself of its sharpness, while his face preserved its malignant expression.

"If I thought—" said he. "But no, perhaps it is as well. What is your name?"

The Englishman gave it.

"Vansittart Smith," the other repeated. "Are you the same Vansittart Smith who gave a paper in London upon El Kab? I saw a report of it. Your knowledge of the subject is contemptible."

"Sir!" cried the Egyptologist.

"Yet it is superior to that of many who make even greater pretensions. The whole keystone of our old life in Egypt was not the inscriptions or monuments of which you make so much, but was our hermetic philosophy and mystic knowledge, of which you say little or nothing."

"Our old life!" repeated the scholar, wide-eyed; and then suddenly: "Good God, look at the mummy's face!"

The strange man turned and flashed his light upon the dead woman, uttering a long, doleful cry as he did so. The action of the air had already undone all the art of the embalmer. The skin had fallen away, the eyes had sunk inward, the discolored lips had writhed away from the yellow teeth and the brown mark upon the forehead alone showed that it was indeed the same face which had shown such youth and beauty a few short minutes before.

The man flapped his hands together in grief and horror. Then mastering himself by a strong effort, he turned his hard eyes once more upon the Englishman.

"It does not matter," he said, in a shaking voice. "It does not really matter. I came here tonight with the fixed determination to do something. It is now done. All else is as nothing. I have found my quest. The old curse is broken. I can rejoin her. What matters about her inanimate shell so long as her spirit is awaiting me at the other side of the veil!"

"These are wild words," said Vansittart Smith. He was becoming more and more convinced that he had to do with a madman.

"Time presses and I must go," continued the other. "The moment is at hand for which I have waited this weary time. But I must show you out first. Come with me."

Taking up the lamp, he turned from the disordered chamber, and led the student swiftly through the long series of the Egyptian, Assyrian and Persian apartments. At the end of the latter he pushed open a small door let into the wall, and descended a winding stone stair. The Englishman felt the cold fresh air of the night upon his brow. There was a door opposite him which appeared to communicate with the street. To the right of this another door stood ajar, throwing a spurt of yellow light across the passage. "Come in here!" said the attendant shortly.

Vansittart Smith hesitated. He had hoped that he had come to the end of his adventures. Yet his curiosity was strong within him. He could not leave the matter unsolved, so he followed his strange companion into the lighted chamber.

It was a small room, such as is devoted to a concierge. A wood fire sparkled in the grate. At one side stood a truckle bed and at the other a coarse wooden chair, with a round table in the center, which bore the remains of a meal. As the visitor's eye glanced around he could not but remark with an ever-recurring thrill that all the small details of the room were of the most quaint design and antique workmanship. The candlesticks, the vases upon the chimney-piece, the fire-irons, the ornaments upon the walls, were all such as he had been wont to associate with the remote past. The gnarled, heavy-eyed man sat himself down upon the edge of the bed and motioned his guest into the chair.

"There may be design in this," he said, still speaking excellent English. "It may be decreed that I should leave some account behind as a warning to all rash mortals who would set their wits up against workings of Nature. I leave it to you. Make such use as you will of it. I speak to you now with my feet upon the threshold of the other world.

"I am, as you surmised, an Egyptian—not one of the down-trodden race of slaves who now inhabit the Delta of the Nile, but a survivor of that fiercer and harder people who tamed the Hebrew, drove the Ethiopian back into the southern deserts and built those mighty works which have been the envy and the wonder of all after generations. It was in the reign of Tuthmosis, sixteen hundred years before the birth of Christ, that I first saw the light. You shrink away from me. Wait and you will see that I am more to be pitied than to be feared.

"My name was Sosra. My father had been the chief priest of Osiris in the great temple of Abaris, which stood in those days upon the Bubastic branch of the Nile. I was brought up in the temple and was trained in all those mystic arts which are spoken of in your own Bible. I was an apt pupil. Before I was sixteen I had learned all which the wisest priest could teach me. From that time on

I studied Nature's secrets for myself, and shared my knowledge with no man.

"Of all the questions which attracted me there were none over which I labored so long as over those which concern themselves with the nature of life. I probed deeply into the vital principle. The aim of medicine had been to drive away disease when it appeared. It seemed to me that a method might be devised which should so fortify the body as to prevent weakness or death from ever taking hold of it. It is useless that I should recount my researches. You would scarce comprehend them if I did. They were carried out partly upon animals, partly upon slaves and partly on myself. Suffice it that their result was to furnish me with a substance which, when injected into the blood, would endow the body with strength to resist the effects of time, of violence or of disease. It would not, indeed, confer immortality, but its potency would endure for many thousands of years. I used it upon a cat, and afterward drugged the creature with the most deadly poisons. That cat is alive in Lower Egypt at the present moment. There was nothing of mystery or magic in the matter. It was simply a chemical discovery, which may well be made again.

"Love of life runs high in the young. It seemed to me that I had broken away from all human care now that I had abolished pain and driven death to such a distance. With a light heart I poured the accursed stuff into my veins. Then I looked around for some one whom I could benefit. There was a young priest of Thoth, Parmes by name, who had won my good will by his earnest nature and his devotion to his studies. To him I whispered my secret and at his request I injected him with my elixir. I should now, I reflected, never be without a companion of the same age as myself.

"After this grand discovery I relaxed my studies to some extent, but Parmes continued his with redoubled energy. Every day I could see him working with his flasks and his distiller in the Temple of Thoth, but he said little to me as to the result of his labors. For my own part, I used to walk through the city and looked around me with exultation as I reflected that all this was destined to pass away, and that only I should remain. The people would bow to me as they passed, for the fame of my knowledge had gone abroad.

"There was war at this time and the great king had sent his soldiers to the eastern boundary to drive away the Hyksos. A governor, too, was sent to Abaris, that he might hold it for the king. I had heard much of the beauty of the daughter of this governor, but one day as I walked out with Parmes we met her, borne upon the shoulders of her slaves. I was struck with love as with lightning. My heart went out from me. I could have thrown myself beneath the feet of her bearers. This was my woman. Life without her was impossible. I swore by the head of Horus that she should be mine. I swore it to the priest of Thoth. He turned away from me with a brow which was as black as midnight.

"There is no need to tell you of our wooing. She came to love me even as I loved her. I learned that Parmes had seen her before I did and had shown her that he too loved her; but I could smile at his passion, for I knew that her heart was mine. The white plague had come upon the city and many were stricken, but I laid my hands upon the sick and nursed them without fear or scathe. She marveled at my daring. Then I told her my secret, and begged her that she would let me use my art upon her.

"'Your flower shall then be unwithered, Atma,' I said. 'Other things may pass away, but you and I, and our great love for each other, shall outlive the tomb of King Chefru.'

"But she was full of timid, maidenly objections. 'Was

" 'In the ring of Thoth!' I repeated; 'where, then, is the ring of Thoth?'

" 'That also you shall never know,' he answered. 'You won her love. Who has won in the end? I leave you to your sordid earth life. My chains are broken. I must go!' He turned upon his heel and fled from the chamber. In the morning came the news that the priest of Thoth was dead.

"My days after that were spent in study. I must find this subtle poison which was strong enough to undo the elixir. From early dawn to midnight I bent over the test tube and the furnace. Above all, I collected the papyri and the chemical flasks of the priest of Thoth. Alas! they taught me little. Here and there some hint or stray expression would raise hope in my bosom, but no good ever came of it. Still, month after month, I struggled on. When my heart grew faint I would make my way to the tomb by the palm trees. There, standing by the dead casket from which the jewel had been rifled, I would feel her sweet presence and would whisper to her that I would rejoin her if mortal wit could solve the riddle.

"Parmes had said that his discovery was connected with the ring of Thoth. I had some remembrance of the trinket. It was a large and weighty circlet, made, not of gold, but of a rarer and heavier metal brought from the mines of Mount Harbal. Platinum, you call it. The ring had, I remembered, a hollow crystal set in it, in which some few drops of liquid might be stored. Now, the secret of Parmes could not have to do with the metal alone, for there were many rings of that metal in the Temple. Was it not more likely that he had stored his precious poison within the cavity of the crystal? I had scarce come to this conclusion before, in hunting through his papers, I came upon one which told me that it was indeed so, and that there was still some of the liquid unused.

"But how to find the ring? It was not upon him when he was stripped for the embalmer. Of that I made sure. Neither was it among his private effects. In vain I searched every room that he had entered, every box and vase, and chattel that he had owned. I sifted the very sand of the desert in the places where he had been wont to walk; but, do what I would, I could come upon no trace of the ring of Thoth. Yet it may be that my labors would have overcome all obstacles had it not been for a new and unlooked-for misfortune.

"A great war had been waged against the Hyksos, and the captains of the great king had been cut off in the desert, with all their bowmen and horsemen. The shepherd tribes were upon us like the locusts in a dry year. From the wilderness of Shur to the great bitter lake there was blood by day and fire by night. Abaris was the bulwark of Egypt, but we could not keep the savages back. The city fell. The governor and his soldiers were put to the sword, and I, with many more, was led away into captivity.

"For years and years I tended cattle in the great plains by the Euphrates. My master died and his son grew old, but I was still as far from death as ever. At last I escaped upon a swift camel and made my way back to Egypt. The Hyksos had settled in the land which they had conquered, and their king ruled over the country. Abaris had been torn down, the city had been burned and of the great temple there was nothing left save an unsightly mound. Everywhere the tombs had been rifled and the monuments destroyed. Of my Atma's grave no sign was left. It was buried in the sands of the desert and the palm trees which marked the spot had long disappeared. The papers of Parmes and the remains of the Temple of Thoth were either destroyed or scattered far and wide over the deserts of Syria. All search after them was vain.

"From that time I gave up all hope of ever finding the ring or discovering the subtle drug. I set myself to live as patiently as might be until the effect of the elixir should wear away. How can you understand how terrible a thing time is, you who have experienced only the narrow course which lies between the cradle and the grave! I know it to my cost, I who have floated down the whole stream of history. I was old when Illium fell. I was very old when Herodotus came to Memphis. I was bowed down with years when the new Gospel came upon earth. Yet you see me much as other men are, with the cursed elixir still sweeting my blood and guarding me against that which I would court. Now at last, at last, I have come to the end of it!

"I have traveled in all lands and I have dwelt with all nations. Every tongue is the same to me. I learned them all to help pass the weary time. I need not tell you how slowly they drifted by, the long dawn of modern civilization, the dreary middle years, the dark times of barbarism. They were behind me now. I have never looked with the eyes of love upon another woman. Atma knows that I have been constant to her.

"It was my custom to read all that the scholars had to say upon ancient Egypt. I have been in many positions, sometimes affluent, sometimes poor, but I have always found enough to enable me to buy the journals which deal with such matters. Some nine months ago I was in San Francisco when I read an account of some discoveries made in the neighborhood of Abaris. My heart leaped into my mouth as I read it. It said that the excavator had busied himself in exploring some tombs recently unearthed. In one there had been found an unopened mummy with an inscription upon the outer case setting forth that it contained the body of the daughter of the governor of the city in the days of Tuthmosis. It added that on removing the outer case, there had been exposed a large platinum ring set with a crystal, which had been laid upon the breast of the embalmed woman. This, then, was where Parmes had hidden the ring of Thoth. He might well say that it was safe, for no Egyptian would ever stain his soul by moving even the outer case of a buried friend.

"That very night I set off from San Francisco, and in a few weeks I found myself once more at Abaris, if a few sand heaps and crumbling walls may retain the name of the great city. I hurried to the Frenchmen who were digging there and asked them for the ring. They replied that both the ring and the mummy had been sent to the Boulak Museum at Cairo. To Boulak I went, but only to be told that Mariette Bey had claimed them and had shipped them to the Louvre. I followed them, and there at last, in the Egyptian chamber, I came, after close upon four thousand years, upon the remains of my Atma, and upon the ring for which I had sought so long.

"But how was I to lay hands upon them? How was I to have them for my very own? It chanced that the office of attendant was vacant. I went to the director. I convinced him that I knew much about Egypt. In my eagerness I said too much. He remarked that a professor's chair would suit me better than a seat in the conciergerie. I knew more, he said, than he did. It was only by blundering and letting him think that he had overestimated my knowledge, that I prevailed upon him to let me move the few effects which I have retained into this chamber. It is my first and my last night here.

"Such is my story, Mr. Vansittart Smith. I need say more to a man of your perception. By a strange chance you have this night looked upon the face of the woman whom I loved in those far-off days. There were many rings with crystals in the case, and I had to test for the platinum to be sure of the one which I wanted. A glance at the crystal has shown me that the liquid is indeed within it, and that I shall at last be able to shake off that accursed health which has been worse to me than the foulest disease. I have nothing more to say to you. I have unburdened myself. You may tell my story or you may withhold it at your pleasure. The choice rests with you. I owe you some amends, for you have had a narrow escape of your life this night. I was a desperate man and not to be balked in my purpose. Had I seen you before the thing was done, I might have put it beyond your power to oppose me or raise an alarm. This is the door. It leads into the Rue de Rivoli. Good night!"

The Englishman glanced back. For a moment the lean figure of Sosra the Egyptian stood framed in the narrow doorway. The next the door had slammed and the heavy rasping of a bolt broke on the silent night.

It was on the second day after his return to London that Mr. John Vansittart Smith saw the following concise narrative in the Paris correspondence of the *Times*:

"Curious Occurrence in the Louvre—Yesterday morning a strange discovery was made in the principal Egyptian chamber. The ouvriers who are employed to clean out the rooms in the morning found one of the attendants lying dead upon the floor with his arms round one of the mummies. So close was his embrace that it was only with the utmost difficulty that they were separated. One of the cases containing valuable rings had been opened and rifled. The authorities are of the opinion that the man was bearing away the mummy with some idea of selling it to a private collector, but that he was struck down in the very act by long-standing disease of the heart. It is said that he was a man of uncertain age and eccentric habits, without any living relations to mourn over his dramatic and untimely end."

A CASE OF IDENTITY

"My dear fellow," said Sherlock Holmes, as we sat on either side of the fire in his lodgings at Baker Street, "life is infinitely stranger than anything which the mind of man could invent. We would not dare to conceive the things which are really mere commonplaces of existence. If we could fly out of that window hand in hand, hover over this great city, gently remove the roofs and peep in at the queer things which are going on, the strange coincidences, the plannings, the cross-purposes, the wonderful chains of events, working through generations, and leading to the most outre results, it would make all fiction, with its conventionalities and foreseen conclusions, most stale and unprofitable."

"And yet I am not convinced of it," I answered.

"The cases which come to light in the papers are, as a rule, bald enough, and vulgar enough. We have in our police reports realism pushed to its extreme limits and yet the result is, it must be confessed, neither fascinating nor artistic."

"A certain selection and discretion must be used in producing a realistic effect," remarked Holmes. "This is wanting in the police report, where more stress is laid perhaps upon the platitudes of the magistrate than upon the details, which to an observer contain the vital essence of the whole matter. Depend upon it, there is nothing so unnatural as the commonplace."

I smiled and shook my head. "I can quite understand your thinking so," I said. "Of course, in your position of unofficial adviser and helper to everybody who is absolutely puzzled, throughout three continents, you are brought in contact with all that is strange and bizarre. But here"—I picked up the morning paper from the ground—"let us put it to a practical test. Here is the first heading upon which I come. 'A husband's cruelty to his wife.' There is half a column of print, but I know without reading it that it is all perfectly familiar to me. There is, of course, the other woman, the drink, the push, the blow, the bruise, the unsympathetic sister or landlady. The crudest of writers could invent nothing more crude."

"Indeed your example is an unfortunate one for your argument," said Holmes, taking the paper and glancing his eye down it. "This is the Dundas separation case and, as it happens, I was engaged in clearing up some small points in conection with it. The husband was a teetotaler, there was no other woman, and the conduct complained of was that he had drifted into the habit of winding up every meal by taking out his false teeth and hurling them at his wife, which you will allow is not an action likely to occur to the imagination of the average story-teller. Take a pinch of snuff, doctor, and acknowledge that I have scored over you in your example."

He held out his snuff box of old gold, with a great amethyst in the center of the lid. Its splendor was in such contrast to his homely ways and simple life that I could not help commenting upon it.

"Ah!" said he, "I forgot that I had not seen you for some weeks. It is a little souvenir from the King of Bohemia, in return for my assistance in the case of the Irene Adler papers."

"And the ring?" I asked, glancing at a remarkable brilliant which sparkled upon his finger.

"It was from the reigning family of Holland, though the matter in which I served them was of such delicacy that I cannot confide it even to you, who have been good enough to chronicle one or two of my little problems."

"And have you any on hand just now?" I asked with interest.

"Some ten or twelve, but none which present any features of interest. They are important, you understand, without being interesting. Indeed I have found that it is usually in unimportant matters that there is a field for the observation, and for the quick analysis of cause and effect which gives the charm to an investigation. The larger crimes are apt to be the simpler, for the bigger the crime, the more obvious, as a rule, is the motive. In these cases, save for one rather intricate matter which has been referred to me from Marseilles, there is nothing which presents any features of interest. It is possible, however, that I may have something better before very many minutes are over, for this is one of my clients or I am much mistaken."

He had risen from his chair and was standing between the parted blinds, gazing down into the dull, neutral-tinted London street. Looking over his shoulder, I saw that on the pavement opposite there stood a large woman with a heavy fur boa round her neck, and a large curling red feather in a broad-brimmed hat which was tilted in a coquettish Duchess-of-Devonshire fashion over her ear. From under this great panoply she peeped up in a nervous, hesitating fashion at our windows, while her body oscillated backward and forward, and her fingers fidgeted with her glove buttons. Suddenly, with a plunge, as of the swimmer who leaves the bank, she hurried across the road and we heard the sharp clang of the bell.

"I have seen those symptoms before," said Holmes, throwing his cigarette into the fire. "Oscillation upon the pavement always means an affaire de cœur. She would like advice, but is not sure that the matter is not too delicate for communication. And yet even here we may discriminate. When a woman has been seriously wronged by a man, she no longer oscillates, and the usual symptom is a broken bell wire. Here we may take it that there is a love matter, but the maiden is not so much angry as perplexed or grieved. But here she comes in person to resolve our doubts."

As he spoke, there was a tap at the door and the boy in buttons entered to announce Miss Mary Sutherland, while the lady herself loomed behind his small black figure like a full-sailed merchantman behind a tiny pilot boat. Sherlock Holmes welcomed her with the easy courtesy for which he was remarkable, and having closed the door and bowed her into an armchair, he looked her over in the minute, and yet abstracted, fashion which was peculiar to him.

"Do you not find," he said, "that with your short sight it is a little trying to do so much typewriting?"

"I did at first," she answered, "but now I know where the letters are without looking." Then suddenly realizing the full purport of his words, she gave a violent start and looked up with fear and astonishment upon her broad, good-humored face. "You've heard about me, Mr. Holmes," she cried, "else how could you know all that?"

"Never mind," said Holmes, laughing, "it is my business to know things. Perhaps I have trained myself to see what others overlook. If not, why should you come to consult me?"

"I came to you, sir, because I heard of you from Mrs. Etherege, whose husband you found so easily when the police and every one had given him up for dead. Oh, Hr. Holmes, I wish you would do as much for me. I'm not rich, but still I have a hundred a year in my own right, besides the little that I make by the machine, and I would give it all to know what has become of Mr. Hosmer Angel."

"Why did you come away to consult me in such a

hurry?" asked Sherlock Holmes, with his finger tips together, and his eyes to the ceiling.

Again a startled look came over the somewhat vacuous face of Miss Mary Sutherland. "Yes, I did bang out of the house," she said, "for it made me angry to see the easy way in which Mr. Windibank—that is, my father—took it all. He would not go to the police and he would not go to you, and so at last, as he would do nothing and kept on saying that there was no harm done, it made me mad and I just on with my things and came right away to you."

"Your father," said Holmes, "your stepfather, surely, since the name is different."

"Yes, my stepfather. I call him father, though it sounds funny, too, for he is only five years and two months older than myself."

"And your mother is alive?"

"Oh, yes; mother is alive and well. I wasn't best pleased, Mr. Holmes, when she married again so soon after father's death and a man who was nearly fifteen years younger than herself. Father was a plumber in the Tottenham Court Road and he left a tidy business behind him, which mother carried on with Mr. Hardy, the foreman; but when Mr. Windibank came he made her sell the business, for he was very superior, being a traveler in wines. They got four thousand seven hundred for the good-will and interest, which wasn't near as much as father could have got if he had been alive."

I had expected to see Sherlock Holmes impatient under this rambling and inconsequential narrative, but, on the contrary, he had listened with the greatest concentration of attention.

"Your own little income," he asked, "does it come out of the business?"

"Oh, no, sir. It is quite separate and was left me by my uncle Ned in Auckland. It is in New Zealand stock, first walk that we took. Hosmer—Mr. Angel—was a cashier in an office in Leadenhall Street—and—"

"What office?"

"That's the worst of it, Mr. Holmes, I don't know."

"Where did he live then?"

"He slept on the premises."

"And you don't know his address?"

"No—except that it was Leadenhall Street."

"Where did you address your letters, then?"

"To the Leadenhall Street Post Office, to be left till called for. He said that if they were sent to the office he would be chaffed by all the other clerks about having letters from a lady, so I offered to typewrite them, like he did his, but he wouldn't have that, for he said that when I wrote them they seemed to come from me, but when they were typewritten he always felt that the machine had come between us. That will just show you how fond he was of me, Mr. Holmes, and the little things that he would think of."

"It was most suggestive," said Mr. Holmes. "It has long been an axiom of mine that the little things are infinitely the most important. Can you remember any other little things about Mr. Hosmer Angel?"

"He was a very shy man, Mr. Holmes. He would rather walk with me in the evening than in the daylight, for he said that he hated to be conspicuous. Very retiring and gentlemanly he was. Even his voice was gentle. He'd had the quinsy and swollen glands when he was young, he told me, and it had left him with a weak throat and a hesitating, whispering fashion of speech. He was always well dressed, very neat and plain, but his eyes were weak, just as mine are, and he wore tinted glasses against the glare."

"Well, and what happened when Mr. Windibank, your stepfather, returned to France?"

"Mr. Hosmer Angel came to the house again and proposed that we should marry before father came back. He was in dreadful earnest and made me swear, with my hands on the Testament, that whatever happened, I would always be true to him. Mother said he was quite right to make me swear and that it was a sign of his passion. Mother was all in his favor from the first, and was even fonder of him than I was. Then, when they talked of marrying within the week, I began to mind about father, but they both said never to mind about father, but just to tell him afterward and mother said she would make it all right with him. I didn't quite like that, Mr. Holmes. It seemed funny that I should ask his leave, as he was only a few years older than me; but I didn't want to do anything on the sly, so I wrote to father at Bordeaux, where the company has its French offices, but the letter came back to me on the very morning of the wedding."

"It missed him, then?"

"Yes, sir, for he had started to England just before it arrived."

"Ha! That was unfortunate. Your wedding was arranged then for the Friday. Was it to be in church?"

"Yes, sir, but very quietly. It was to be at St. Saviour's, near King's Cross, and we were to have breakfast afterward at the St. Pancras Hotel. Hosmer came for us in a hansom, but as there were two of us, he put us both into it and stepped himself into a four-wheeler, which happened to be the only other cab in the street. We got to the church first and when the four-wheeler drove up we waited for him to step out, but he never did, and when the cabman got down from the box and looked, there was no one there! The cabman said that he could not imagine what had become of him, for he had seen him get in with his own eyes. That was last Friday, Mr. Holmes, and I have never seen or heard anything since then to throw any light upon what became of him."

Then he took down from the rack the old and oily clay pipe, which was to him as a counselor and, having lighted it, he leaned back in his chair, with thick blue cloud wreaths spinning up from him and a look of infinite languour in his face.

"Quite an interesting study, that maiden," he observed. "I found her more interesting than her little problem, which, by the way, is rather a trite one. You will find parallel cases, if you consult my index, in Andover in '77, and there was something of the sort at the Hague last year. Old as is the idea, however, there were one or two details which were new to me. But the maiden herself was most instructive."

"You appeared to read a good deal upon her which was not quite visible to me," I remarked.

"Not invisible, but unnoticed, Watson. You did not know where to look and so you missed all that was important. I can never bring you to realize the importance of sleeves, the suggestiveness of thumb nails, or the great issues that may hang from a boot lace. Now what did you gather from that woman's appearance? Describe it."

"Well, she had a slate-colored, broad-brimmed straw hat, with a feather of a brickish red. Her jacket was black, with black beads sewed upon it and a fringe of little black jet ornaments. Her dress was brown, rather darker than coffee color, with a little purple plush at the neck and sleeves. Her gloves were grayish and were worn through at the right forefinger. Her boots I didn't observe. She had small round, hanging gold earrings and a general air of being fairly well to do, in a vulgar, comfortable, easy-going way."

Sherlock Holmes clapped his hands softly together and chuckled.

"'Pon my word, Watson, you are coming along wonderfully. You have really done very well indeed. It is true that you have missed everything of importance, but you have hit upon the method and you have a quick eye for color. Never trust to general impressions, my boy, but concentrate yourself upon details. My first glance is always at a woman's sleeve. In a man it is perhaps better first to take the knee of the trouser. As you observe, this woman had plush upon her sleeves, which is a most useful material for showing traces. The double line a little above the wrist, where the typewritist presses against the table, was beautifully defined. The sewing machine, of the hand type, leaves a similar mark, but only on the left arm, and on the side of it furthest from the thumb, instead of being right across the broadest part, as this was. I then glanced at her face and, observing the dint of a pince-nez at either side of her nose, I ventured a remark upon short sight and typewriting, which seemed to surprise her."

"It surprised me."

"But surely it was very obvious. I was then much surprised and interested on glancing down to observe that, though the boots which she was wearing were not unlike each other, they were really odd ones, the one having a slightly decorated toe cap and the other a plain one. One was buttoned only in the two lower buttons out of five and the other at the first, third and fifth. Now when you see that a young lady, otherwise neatly dressed, has come away from home with odd boots, half-buttoned, it is no great deduction to say that she came away in a hurry."

"And what else?" I asked, keenly interested, as I always was, by my friend's incisive reasoning.

"I noted, in passing, that she had written a note before leaving home, but after being fully dressed. You observed that her right glove was torn at the forefinger, but you did not, apparently, see that both glove and finger were stained with violet ink. She had written in a hurry, and dipped her pen too deep. It must have been this

"Well, have you solved it?" I asked as I entered.

"Yes. It was the bisulphate of baryta."

"No, no; the mystery!" I cried.

"Oh, that! I thought of the salt that I have been working upon. There was never any mystery in the matter, though, as I said yesterday, some of the details are of interest. The only drawback is that there is no law, I fear, that can touch the scoundrel."

"Who was he then and what was his object in deserting Miss Sutherland?"

The question was hardly out of my mouth and Holmes had not yet opened his lips to reply, when we heard a heavy footfall in the passage, and a tap at the door.

"This is the girl's stepfather, Mr. James Windibank," said Holmes. "He has written me to say that he would be here at six. Come in!"

The man who entered was a sturdy, middle-sized fellow, some thirty years of age, clean shaven and sallow skinned, with a bland, insinuating manner and a pair of wonderfully sharp and penetrating gray eyes. He shot a questioning glance at each of us, placed his shiny top hat upon the sideboard and, with a slight bow, sidled down into the nearest chair.

"Good evening, Mr. James Windibank," said Holmes. "I think this typewritten letter is from you, in which you made an appointment with me for six o'clock."

"Yes, sir. I am afraid that I am a little late, but I am not quite my own master, you know. I am sorry that Miss Sutherland has troubled you about this little matter, for I think it is far better not to wash linen of that sort in public. It was quite against my wishes that she came, but she is a very excitable, impulsive girl, as you may have noticed, and she is not easily controlled when she has made up her mind on a point. Of course, I did not mind you so much, as you are not connected with the official police, but it is not pleasant to have a family misfortune like this noised abroad. Besides, it is a useless expense, for how could you possibly find this Hosmer Angel?"

"On the contrary," said Holmes, quietly, "I have every reason to believe that I will succeed in discovering Mr. Hosmer Angel."

Mr. Windibank gave a violent start and dropped his gloves. "I am delighted to hear it," he said.

"It is a curious thing," remarked Holmes, "that a typewriter has really as much individuality as a man's handwriting. Unless they are quite new no two of them write exactly alike. Some letters get more worn than others and some wear only on one side. Now you remark in this note of yours, Mr. Windibank, that in every case there is some little slurring over the *e*, and a slight defect in the tail of the *r*. There are fourteen other characteristics, but those are the more obvious."

"We do all our correspondence with this machine at the office and no doubt it is a little worn," our visitor answered, glancing keenly at Holmes with his bright little eyes.

"And now I will show you what is really a very interesting study, Mr. Windibank," Holmes continued. "I think of writing another little monograph some of these days on the typewriter and its relation to crime. It is a subject to which I have devoted some little attention. I have here four letters which purport to come from the missing man. They are all typewritten. In each case, not only are the *e's* slurred and the *r's* tailless, but you will observe, if you care to use my magnifying lens, that the fourteen other characteristics to which I have alluded are there as well."

Mr. Windibank sprang out of his chair and picked up his hat. "I cannot waste time over this sort of fantastic talk, Mr. Holmes," he said. "If you can catch the man, catch him, and let me know when you have done it."

of something happening on the very morning of the wedding. James Windibank wished Miss Sutherland to be so bound to Hosmer Angel and so uncertain as to his fate that for ten years to come, at any rate, she would not listen to another man. As far as the church door he brought her and then, as he could go no further, he conveniently vanished away by the old trick of stepping in at one door of a four-wheeler and out at the other. I think that that was the chain of events, Mr. Windibank!"

Our visitor had recovered something of his assurance while Holmes had been talking and he rose from his chair now with a cold sneer upon his pale face.

"It may be so or it may not, Mr. Holmes," said he; "but if you are so very sharp you ought to be sharp enough to know that it is you who are breaking the law now, and not me. I have done nothing actionable from the first, but as long as you keep that door locked you lay yourself open to an action for assault and illegal constraint."

"The law cannot, as you say, touch you," said Holmes, unlocking and throwing open the door, "yet there never was a man who deserved punishment more. If the young lady had a brother or a friend, he ought to lay a whip across your shoulders. By Jove!" he continued, flushing up at the sight of the bitter sneer upon the man's face, "it is not part of my duties to my client, but here's a hunting crop handy, and I think I shall just treat myself to—" He took two swift steps to the whip but before he could grasp it there was a wild clatter of steps upon the stairs, the heavy hall door banged and from the window we could see Mr. James Windibank running at the top of his speed down the road.

"There's a cold-blooded scoundrel!" said Holmes, laughing as he threw himself down into his chair once more. "That fellow will rise from crime to crime until he does something very bad and ends on a gallows. The case has, in some respects, been not entirely devoid of interest."

"I cannot now entirely see all the steps of your reasoning," I remarked.

"Well, of course, it was obvious from the first that this Mr. Hosmer Angel must have some strong object for his curious conduct and it was equally clear that the only man who really profited by the incident, as far as we could see, was the stepfather. Then the fact that the two men were never together, but that the one always appeared when the other was away, was suggestive. So were the tinted glasses and the curious voice, which both hinted at a disguise, as did the bushy whiskers. My suspicions were all confirmed by his peculiar action in typewriting his signature, which, of course, inferred that his handwriting was so familiar to her that she would recognize even the smallest sample of it. You see all these isolated facts, together with many minor ones, all pointed in the same direction."

"And how did you verify them?"

"Having once spotted my man, it was easy to get corroboration. I knew the firm for which this man worked. Having taken the printed description, I eliminated everything from it which could be the result of a disguise—the whiskers, the glasses, the voice and I sent it to the firm with a request that they would inform me whether it answered to the description of any of their travelers. I had already noticed the peculiarities of the typewriter and I wrote to the man himself at his business address, asking him if he would come here. As I expected, his reply was typewritten and revealed the same trivial but characteristic defects. The same post brought me a letter from Westhouse & Marbank, of Fenchurch Street, to say that the description tallied in every respect with that of their employe, James Windibank. *Voila tout!*"

"And Miss Sutherland?"

which I had not set foot, and scarcely any joy or sorrow
of which I had not tasted. Among the first of Europeans,
I had penetrated to the desolate shores of Lake Tan-
ganyika; I had twice made my way to those unvisited and
impenetrable jungles which skirt the great tableland of
Roraima. As a soldier of fortune I had served under
many flags. I was with Jackson in the Shenandoah Valley, and I fought with Chanzy in the army of the Loire.
It may well seem strange that, after a life so exciting, I
could give myself up to the dull routine and trivial interests of the West Riding hamlet. And yet there are ex-
citements of the mind to which mere bodily peril or the
exaltation of travel is mean and commonplace. For
years I had devoted myself to the study of the mystic and
hermetic philosophies, Egyptian, Indian, Grecian and medieval, until out of the vast chaos there had dimly dawned
upon me a huge symmetrical design; and I seemed to
grasp the key of that symbolism which was used by those
learned men to screen their precious knowledge from the
vulgar and the wicked. Gnostics and Neo-platonists,
Chaldeans, Rosicrucians and Indian Mystics, I saw and
understood in which each played a part. To me a jar-
gon of Paracelsus, the mysteries of the alchemists and
the visions of Swedenborg were all pregnant with meaning. I had deciphered the mysterious inscriptions of El
Biram; and I knew the import of those strange characters which have been engraved by an unknown race upon
the cliffs of Southern Turkestan. Immersed in these
great and engrossing studies, I asked nothing from life
save a garret for myself and for my books, where I might
pursue my studies without interference or interruption.

But even in this little moorside village I found that it
was impossible to shake off the censorship of one's fellow-
mortals. When I went forth, the rustics would eye me
askance, and mothers would whip up their children as I
passed down the village street. At night I have glanced

through my diamond-paned lattice to find that a group of foolish, staring peasants had been craning their necks in an ectasy of fear and curiosity to watch me at my solitary task. My landlady, too, became garrulous with a clatter of questions under every small pretext, and a hundred small ruses and wiles by which to tempt me to speak to her of myself and of my plans. All this was ill to bear; but when at last I heard that I was no longer to be sole lodger and that a lady, a stranger, had engaged the other room, I felt that indeed it was time for one who sought the quiet and the peace of study to seek some more tranquil surrounding.

In my frequent walks I had learned to know well the wild and desolate region where Yorkshire borders on both Lancashire and Westmoreland. From Kirkby-Malhouse I had frequently made my way to this lonesome wilderness, and had traversed it from end to end. In the gloomy majesty of its scenery and the appalling stillness and loneliness of its rock-strewn, melancholy solitudes, it seemed to offer me a secure asylum from espionage and criticism. As it chanced, I had in my rambles come upon an isolated dwelling in the very heart of these lonely moors, which I at once determined should be my own. It was a two-roomed cottage, which had once belonged to some shepherd, but which had long been deserted and was crumbling rapidly to ruin. In the winter floods, the Gaster Beck, which runs down Gaster Fell, where the little shieling stood, had overswept its bank and torn away a portion of the wall. The roof, too, was in ill case, and the scattered slates lay thick amongst the grass. Yet the main shell of the house stood firm and true; and it was no great task for me to have all that was amiss set right. Though not rich, I could yet afford to carry out so modest a whim in a lordly way. There came slaters and masons from Kirkby-Malhouse and soon the

lonely cottage upon Gaster Fell was as strong and
weather-tight as ever.

The two rooms I laid out in a widely different manner
—my own tastes are of a Spartan turn and the outer
chamber was so planned as to accord with them. An oil
stove by Rippingille, of Birmingham, furnished me with
the means of cooking; while two great bags, the one of
flour and the other of potatoes, made me independent of
all supplies from without. In diet I had long been a
Pythagorean, so that the scraggy long-limbed sheep
which browsed upon the wiry grass by the Gaster Beck
had little to fear from their new companion. A nine-
gallon cask of oil served me as a sideboard; while a
square table, a deal chair and a truckle bed completed the
list of my domestic fittings. At the head of my couch
hung two unpainted shelves—the lower for my dishes and
cooking utensils, the upper for the few portraits which
took me back to the little that was pleasant in the long,
wearisome toiling for wealth and for pleasure which had
marked the life I had left behind.

If this dwelling room of mine were plain even to
squalor, its poverty was more than atoned for by the
luxury of the chamber which was destined to serve me as
my study. I had ever held that it was best for the mind
to be surrounded by such objects as would be in harmony
with the studies which occupied it, and that the loftiest
and most ethereal conditions of thoughts are only possible
amid surroundings which please the eye and gratify the
senses. The room which I had set apart for my mystic
studies was set forth in a style as gloomy and majestic as
the thoughts and aspirations with which it was to har-
monize. Both walls and ceilings were covered with a
paper of the richest and glossiest black, on which were
traced a lurid and arabesque pattern of dead gold. A
black velvet curtain covered the single diamond-paned
window, while a thick, yielding carpet of the same ma-

terial prevented the sound of my footfalls, as I paced backward and forward, from breaking the current of my thoughts. Along the cornices ran gold rods, from which suspended six pictures, all of the somber and imaginative caste, which chimed best with my fancy. Two, as I remember, were from the brush of Fuseli; one from Noel Paton; one from Gustave Dore; two from Martin; with a little water color by the incomparable Blake. From the center of the ceiling hung a single gold thread, so thin as to be scarce visible, but of great toughness. From this swung a dove of the same metal, with wings outstretched. The bird was hollow and contained perfumed oil; while a sylph-like figure, curiously fashioned from pink crystal, hovered over the lamp and imparted a soft and rich glow to the light. A brazen fireplace backed with malachite, two tiger skins upon the carpet, a buhl table and two reclining chairs in amber plush and ebony, completed the furniture of my bijou study, save only that under the window stretched the long book shelves, which contained the choicest works of those who have busied themselves with the mystery of life.

Boehme, Swedenborg, Damton, Berto, Lacci, Sinnett, Hardinge, Britten, Dunlop, Amberley, Winwood Read, Des Mousseux, Alan Kardec, Lepsius, Sepher, Toldo and the Abbe Dubois—these were some of those who stood marshaled between my oaken shelves. When the lamp was lighted of a night and the lurid, flickering light played over the somber and bizarre surroundings, the effect was all that I could wish. Nor was it lessened by the howling of the wind as it swept over the melancholy waste around me. Here, at last, I thought, is a back-eddy in life's hurried stream, where I may lie in peace, forgetting and forgotten.

And yet it was destined that ere ever I reached this quiet harbor I should learn that I was still one of humankind, and that it is an ill thing to strive to break the bond which binds us to our fellows. It was but two nights before the date I had fixed upon for my change of dwelling when I was conscious of a bustle in the house beneath, with the bearing of heavy burdens up the creaking stair and the harsh voice of my landlady, loud in welcome and protestations of joy. From time to time, amid her whirl of words, I could hear a gentle and softly modulated voice, which struck pleasantly upon my ear after the long weeks during which I had listened only to the rude dialect of the dalesmen. For an hour I could hear the dialogue beneath—the high voice and the low, with clatter of cup and clink of spoon, until at last a light quick step passed my study door and I knew that my new fellow lodger had sought her room. Already my fears had been fulfilled, and my studies the worse for her coming. I vowed in my mind that the second sunset should find me installed, safe from all such petty influences in my sanctuary at Gester Fell.

On the morning after this incident I was up betimes, as is my wont; but I was surprised, on glancing from my window, to see that our new inmate was earlier still. She was walking down the narrow pathway which zigzags over the fell—a tall woman, slender, her head sunk upon her breast, her arms filled with a bristle of wild flowers, which she had gathered in her morning rambles. The white and pink of her dress, and the touch of deep red ribbon in her broad drooping hat, formed a pleasant dash of color against the dun-tinted landscape. She was some distance off when I first set eyes upon her, yet I knew that this wandering woman could be none other than our arrival of last night, for there was a grace and refinement in her bearing which marked her from the dwellers of the fells. Even as I watched, she passed swiftly and lightly down the pathway, and turning through the wicket gate, at the further end of our cottage garden, she seated herself upon the green bank which faced my window and strewing her flowers in front of her, set herself to arrange them.

As she sat there, with the rising sun at her back, and the glow of the morning spreading like an aureole around her stately and well-poised head, I could see that she was a woman of extraordinary personal beauty. Her face was Spanish rather than English in its type—oval, olive, with black sparkling eyes and a sweetly sensitive mouth. From under the broad straw hat two thick coils of blue-black hair curved down on either side of her graceful, queenly neck. I was surprised, as I watched her, to see that her shoes and skirt bore witness to a journey rather than to a mere morning ramble. Her light dress was stained, wet and bedraggled; while her boots were thick with the yellow soils of the fells. Her face, too, wore a weary expression and her young beauty seemed to be clouded over by the shadow of inward trouble. Even as I watched her. she burst suddenly into wild weeping, and throwing down her bundle of flowers, ran swiftly into the house.

Distrait as I was and weary of the ways of the world, I was conscious of a sudden pang of sympathy and grief as I looked upon the spasm of despair which seemed to convulse this strange and beautiful woman. I bent to my books and yet my thoughts would ever turn to her proud, clear-cut face, her weather-stained dress, her drooping head and the sorrow which lay in each line and feature of her pensive face. Again and again I found myself standing at my casement and glancing out to see if there were signs of her return. There on the green bank was the litter of golden gorse and purple marsh-mallow where she had left them; but through the whole morning I neither saw nor heard anything from her who had so suddenly aroused my curiosity and stirred my long-slumbering emotions.

Mrs. Adams, my landlady, was wont to carry up my frugal breakfast; yet it was very rarely that I allowed

her to break the current of my thoughts or to draw my
mind by her idle chatter from weightier things. This
morning, however, for once she found me in a listening
mood, and with little prompting, proceeded to pour into
my ears all she knew of our beautiful visitor.

"Miss Eva Cameron be her name, sir,'" she said; "but
who she be, or where she come fra, I know little more
than yoursel'. Maybe it was the same reason that brought
her to Kirkby-Malhouse as fetched you there yoursel',
sir."

"Possibly," said I, ignoring the covert question; "but
I should hardly have thought that Kirkby-Malhouse was
a place which offered any great attractions to a young
lady."

"It's a gay place when the fair is on," said Mrs. Adams;
"yet maybe it's just health and rest as the young lady is
seeking."

"Very likely," said I, stirring my coffee; "and no doubt
some friend of yours has advised her to seek them in your
very comfortable apartments."

"Heh, sir!" she cried, "there's the wonder of it. The
leddy has just come fra France; and how her folk came
to learn of me is just a wonder. A week ago, up comes
a man to my door—a fine man, sir, and a gentleman, as
one could see with half an eye. 'You are Mrs. Adams,'
says he. 'I engage your rooms for Miss Cameron,' says
he. 'She will be here in a week,' says he; and then off
without a word of terms. Last night there comes the
young lady hersel'—soft-spoken and downcast, with a
touch of the French in her speech. But my sakes, sir! I
must away and mak' her some tea, for she'll feel lone-
some-like, poor lamb, when she wakes under a strange
roof."

CHAPTER II

HOW I WENT FORTH TO GASTER FELL

I WAS still engaged upon my breakfast when I heard the clatter of dishes and the landlady's footfall as she passed toward her new lodger's room. An instant afterward she had rushed down the passage and burst in upon me with uplifted hand and startled eyes. "Lord 'a mercy, sir!" she cried, "and asking your pardon for troubling you, but I'm feared o' the young leddy, sir; she is not in her room."

"Why, there she is," said I, standing up and glancing through the casement. "She has gone back for the flowers she left upon the bank."

"Oh, sir, see to her boots and her dress!" cried the landlady, wildly. "I wish her mother was here, sir—I do. Where she has been is more than I ken, but her bed has not been lain on this night."

"She has felt restless, doubtless, and went for a walk, though the hour was certainly a strange one."

Mrs. Adams pursed her lip and shook her head. But even as she stood at the casement, the girl beneath looked smilingly up at her and beckoned to her with a merry gesture to open the window.

"Have you my tea there?" she asked in a rich, clear voice, with a touch of the mincing French accent.

"It is in your room, miss."

"Look at my boots, Mrs. Adams!" she cried, thrusting them out from under her skirt. "These fells of yours are

dreadful places—effroyable—one inch, two inch; never
have I seen such mud! My dress, too—voila!"

"Eh, miss, but you are in a pickle," cried the landlady, as she gazed down at the bedraggled gown. "But
you must be main weary and heavy for sleep."

"No, no," she answered, laughing, "I care not for sleep.
What is sleep? It is a little death—voila tout. But for
me to walk, to run, to breathe the air—that is to live. I
was not tired and so all night I have explored these fells
of yours."

"Lord 'a mercy, miss, and where did you go?" asked
Mrs. Adams.

She waved her hand round in a sweeping gesture which
included the whole western horizon. "There," she cried.
"O comme elles sont tristes et sauvages, ces collines!
But I have flowers here. You will give me water, will you
not? They will wither else." She gathered her treasures
into her lap, and a moment later we heard her light,
springy footfall upon the stair.

So she had been out all night, this strange woman.
What motive could have taken her from her snug room on
to the bleak, wind-swept hills? Could it be merely the
restlessness, the love of adventure of a young girl? Or
was there, possibly, some deeper meaning in this nocturnal journey?

I thought, as I paced my chamber, of her drooping
head, the grief upon her face, and the wild burst of sobbing which I had overseen in the garden. Her nightly
mission, then, be it what it might, had left no thought of
pleasure behind it. And yet, even as I walked, I could
hear the merry tinkle of her laughter and her voice up-
raised in protest against the motherly care wherewith Mrs.
Adams insisted upon her changing her mud-stained gar-
ments. Deep as were the mysteries which my studies had
taught me to solve, here was a human problem which for
the moment at least was beyond my comprehension. I

had walked out on the moor in the forenoon, and on my return, as I topped the brow that overlooks the little town, I saw my fellow lodger some little distance off among the gorge. She had raised a light easel in front of her and with papered board laid across it, was preparnig to paint the magnificent landscape of rock and moor which stretched away in front of her. As I watched her I saw that she was looking anxiously to right and left. Close by me a pool of water had formed in a hollow. Dipping the cup of my pocket flask into it, I carried it across to her. "This is what you need, I think," said I, raising my cap and smiling.

"Merci, bien!" she answered, pouring the water into her saucer, "I was indeed in search of some."

"Miss Cameron, I believe," said I. "I am your fellow lodger. Upperton is my name. We must introduce ourselves in these wilds if we are not to be forever strangers."

"Oh, then, you live also with Mrs. Adams!" she cried. "I had thought that there were none but peasants in this strange place."

"I am a visitor, like yourself," I answered. "I am a student and have come for the quiet and repose which my studies demand."

"Quiet indeed!" said she, glancing round at the vast circle of silent moors, with the one tiny line of gray cottages which sloped down beneath us.

"And yet not quiet enough," I answered, laughing, "for I have been forced to move further into the fells for the absolute peace which I require."

"Have you, then, built a house upon the fells?" she asked, arching her eyebrows.

"I have and hope with a few days to occupy it."

"Ah, but that is triste," she cried. "And where is it, then, this house which you have built?"

"It is over yonder," I answered. "See that stream

which lies like a silver band upon the distant moor? It is the Gaster Beck and it runs through Gaster Fell."

She started and turned upon me her great dark, questioning eyes with a look in which surprise, incredulity and something akin to horror seemed to be struggling for mastery.

"And you will live on the Gaster Fell?" she cried.

"So I have planned. But what do you know of Gaster Fell, Miss Cameron?" I asked. "I had thought that you were a stranger in these parts."

"Indeed, I have never been here before," she answered. "But I have heard my brother talk of these Yorkshire moors; and, if I mistake not, I have heard him name this very one as the wildest and most savage of them all."

"Very likely," said I, carelessly. "It is indeed a dreary place."

"Then why live there?" she cried eagerly. "Consider the loneliness, the barrenness, the want of all comfort and of all aid, should aid be needed."

"Aid! What aid should be needed on Gaster Fell?"

She looked down and shrugged her shoulders. "Sickness may come in all places," said she. "If I were a man, I do not think I would live alone on Gaster Fell."

"I have braved worse dangers than that," said I, laughing; "but I fear that your picture will be spoiled, for the clouds are banking up and already I feel a few rain drops."

Indeed, it was high time we were on our way to shelter, for even as I spoke there came the sudden, steady swish of the shower. Laughing merrily, my companion threw her light shawl over her head and, seizing picture and easel, ran with the lithe grace of a young fawn down the furze-clad slope, while I followed after with camp stool and paint box.

*   *   *   *   *   *

Deeply as my curiosity had been aroused by this strange

waif which had been cast up in our West Riding hamlet, I found that with fuller knowledge of her my interest
was stimulated rather than satisfied. Thrown together as
we were, with no thought in common with the good people
who surrounded us, it was not long before a friendship
and confidence arose between us. Together we strolled
over the moors in the mornings or stood upon the Moor-
stone Crag to watch the red sun sinking beneath the distant waters of Morecambe. Of herself she spoke frankly
and without reserve. Her mother had died young and
her youth had been spent in the Belgian convent from
which she had just finally returned. Her father and one
brother, she told me, constituted the whole of her family.
Yet when the talk chanced to turn upon the causes which
had brought her to so lonely a dwelling, a strange reserve possessed her and she would either relapse into
silence or turn the talk into another channel. For the
rest, she was an admirable companion—sympathetic, well
read, with the quick, piquant daintiness of thought which
she had brought with her from her foreign training. Yet
the shadow which I had observed in her on the first morning that I had seen her was never far from her mind, and
I have seen her merriest laugh frozen suddenly upon her
lips, as though some dark thought lurked within her, to
choke down the mirth and gaiety of her youth.

It was the eve of my departure from Kirkby-Malhouse
that we sat upon the green bank in the garden, she with
dark, dreamy eyes looking sadly out over the somber fells;
while I, with a book upon my knee, glanced covertly at
her lovely profile, and marveling to myself how twenty
years of life could have stamped so sad and wistful an
expression upon it.

"You have read much?" I remarked at last. "Women
have opportunities now such as their mothers never knew.
Have you ever thought of going further—or seeking a
course of college or even a learned profession?"

She smiled wearily at the thought.

"I have no aim, no ambition," she said. "My future is black—confused—a chaos. My life is like to one of these paths upon the fells. You have seen them, Monsieur Upperton. They are smooth and straight and clear where they begin; but soon they wind to left and wind to right and so mid rocks and over crags until they lose themselves in some quagmire. At Brussels my path was straight; but now, *mon Dieu!* who is there can tell me where it leads?"

"It might take no prophet to do that, Miss Cameron," quote I, with the fatherly manner which two score years may show toward one. "If I may read your life, I would venture to say that you were destined to fulfil the lot of women—to make some good man happy and to shed around, in some wider circle, the pleasure which your society has given me since first I knew you."

"I will never marry," said she, with a sharp decision, which surprised and somewhat amused me.

"Not marry—and why?"

A strange look passed over her sensitive features, and she plucked nervously at the grass on the bank beside her.

"I dare not," said she in a voice that quivered with emotion.

"Dare not?"

"It is not for me. I have other things to do. That path of which I spoke is one which I must tread alone."

"But this is morbid," said I. "Why should your lot, Miss Cameron, be separate from that of my own sisters or the thousand other young ladies whom every season brings out into the world? But perhaps it is that you have a fear and distrust of mankind. Marriage brings a risk as well as a happiness."

"The risk would be with the man who married me," she cried. And then in an instant, as though she had said too much, she sprang to her feet and drew her mantle round her. "The night air is chill, Mr. Upperton," said she, and so swept swiftly away, leaving me to muse over the strange words which had fallen from her lips.

I had feared that this woman's coming might draw me from my studies, but never had I anticipated that my thoughts and interests could have been changed in so short a time. I sat late that night in my little study, pondering over my future course. She was young, she was fair, she was alluring, both from her own beauty and from the strange mystery that surrounded her. And yet what was she, that she should turn me from the high studies that filled my mind, or change me from the line of life which I had marked out for myself? I was no boy, that I should be swayed and shaken by a dark eye or a woman's smile, and yet three days had passed and my work lay where I had left it. Clearly it was time that I should go. I set my teeth and vowed that another day should not have passed before I should have snapped this newly formed tie and sought the lonely retreat which awaited me upon the moors. Breakfast was hardly over in the morning before a peasant dragged up to the door the rude hand cart which was to convey my few personal belongings to my new dwelling. My fellow lodger had kept her room; and steeled as my mind was against her influence, I was yet conscious of a little throb of disappointment that she allow me to depart without a word of farewell. My hand cart with its load of books had already started and I, having shaken hands with Mrs. Adams, was about to follow it, when there was a quick scurry of feet on the stair, and there she was beside me all panting with her own haste.

"Then you go—you really go?" said she.

"My studies call me."

"And to Gaster Fell?" she asked.

"Yes; to the cottage which I have built there."

"And you will live alone there?"

"With my hundred companions who lie in that cart."

"Ah, books!" she cried, with a pretty shrug of her graceful shoulders. "But you will make me a promise?"

"What is it?" I asked, in surprise.

"It is a small thing. You will not refuse me?"

"You have but to ask it."

She bent forward her beautiful face with an expression of the most intense earnestness. "You will bolt your door at night?" said she; and was gone ere I could say a word in answer to her extraordinary request.

It was a strange thing for me to find myself at last duly installed in my lonely dwelling. For me, now, the horizon was bounded by the barren circle of wiry, unprofitable grass, patched over with furze bushes and scarred by the profusion of Nature's gaunt and granite ribs. A duller, wearier waste I have never seen; but its dullness was its very charm. What was there in the faded, rolling hills, or in the blue, silent arch of heaven to distract my thoughts from the high thoughts which engrossed them? I had left the drove of mankind and had wandered away, for better or worse, upon a side path of my own. With them I had hoped to leave grief, disappointment and emotion and all other petty human weaknesses. To live for knowledge, and knowledge alone, that was the highest aim which life could offer. And yet upon the very first night which I spent at Gaster Fell there came a strange incident to lead my thoughts back once more to the world which I had left behind me.

It had been a sullen and sultry evening, with great livid cloud banks mustering in the west. As the night wore on, the air within my little cabin became closer and more oppressive. A weight seemed to rest upon my brow and my chest. From far away the low rumble of thunder came moaning over the moor. Unable to sleep, I dressed and standing at my cottage door, looked on the black solitude which surrounded me. There was no breeze below;

but above, the clouds were sweeping majestically across the sky, with half a moon peeping at times between the rifts. The ripple of the Gaster Beck and the dull hooting of a distant owl were the only sounds which broke upon my ear. Taking the narrow sheep path which ran by the stream, I strolled along it for some hundred yards and had turned to retrace my steps, when the moon was finally buried beneath an ink-black cloud, and the darkness deepened so suddenly that I could see neither the path at my feet, the stream upon my right, nor the rocks upon my left. I was standing groping about in the thick gloom, when there came a crash of thunder with a flash of lightning which lighted up the whole vast fell, so that every bush and rock stood out clear and hard in the livid light. It was but for an instant, and yet that momentary view struck a thrill of fear and astonishment through me, for in my very path, not twenty yards before me, there stood a woman, the livid light beating upon her face and showing up every detail of her dress and features. There was no mistaking those dark eyes, that tall, graceful figure. It was she—Eva Cameron, the woman whom I thought I had forever left. For an instant I stood petrified, marveling whether this could indeed be she or whether it was some figment conjured up by my excited brain. Then I ran swiftly forward in the direction where I had seen her, calling loudly upon her, but without reply. Again I called and again no answer came back, save the melancholy wail of the owl. A second flash illuminated the landscape and the moon burst out from behind its cloud. But I could not, though I climbed upon a knoll which overlooked the whole moor, see any sign of this strange midnight wanderer. For an hour or more I traversed the fell and at last found myself back at my little cabin, still uncertain as to whether it had been a woman or a shadow upon which I gazed.

For the three days which followed this midnight storm,

I bent myself doggedly to my work. From early morn till late at night I immured myself in my little study, with my whole thoughts buried in my books and my parchments. At last it seemed to me that I had reached that haven of rest, that oasis of study for which I had so often sighed. But, alas! for my hopes and my plannings! Within a week of my flight from Kirkby-Malhouse a strange and most unforeseen series of events not only broke in upon the calm of my existence, but filled me with emotions so acute as to drive all other considerations from my mind.

CHAPTER III

OF THE GRAY COTTAGE IN THE GLEN

It was either on the fourth or the fifth day after I had taken possession of my cottage that I was astonished to hear footsteps upon the grass outside, quickly followed by a crack, as from a stick, upon the door. The explosion of an infernal machine would hardly have surprised or discomfited me more. I had hoped to have shaken off all intrusion forever, yet here was somebody beating at my door with as little ceremony as if it had been a village ale house. Hot with anger, I flung down my book, withdrew the bolt just as my visitor had raised his stock to renew his rough application for admittance. He was a tall, powerful man, tawny-bearded and deep-chested, clad in a loose-fitting suit of tweed, cut for comfort rather than elegance. As he stood in the shimmering sunlight, I took in every feature of his face. The large, fleshy nose; the steady blue eyes, with their thick thatch of overhanging brows; the broad forehead, all knitted and lined with furrows, which were strangely at variance with his youthful bearing. In spite of his weather-stained felt hat and the colored handkerchief slung around his muscular brown neck, I could see at a glance he was a man of breeding and education. I had been prepared for some wandering shepherd or uncouth tramp, but this apparition fairly disconcerted me.

"You look astonished," said he, with a smile. "Did you think, then, that you were the only man in the world with a taste for solitude? You see that there are other hermits in the wilderness besides yourself."

"Do you mean to say that you live here?" I asked in no conciliatory voice.

"Up yonder," he answered, tossing his head backward. "I thought as we were neighbors, Mr. Upperton, that I could not do less than look in and see if I could assist you in any way."

"Thank you," said I, coldly, standing with my hand upon the latch of the door. "I am a man of simple tastes and you can do nothing for me. You have the advantage of me in knowing my name."

"I learned it from the masons who were at work here," he said. "As for me, I am a surgeon, the surgeon of Gaster Fell. That is the name I have gone by in these parts and it serves as well as another."

"Not much room for practise here?" I observed.

"Not a soul except yourself for miles on either side."

"You appear to have had need of some assistance yourself?" I remarked, glancing at a broad white splash, as from the recent action of some powerful acid, upon his sunburnt cheek.

"That is nothing," he answered, curtly, turning his face half round to hide the mark. "I must get back, for I have a companion who is waiting for me. If I can ever do anything for you, pray let me know. You have only to follow the beck upward for a mile or so to find my place. Have you a bolt on the inside of your door?"

"Yes," I answered, rather startled at this question.

"Keep it bolted then," he said. "The fell is a strange

place. You never know who may be about. It is as well to be on the safe side. Good-by." He raised his hat, turned on his heel and lounged away along the bank of the little stream.

I was still standing with my hand upon the latch, gazing after my unexpected visitor, when I became aware of yet another dweller in the wilderness. Some distance along the path which the stranger was taking there lay a great gray boulder, and leaning against this was a small, wizened man, who stood erect as the other approached and advanced to meet him. The two talked for a minute or more, the taller man nodding his head frequently in my direction, as though describing what had passed between us. Then they walked on together and disappeared in a dip of the fell. Presently I saw them ascending once more some rising ground further on. My acquaintance had thrown his arm round his elderly friend, either from affection or from a desire to aid him up the steep incline. The square, burly figure and its shriveled, meager companion stood out against the sky line and, turning their faces, they looked back at me. At the sight, I slammed the door, lest they should be encouraged to return. But when I peeped from the window some minutes afterward, I perceived that they were gone.

For the remainder of that day I strove in vain to recover that indifference to the world and its ways which is essential to mental abstraction. Do what I would, my thoughts ran upon the solitary surgeon and his shriveled companion. What did he mean by his question as to my bolt? and how came it that the last words of Eva Cameron were to the same sinister effect? Again and again I speculated as to what train of causes could have led two men so dissimilar in age and appearance to dwell together on the wild, inhospitable fells. Were they, like myself, immersed in some engrossing study? or could it be that a companionship in crime had forced them from the haunts of men? Some cause there must be, and that a potent one, to induce the man of education to turn to such an existence. It was only now that I began to realize that the crowd of the city is infinitely less disturbing than the unit of the country.

All day I bent over the Egyptian papyrus upon which I was engaged; but neither the subtle reasonings of the ancient philosopher of Memphis, nor the mystic meaning which lay in his pages, could raise my mind from the things of earth. Evening was drawing in before I threw my work aside in despair. My heart was bitter against this man for his intrusion. Standing by the beck which purled past the door of my cabin, I cooled my heated brow, and thought the matter over. Clearly it was the small mystery hanging over these neighbors of mine which had caused my mind to run so persistently on them. That cleared up, they would no longer cause an obstacle to my studies. What was to hinder me, then, from walking in the direction of their dwelling and observing for myself, without permitting them to suspect my presence, what manner of men they might be? Doubtless, their mode of life would be found to admit of some simple and prosaic explanation. In any case, the evening was fine and a walk would be bracing for mind and body. Lighting my pipe, I set off over the moors in the direction which they had taken. The sun lay low and red in the west, flushing the heather with a deeper pink, and mottling the broad heaven with every hue from the palest green at the zenith to the richest crimson along the fair horizon. It might have been the great palette upon which the world-painter had mixed his primeval colors. On either side, the giant peaks of Ingleborough and Pennigent looked down upon the gray, melancholy country which stretches between them. As I advanced, the rude fells ranged themselves upon right and left, forming a well-defined valley, down the center of which meandered the little brooklet.

On either side, parallel lines of gray rock marked the level of some ancient glacier, the moraine of which had formed the broken ground about my dwelling. Ragged boulders, precipitous scarps, and twisted, fantastic rocks, all bore witness to the terrible power of the old ice field, and showed where its frosty fingers had ripped and rent the solid limestones.

About halfway down this wild glen there stood a small clump of gnarled and stunted oak trees. From behind these, a thin column of smoke rose into the still evening air. Clearly this marked the position of my neighbor's house. Trending away to the left, I was able to gain the shelter of a line of rocks and so reach a spot from which I could command a view of the building without exposing myself to any risk of being observed. It was a small, slate-covered cottage, hardly larger than the boulders among which it lay. Like my own cabin, it showed signs of having been constructed for the use of some shepherd; but, unlike mine, no pains had been taken by the tenants to improve and enlarge it. Two little peeping windows, a cracked and weather-beaten door and a discolored barrel for catching the rain water, were the only external objects from which I might draw deductions as to the dwellers within. Yet even in these there was food for thought; for as I drew nearer, still concealing myself behind the ridge, I saw that thick bars of iron covered the windows, while the old door was slashed and plated with the same metal. These strange precautions, together with the wild surroundings and unbroken solitude, gave an indescribably ill omen and fearsome character to the solitary building. Thrusting my pipe into my pocket, I crawled upon my hands and knees through the gorse and ferns until I was within a hundred yards of my neighbor's door. There, finding that I could not approach nearer without fear of detection, I crouched down and set myself to watch.

I had hardly settled into my hiding place when the door

of the cottage swung open and the man who had introduced himself to me as the surgeon of Gaster Fell came out, bareheaded, with a spade in his hands. In front of the door there was a small cultivated patch containing potatoes, peas, and other forms of green stuff, and here he proceeded to busy himself, trimming, weeding and arranging, singing the while in a powerful though not very musical voice. He was all engrossed in his work, with his back to the cottage, when there emerged from the half-opened door the same attenuated creature whom I had seen in the morning. I could perceive now that he was a man of sixty, wrinkled, bent and feeble, with sparse, grizzled hair, and long, colorless face. With a cringing, sidelong gait, he shuffled toward his companion, who was unconscious of his approach until he was close upon him. His light footfall or his breathing may have finally given notice of his proximity, for the worker sprang round and faced him. Each made a quick step toward the other, as though in greeting, and then—even now I feel the horror of the instant—the tall man rushed upon and knocked his companion to the earth, then whipping up his body, ran with great speed over the intervening ground and disappeared with his burden into the house.

Case-hardened as I was by my varied life, the suddenness and violence of the thing made me shudder. The old man's age, his feeble frame, his humble and deprecating manner, all cried shame against the deed. So hot was my anger that I was on the point of striding up to the cabin, unarmed as I was, when the sound of voices from within showed me that the victim had recovered. The sun had sunk beneath the horizon and all was gray, save a red feather in the cap of Pennigent. Secure in the failing light, I approached near and strained my ears to catch what was passing. I could hear the high, querulous voice of the elder man and the deep, rough monotone of his assailant, mixed with a strange metallic jangling and clanking. Presently the surgeon came out, locking the door behind him and stamped up and down in the twilight, pulling at his hair and brandishing his arms, like a man demented. Then he set off, walking rapidly up the valley, and I soon lost sight of him among the rocks. When the sound of his feet had died away in the distance, I drew nearer to the cottage. The prisoner within was still pouring forth a stream of words and moaning from time to time like a man in pain. These words resolved themselves, as I approached, into prayers —shrill, voluble prayers, pattered forth with the intense earnestness of one who sees impending an imminent danger. There was to me something inexpressibly awesome in this gush of solemn entreaty from the lonely sufferer, meant for no human ear and jarring upon the silence of the night. I was still pondering whether I should mix myself in the affair or not, when I heard in the distance the sound of the surgeon's returning footfall. At that I drew myself up quickly by the iron bars and glanced in through the diamond-paned window. The interior of the cottage was lighted up by a lurid glow, coming from what I afterward discovered to be a chemical furnace. By its rich light I could distinguish a great litter of retorts, test tubes and condensers, which sparkled over the table and threw strange, grotesque shadows on the wall. On the further side of the room was a wooden framework resembling a hencoop, and in this, still absorbed in prayer, knelt the man whose voice I heard. The red glow beating upon his upturned face made it stand out from the shadow like a painting from Rembrandt, showing up every wrinkle upon the parchment-like skin. I had but time for a fleeting glance; then dropping from the window I made off through the rocks and the heather, nor slackened my pace until I found myself back in my cabin once more. There I threw myself upon my couch, more disturbed and shaken than I had ever thought to feel again.

Long into the watches of the night I tossed and tumbled on my uneasy pillow. A strange theory had framed itself within me, suggested by the elaborate scientific apparatus which I had seen. Could it be that this surgeon had some profound and unholy experiments on hand, which necessitated the taking, or at least the tampering with the life of his companion? Such a supposition would account for the loneliness of his life; but how could I reconcile it with the close friendship which had appeared to exist between the pair no longer ago than that very morning? Was it grief or madness which had made the man tear his hair and wring his hands when he emerged from the cabin? And sweet Eva Cameron, was she also a partner to this somber business? Was it to my grim neighbors that she made her nocturnal journeys? and if so, what bond could there be to unite so strangely assorted a trio? Try as I might, I could come to no satisfactory conclusion upon these points. When at last I dropped into a troubled slumber, it was only to see once more in my dreams the strange episodes of the evening and to wake at dawn unrefreshed and weary.

Such doubts as I might have had as to whether I had indeed seen my former fellow lodger upon the night of the thunder storm, were finally resolved that morning. Strolling along down the path which led to the fell, I saw in one spot where the ground was soft the impression of a foot—the small, dainty foot of a well-booted woman. That tiny heel and high instep could have belonged to none other than my companion of Kirkby-Malhouse. I followed her trail for some distance till it lost itself among hard and stony ground; but it still pointed, as far as I could discern it, to the lonely and ill-omened cottage. What power could there be to draw this tender girl, through wind and rain and darkness, across the fearsome moors to that strange rendezvous?

But why should I let my mind run upon such things?

Had I not prided myself that I lived a life of my own, beyond the sphere of my fellow mortals? Were all my plans and my resolutions to be shaken because the ways of my neighbors were strange to me? It was unworthy, it was puerile. By constant and unremitting effort, I set myself to cast out these distracting influences and to return to my former calm. It was no easy task. But after some days, during which I never stirred from my cottage, I had almost succeeded in regaining my peace of mind, when a fresh incident whirled my thoughts back into their old channel.

I have said that a little beck flowed down the valley and past my very door. A week or so after the doings which I have described, I was seated by my window, when I perceived something white drifting slowly down the stream. My first thought was that it was a drowning sheep; but picking up my stick, I strolled to the bank and hooked it ashore. On examination it proved to be a large sheet, torn and tattered, with the initials J. C. in the corner. What gave it its sinister significance, however, was that from hem to hem it was all dabbled and discolored with blood. In parts where the water had soaked it, this was but a discoloration; while in others the stains showed they were of recent origin. I shuddered as I gazed at it. It could but have come from the lonely cottage in the glen. What dark and violent deed had left this gruesome trace behind it? I had flattered myself that the human family was as nothing to me and yet my whole being was absorbed now in curiosity and resentment. How could I remain neutral when such things were doing within a mile of me? I felt that the old Adam was too strong in me and that I must solve this mystery. Shutting the door of my cabin behind me, I set off up the glen in the direction of the surgeon's cabin. I had not gone far before I perceived the very man himself. He was walking rapidly along the hillside, beating the furze bushes with a cudgel and bellowing like a madman. Indeed, at the sight of him, the doubts as to his sanity which had arisen in my mind were strengthened and confirmed. As he approached, I noticed that his left arm was suspended in a sling. On perceiving me, he stood irresolute, as though uncertain whether to come over to me or not. I had no desire for an interview with him, however; so I hurried past him, on which he continued on his way, still shouting and striking about with his club. When he had disappeared over the fells, I made my way down to his cottage, determined to find some clew to what had occurred. I was surprised, on reaching it, to find the iron-plated door flung wide open. The ground immediately outside it was marked with the signs of a struggle. The chemical apparatus within and the furniture were all dashed about and shattered. Most suggestive of all, the sinister wooden cage was stained with bloodmarks, and its unfortunate occupant had disappeared. My heart was heavy for the little man, for I was assured that I should never see him in this world more. There were many gray cairns of stones scattered over the valley. I ran my eye over them and wondered which of them concealed the traces of this last act which ended the long tragedy.

There was nothing in the cabin to throw any light upon the identity of my neighbors. The room was stuffed with chemicals and delicate philosophical instruments. In one corner, a small bookcase contained a choice selection of works of science. In another was a pile of geological specimens collected from the limestone. My eye ran rapidly over these details; but I had no time to make a more thorough examination, for I feared lest the surgeon should return and find me there. Leaving the cottage, I hastened homeward with a weight at my heart. A nameless shadow hung over the lonely gorge—the heavy shadow of unexpiated crime, making the grim fells look grimmer, and the wild moors more dreary and forbidding.

My mind wavered whether I should send to Lancaster to
acquaint the police of what I had seen. My thoughts recoiled at the prospect of becoming a witness in a *cause
celebre*, and having an overbusy counsel or an officious
press peeping and prying into my own modes of life.
Was it for this I had stolen away from my fellow mortals and settled in these lonely wilds? The thought of
publicity was repugnant to me. It was best, perhaps, to
wait and watch without taking any decided step until I
had come to a more definite conclusion as to what I had
heard.

I caught no glimpse of the surgeon upon my homeward
journey; but when I reached my cottage, I was astonished
and indignant to find that somebody had entered it in my
absence. Boxes had been pulled out from under the
bed, the curtains disarranged, the chairs drawn out from
the wall. Even my study had not been safe from this
rough intruder, for the prints of a heavy foot were
plainly visible on the ebony-black carpet. I am not a
patient man at the best of times; but this invasion and
systematic examination of my household effects stirred
up every drop of gall in my composition. Swearing under
my breath, I took my old cavalry saber down from its nail
and passed my finger along the edge. There was a great
notch in the center where it had jarred up against the
collar bone of a Bavarian artilleryman the day we beat
Van Der Tann back from Orleans. It was still sharp
enough, however, to be serviceable. I placed it at the
head of my bed, within reach of my arm, ready to give a
keen greeting to the next uninvited visitor who might
arrive.

CHAPTER IV

OF THE MAN WHO CAME IN THE NIGHT

THE night set in gusty and tempestuous and the moon was all girt with ragged clouds. The wind blew in melancholy gusts, sobbing and sighing over the moor and setting all the gorse bushes a-groaning. From time to time a little sputter of rain pattered up against the window pane. I sat until near midnight glancing over the fragment of immortality by Iamblichus, the Alexandrian platonist, of whom the Emperor Julian said that he was posterior to Plato in time, but not in genius. At last, shutting up my book, I opened my door and took a last look at the dreary fell and still more dreary sky. As I protruded my head, a swoop of wind caught me and sent the red ashes of my pipe sparkling and dancing through the darkness. At the same moment the moon shone brilliantly out from between two clouds, and I saw, sitting on the hillside, not two hundred yards from my door, the man who called himself the surgeon of Gaster Fell. He was squatted among the heather, his elbows upon his knees and his chin resting upon his hands, as motionless as a stone, with his gaze fixed steadily upon the door of my dwelling.

At the sight of this ill-omened sentinel, a chill of horror and of fear shot through me, for his gloomy and mysterious associations had cast a glamour round the man and the hour and place were in keeping with his sinister presence. In a moment, however, a manly glow of resentment and self-confidence drove this pretty emotion from my mind and I strode fearlessly in his direction. He rose as I approached and faced me, with the moon shining on his grave, bearded face and glittering on his eyeballs. "What is the meaning of this?" I cried, as I came upon him. "What right have you to play the spy on me?"

I could see the flush of anger rise on his face. "Your stay in the country has made you forget your manners," he said. "The moor is free to all."

"You will say next that my house is free to all," I said, hotly. "You have had the impertinence to ransack it in my absence this afternoon."

He started and his features showed the most intense excitement. "I swear to you that I had no hand in it," he cried. "I have never set foot in your house in my life. Oh, sir, sir, if you will but believe me, there is a danger hanging over you, and you would do well to be careful."

"I have had enough of you," I said. "I saw the cowardly blow you struck when you thought no human eye rested upon you. I have been to your cabin, too, and know all that it has to tell. If there is a law in England, you shall hang for what you have done. As to me, I am an old soldier, sir, and I am armed. I shall not fasten my door. But if you or any other villain attempt to cross my threshold, it shall be at your risk." With these words I swung round upon my heel and strode into my cabin. When I looked back at him from the door he was still looking at me, a gloomy figure among the heather, with his head sunk low upon his breast. I slept fitfully all that night; but I heard no more of this strange sentinel without, nor was he to be seen when I looked out in the morning.

For two days the wind freshened and increased with constant squalls of rain, until on the third night the most furious storm was raging which I can ever recollect in England. The thunder roared and rattled overhead, while the incessant lightning flashes illuminated the heavens. The wind blew intermittently, now sobbing away into a calm and then, of a sudden, beating and howling at my window panes until the glasses rattled in their frames. The air was charged with electricity and its peculiar influence, combined with the strange episodes with which I had been recently connected, made me morbidly wakeful and acutely sensitive. I felt that it was useless to go to bed, nor could I concentrate my mind sufficiently to read a book. I turned my lamp half down to moderate the glare, and leaning back in my chair, I gave myself up to reverie. I must have lost perception of time, for I have no recollection how long I sat there on the borderland betwixt thought and slumber. At last, about three or possibly four o'clock, I came to myself with a start—not only came to myself, but with every sense and nerve upon the strain. Looking round my chamber in the dim light, I could not see anything to justify my sudden trepidation. The homely room, the rain-blurred window and the rude wooden door were all as they had been. I had begun to persuade myself that some half-formed dream had sent that vague thrill through my nerves, when in a moment I became conscious of what it was. It was a sound—the sound of a human step outside my solitary cottage.

Amid the thunder and the rain and the wind, I could hear it—a dull, stealthy footfall, now on the grass, now on the stones—occasionally stopping entirely, then resumed, and ever drawing nearer. I sat breathlessly, listening to the eerie sound. It had stopped now at my very door and was replaced by a panting and gasping, as of one who has traveled fast and far. Only the thickness of the door separated me from this hard-breathing, light-treading night walker. I am no coward; but the wildness of the night, and the vague warning which I had had, and the proximity of this strange visitor, so unnerved me that my mouth was too dry for speech. I stretched out my hand, however, and grasped my saber, with my eyes still bent upon the door. I prayed in my heart that the thing, whatever it might be, would but knock or threaten or hail me, or give any clew as to its character. Any known danger was better than this awful silence, broken only by the rhythmic panting.

By the flickering light of the expiring lamp I could see that the latch of my door was twitching, as though a gentle pressure was exerted on it from without. Slowly, slowly, it rose, until it was free of the catch, and then there was a pause of a quarter minute or more, while I still sat silent, with dilated eyes and drawn saber. Then, very slowly, the door began to revolve upon its hinges and the keen air of the night came whistling through the slit. Very cautiously it was pushed open, so that never a sound came from the rusty hinges. As the aperture enlarged, I became aware of a dark, shadowy figure upon my threshold, and of a pale face that looked in at me. The features were human, but the eyes were not. They seemed to burn through the darkness with a greenish brilliancy of their own; and in their baleful, shifty glare I was conscious of the very spirit of murder. Springing from my chair, I had raised my naked sword, when, with a wild shouting, a second figure dashed up to my door. At its approach my shadowy visitant uttered a shrill cry and fled away across the fells, yelping like a beaten hound. The two creatures were swallowed up in the tempest from which they had emerged as if they were the very genii of the beating wind and the howling rain.

Tingling with my recent fear, I stood at my door, peering through the night with the discordant cry of the fugitives still ringing in my ears. At that moment a vivid flash of lightning illuminated the whole landscape and made it as clear as day. By its light I saw far away upon the hillside two dark figures pursuing each other with extreme rapidity across the fells. Even at that distance the contrast between them forbid all doubts as to their identity. The first was the small, elderly man whom I had supposed to be dead; the second was my neighbor, the surgeon. For an instant they stood out clear and hard in the unearthly light; in the next, the darkness had closed over them, and they were gone. As I turned to re-enter my chamber, my foot rattled against something on my threshold. Stooping, I found it was a straight knife, fashioned entirely of lead and so soft and brittle that it was a strange choice for a weapon. To render it more harmless, the top had been cut square off. The edge, however, had been assiduously sharpened against a stone, as was evident from the markings upon it, so that it was still a dangerous implement in the grasp of a determined man. It had evidently been dropped from the fellow's hand at the moment when the sudden coming of the surgeon had driven him to flight. There could no longer be a doubt as to the object of his visit.

And what was the meaning of it all? you ask. Many a drama which I have come across in my wandering life, some as strange and as striking as this one, has lacked the ultimate explanation which you demand. Fate is a grand weaver of tales; but she ends them, as a rule, in defiance of all artistic laws and with an unbecoming want of regard for literary propriety. As it happens, however, I have a letter before me as I write which I may add without comment and which will clear all that may remain dark.

> "Kirkby Lunatic Asylum,
> "Sept. 4, 1885.

"Sir—I am deeply conscious that some apology and explanation is due to you for the very startling and, in your eyes, mysterious events which have recently occurred, and which have so seriously interfered with the retired existence which you desire to lead. I should have called upon you on the morning after the recapture of my father; but my knowledge of your dislike to visitors, and also of—you will excuse my saying it—your very violent temper, led me to think that it was better to communicate with you by letter. On the occasion of our last interview I should have told you what I tell you now; but your allusions to some crime of which you considered me guilty, and your abrupt departure, prevented me from saying much that was on my lips.

"My poor father was a hard-working general practitioner in Birmingham, where his name is still remembered and respected. About ten years ago he began to show signs of mental aberration, which we were inclined to put down to overwork and the effect of a sunstroke. Feeling my own incompetence to pronounce upon a case of such importance, I at once sought the highest advice in Birmingham and London. Among others we consulted the eminent alienist, Mr. Fraser Brown, who pronounced my father's case to be intermittent in its nature, but dangerous during the paroxysms. 'It may take a homicidal, or it may take a religious turn,' he said; 'or it may prove to be a mixture of both. For months he may be as well as you or me, and then in a moment he may break out. You will incur a great responsibility if you leave him without supervision.'

"The result showed the justice of the specialist's diagnosis. My poor father's disease rapidly assumed both a religious and homicidal turn, the attacks coming on without warning after months of sanity. It would weary you were I to describe the terrible experiences which his family have undergone. Suffice it that, by the blessing of God, we have succeeded in keeping his poor crazed fingers clear of blood. My sister Eva I sent to Brussels and I devoted myself entirely to his case. He has an intense dread of madhouses; and in his sane intervals would beg and pray so piteously not to be condemned to one, that I could never find the heart to resist him. At last, however, his attacks became so acute and dangerous that I determined, for the sake of those about me, to remove him from the town to the loneliest neighborhood that I could find. This proved to be Gaster Fell; and there he and I set up house together.

"I had a sufficient competence to keep me and being devoted to chemistry, I was able to pass the time with a fair degree of comfort and profit. He, poor fellow, was as submissive as a child, when in his right mind; and a better, kinder companion no man could wish for. We constructed together a wooden compartment, into which he could retire when the fit was upon him; and I had arranged the window and door so that I could confine him to the house if I thought an attack was impending. Looking back, I can safely say that no possible precaution was neglected; even the necessary table utensils were leaden and pointless, to prevent his doing mischief with them in his frenzy.

"For months after our change of quarters he appeared to improve. Whether it was the bracing air, or the absence of any incentive to violence, he never showed during that time any signs of his terrible disorder. Your arrival first upset his mental equilibrium. The very sight of you in the distance awoke all those morbid impulses which had been sleeping. That very evening he approached me stealthily with a stone in his hand and would have slain me, had I not, as the lesser of two evils, struck him to the ground and thrust him into his cage before he had time to regain his senses. This sudden relapse naturally plunged me into the deepest sorrow. For two days I did all that lay in my power to soothe him. On the third day he appeared to be calmer; but, alas! it was but the cunning of a madman. He had contrived to loosen two bars of his cage; and when thrown off my guard by his apparent improvement—I was engrossed in my chemistry —he suddenly sprang out at me, knife in hand. In the scuffle, he cut me across the foreman and escaped from the hut before I recovered myself, nor could I find out which direction he had taken. My wound was a trifle and for several days I wandered over the fells, beating through every clump of bushes in my fruitless search. I was convinced that he would make an attempt on your life, a conviction that was strengthened when I heard that some one in your absence had entered your cottage. I therefore kept a watch over you at night. A dead sheep which I found upon the moor, terribly mangled, showed me that he was not without food, and that the homicidal impulse was still strong in him. At last, as I had expected, he made his attempt upon you which, but for my intervention, would have ended in the death of one or the other of you. He ran, and struggled like a wild animal; but I was as desperate as he and succeeded in bringing him down and conveying him to my cottage. Convinced by this failure that all hope of permanent improvement was gone, I brought him next morning to this establishment, and he is now, I am glad to say, returning to his senses.

"Allow me once more, sir, to express my sorrow that you should have been subjected to this ordeal, and believe me to be faithfully yours,

"JOHN LIGHT CAMERON."

"P. S.—My sister Eva bids me send you her kind regards. She told me how you were thrown together at Kirkby-Malhouse and also that you met one night upon the fells. You will understand from what I have already told you that when my dear sister came back from Brussels I did not dare to bring her home, but preferred that she should lodge in safety in the village. Even then I did not venture to bring her into the presence of her father, and it was only at night, when he was asleep, that we could plan a meeting."

And this was the story of this strange group whose path

through life had crossed my own. From that last terrible night I have neither seen nor heard of any of them, save for this one letter which I have transcribed. Still I dwell on Gaster Fell and still my mind is buried in the secrets of the past. But when I wander forth upon the moor, and when I see the deserted little gray cottage among the rocks, my mind is still turned to the strange drama and to the singular couple who broke in upon my solitude.